HIT ME

ALEX BROWN

**Class Moustache
Books**

First Published in Great Britain by Alex Brown and Class Moustache Books
This paperback edition published in 2018 by Alex Brown and Class Moustache Books
www.hitmebook.co.uk
www.classmoustache.com

With S.T. Cairns
Edited and Brought to Print by Ethos Writing Agency
www.ethoswriting.com

A CIP catalogue record for this book is available from the British Library

ISBN: 978-1-9995833-1-6 (paperback)
ISBN: 978-1-9995833-2-3 - Hit Me (hardback)
ISBN: 978-1-9995833-3-0 - Hit Me (ebook)

10 9 8 7 6 5 4 3 2 1

Cover Illustration © 2018 by Copy Made, Edinburgh
Typeset by Kelvin Carlos Typesetters
Printed and bound in Great Britain by Clays Ltd, Elcograf S.p.A.

A very special thanks to Stephen Cairns and Ana Petrusevski from Ethos Writing for all their help and guidance, and also giving me the confidence when I had my doubts to see the project through.

Special thanks to Stuart, Grant and Tomas from Copy Made Ltd. for their work on all images and in creating the excellent book cover.

Special thanks to Brad Welsh at Holyrood Boxing Gym for all his efforts in the promotional work.

The biggest thanks of all is to my wife Monica, my family and friends for putting up with constantly hearing me go on about the book over the last few years.

Finally it is done!

In loving memory of my mum June, my dad Alex,

and my brother Stephen

All passed away far too soon and inspired this book.

Always Missed & Never Ever Forgotten

To Helen McMillan

AUTHOR'S WORDS ABOUT SOME SUBJECT MATTER IN THE BOOK

Alex Ferguson

It's very hard for family and friends to cope when a loved one has cancer. The best thing you can do is treat them as you always have, like a father, a mother, a brother or a sister, a son or daughter, a friend or neighbour.

Love them, talk to them, agree with them, or better still *disagree* with them, but treat them the same as always and be with them.

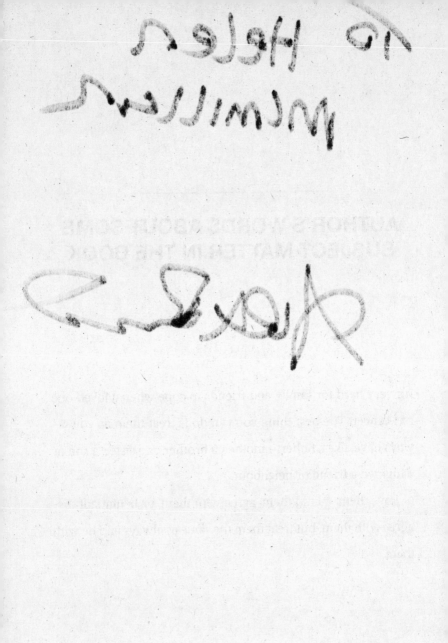

"Our greatest glory is not in never falling

but in getting up every time we do."

– Confucius
5TH century Chinese philosopher

PROLOGUE

Callum walked through the dismal hospital court yard to the covered area behind the canteen, where old generators rumbled against depressing brown brickwork dressed in layers of mould.

Hidden from view and prying eyes, he took out a tiny spliff from a tin box in his trouser pocket. The thought of a smoke had kept him going since the start of his shift. Finally, he'd made it to his morning break.

"Here's a wee gift for ma loyal customer," Tam had said, a few days before. "Special concoction, created by yours truly."

Callum had eyed the tampon sized joint with a certain distrust. "It's a bit small," he said.

"Aye, bet that's what all the lassies tell ye," said Tam. "But din-nae let the size fool you. This is pure *rocket* fuel."

Tam's warning was given about as much respect as the patients' blood tests he was supposed to check and then re-check before putting into the container fridges for testing. With a flick of his silver zippo, Callum sparked up and got the burn going on the white paper. Inhaling deeply, the warm smoke filled his lungs, which were totally unprepared for the cosmic blast that hit them. A flash of blinding light in his minds' eye, and then... some sort of eternity.

When his neurological systems eventually returned to a more *normal* state, Callum found himself sitting down with his back to the damp brick wall, knees up to his chest. His spliff had disintegrated, leaving a blackened burn between his forefinger and thumb. He blew the dust away and then licked the fingers of his other hand to give the ashen mark a wipe.

On checking his watch, he observed all four digital numbers spinning through the zero to nine sequence over and over again. He blinked a few times and waited until they stopped, one after another, to show he was five minutes late. Shit.

Dr. Cole wasn't going to be happy. But then again, Dr. Cole never was. Callum's last appraisal consisted of being told to improve his scruffy appearance and place a greater importance on punctuality. His general lack of interest was also an issue; something he'd need to attend to if he wanted to keep his job.

As he clambered back into the building, Callum found he had bigger things to worry about. His left and right brain had somehow swapped sides and simply walking along the corridor required the utmost concentration. If he hadn't been at work, he might actually be enjoying it.

A hospital cleaner pushing a rattling trolley with a wonky wheel gave him a nod. Callum tried his best to smile back but his facial muscles malfunctioned and returned the picture of a man who'd just sharted. The porter shook his head and continued on his rounds.

Walking with what felt like an entire body stutter on Elvis' legs, Callum somehow made it to the lab without passing anyone else along the way.

His luck was in.

The patronising Dr. Cole must have been called away, and only a tray of test tubes and blood samples remained. A note read:

Callum, please continue to sort these out.

They're being picked up at 11.45am.

I'll be back after lunch. Dr. Cole.

Callum sighed and leaned over the samples. The correct names and dates of the patients whom they belonged to started to disappear and re-appear on different cards and stickers. He shook his head, blinked and wiped his eyes. All he really had to do was move each specimen from the green tray into the corresponding named slot in the blue tray. However, the effects of Tam's *pocket rocket* hadn't let go of him just yet...

Barney was a young amateur in only his third fight. The bigger and more experienced boy had won the first two rounds with ease. George, his coach, told him just to go out and enjoy the final two minutes. No point in telling the kid to try for the knockout. Not with arms as skinny as those. It'd be good experience for him anyway. When the bell rang, the older boy bullied Barney into his corner and began bashing away. It was impossible to see Barney behind his opponent and the giant guard of those oversized gloves. After about a dozen shots without reply, Barney swung a left hook just as the older boy slipped on water his corner man had spilled between rounds. The boy went down hard on his arm. Old McTaggart, the diehard referee, whose glasses were thicker than the perspex in a car's front headlights, started the count. The boy pushed himself up and then collapsed in pain. His wrist had snapped in two places. Old McTaggart didn't notice and so counted him out, raising Barney's hand in victory. The result stood. "Lucky" Barney Wild, George had said afterwards. The name stuck.

CHAPTER 1

NEVER SAW IT COMING

The last time Barney had been this nervous was when he'd gone with his brother, Stephen, to get the results for the cancer. And now here he was. Same place. Same chair in fact. Different doctor, but same double knot in his stomach pulling tighter the longer the doctor took to say what he had to say. It'd been a job just to get here again. His fear of hospitals and illness was a recognised phobia and he'd been sick several times when the samples were taken the week before.

"Sorry I couldn't do this over the phone," said Doctor Noble, "I am aware of your *difficulties* with hospitals but there are regulations with these type of test results. As you know, your GP felt there might be some other factors contributing to you passing out at the end of your recent marathon, which is why you were booked in for these tests."

In the past four years, Barney had completed six marathons, raising over a hundred grand for charities. However, the last one had been excruciating, nothing like the others. He'd coughed the whole way through and hit the wall far too early. It was only the pride of a fighter that had enabled him to cross the chequered finish line. A few strides later, he'd collapsed to his knees and then blacked out. When he came to, he was breathing through an oxygen mask and looking up at the concerned faces of the St. John's ambulance crew. He'd convinced himself it was just a chest infection or maybe a bad cold.

Barney's hands were cupped between his legs and he slid one thumb over the other again and again as Doctor Noble went on. The doctor's fine brown hair was wisped at the front like the plume of an eagle, and his dark staring eyes made his resemblance to a predatory bird all the more real and unsettling.

Barney swallowed hard, eyes fixated on the doctor, almost pleading for him not to say the one word he feared the most. The word that conjured up so many images and memories of Stephen when he was ill. His wee brother, fading away on a hospital bed in a room full of terminally ill patients. Barney thought he'd known pain as a teenager when his gran died, but watching Stephen succumb to cancer had ripped his heart in two. The smell of the ward was something he'd grown to dread.

Stale, musty, and decaying; like old meat left in a hot room. It took his breath away, and he'd often have to cover his nose and mouth. Sometimes he'd say he was going to get a bottle of juice and a newspaper, only to run down the hallway and spew up in the toilets.

After Stephen's death, Barney's fear of cancer had grown into something his GP called a phobia. Now he didn't so much as speak the word, closing any newspapers or magazines where it was written, or quickly changing conversation if it was brought up.

Doctor Noble turned a page in Barney's file. "As you know, we took a number of tests last week. These were delivered yesterday afternoon. That's the reason I called you in on such short notice."

Barney could feel his heart beating faster.

"There's no easy way to say this," Doctor Noble said.

"Best just to say it," said Barney.

"It's lung cancer."

The words hit Barney like five rapid to the gut, followed by an uppercut that snapped his head back. Doctor Noble allowed him some time.

Barney had stopped twiddling his thumbs. "You're sure?" he asked.

"Yes," said the doctor.

"How far?" Barney asked, the nausea creeping up from his guts into his throat.

"It's advanced. Stage four. We could start a course of treatment immediately but I have to tell you now, it's unlikely to be effective."

Barney had seen other people go through chemo. Even if you did beat it, it tended to come back for a rematch. Most people didn't have the energy, or the will, to beat it a second time.

"How long have I got?"

"Six to eight weeks." Doctor Noble paused. "Though that's just an estimate. Possibly longer if you respond to the treatment."

Barney raised his eyebrows.

"I'd rather not build up your hopes. The truth is, it's not good. And if I were you, I'd start making arrangements sooner rather than later."

"I don't even smoke," Barney said, almost to himself.

"It's not only smoking that causes this type of cancer, I'm afraid. Passive smoking can contribute. There are hereditary factors to consider. Some people are just unlucky."

Unlucky? No one had ever said that to Barney before. He put his hand to his mouth. An unnatural heat was causing him to sweat. "Well, that explains all the coughing," he said, trying to ease the tension inside himself.

"Are you married?" continued the doctor, in his clinical fashion.

"No," replied Barney.

"Do you have family or people you can speak to?" Doctor Noble opened a drawer. "I have these leaflets which might help," he said, holding them out.

But Barney was still thinking about the doctor's first question.

The one thing he hadn't yet found was love. He'd had his fair share of women, of course, but the right woman, the one he dreamed about, hadn't turned up. He'd never given up hope of finding her though. In fact, until today, he was sure she was probably just around the corner of next week, ready to welcome him home. That's the way he'd pictured it anyway. But now that was gone. Gone too were his dreams of starting a family of his own.

Barney wasn't really aware of the rest of the conversation. Doctor Noble had asked if he'd wanted to start treatment the next week, but Barney had told him he needed time to think about it. Treatment, he knew all too well, meant the kind of radiation that knocked you down and made your hair fall out before kicking you in the balls just to make sure you knew it was serious. It was akin to having a bad flu that got worse every day. And if it wasn't going to work, only delay the inevitable, then what was the point in putting yourself through it?

Barney's Granny sat him on her knee and told him there were two types of people in the world: McGees and McTacks.

"What's a McGee?" Barney asked.

"McGees are givers,' said his Granny, giving him a kiss. "They think of others."

"And McTacks?"

"McTacks are takers," she said, bumping Barney up and down like he was on a horse. Barney laughed. "McTacks are only out for themselves. And the happiest people in the world are those who do the most for others. You remember that, son. And you'll always be happy."

Even at four years old, Barney knew his Granny was wise. That bit of advice had stuck with him all his life.

CHAPTER 2

ROCKED BY A LOW BLOW

Barney walked down the hospital steps in a kind of dream, only this one he couldn't wake up from. How the hell had he not noticed he was so ill? Advanced stages of lung cancer. Doctor Noble had said it could be subtle but even he had seemed surprised at Barney's physical state. For all purposes he looked a healthy forty-four year old man. Barney thought of Stephen in his hospital bed near the end. He'd looked so gaunt, as if his soul had been sucked out of his body until there was no more left. And what about the boxing gym? He'd have to sort out a good few things before he signed off. Stephen came into his head again.

He couldn't go like that.

It wasn't a case of simply dying. It was pissing and shitting yourself and being too sore to eat, drink or even move. It was relying on others to wash you and wipe your arse. To be trapped in the one place you didn't want to be. To know that people didn't really want to come and see you like that. And their faces if they did come. Trying to conceal the horror at your appearance. Giving useless words of encouragement while dropping off flowers and grapes. No point in bringing a 'get well' card. Have you got a newspaper? Do you want me to change the channel? Moans from the other beds, respectfully ignored. Draw the curtain, would you? People in real pain. Torture. And the stink. Shite and vomit. Sickness and death. Oh god, the stink.

The drive back to his house was a meaningless blur in time. Barney locked his car and stood daydreaming at his reflection in the window.

His illness would be the big topic of conversation where he lived. People would only have one thing to say to him from now on. And if they didn't, he'd see the pity in their eyes. He could picture it plastered all over social media too. All the well wishers and advice and gossip.

He shook his head. Fuck that. Not him. No fucking way.

CHAPTER 3

REELING FROM THE PUNCH (PART 1)

Barney had never been a big drinker but it'd seemed natural to head straight in through the doors of his local pub, the White House, to take stock of the doctor's diagnosis.

"Alright Barney," said Doug, the barman. "Not seen you in a while, mate. What'll it be?"

"Whisky," said Barney in a low voice. "A large one."

"Tough day, pal?"

Barney pulled out a high stool at the end of the bar. "Aye, you could say that."

"Anything you want tae get off your chest?" asked Doug, not knowing he'd just hit the nail on the head. "It seems half the reason I'm here these days. Should get ma'sel a degree in psychology and charge professional rates for listening tae punters' woes."

Barney shook his head and Doug was savvy enough not to press him further. Pouring out an Old Putney with a dash of water, he slid the glass to Barney. "On the hoose, mate."

"Oh, cheers," said Barney, taking a sip. The drink made a small fire inside him. He coughed and tapped his chest. Was that the whiskey or the cancer?

Doug moved back up the bar but kept his eye on Barney, who put down his glass, tilting and rolling its edge on the old wooden counter. For a long time he did nothing except stare into the golden brown liquid.

"Hi Barney, pal," said a voice. When Barney looked up, he saw two of the old regulars, Mick and Willie sitting at the other end of the room. Barney nodded but said nothing, returning to his drink.

Ten years before, Mick and Willie had been part of the famous 'happy day', when an opportunistic clientele decided to lock a mouthy new barman in the cellar and – over a mere twenty-four hours – drink the place dry.

"That's no like Barney," said Mick. "Seems a bit upset."

Willie's eyes were like two piss holes in the snow and he had a nose that wouldn't have looked out of place pulling a sleigh. He was already too bloated with drink to see anything other than happy hour which, according to his calculations, was about one more drink away. "You git thizz roond, Mick... and I'll git the next," he said with a hiccup.

"Aye, right," said Mick. "I ken what yer up tae. By the time we finish ma roond it'll be happy 'oor, and ye'll have saved yersel some dosh. Short arms and deep pockets. That's your trouble."

Doug laughed and continued drying glasses as Willie smiled and swayed from side to side.

Like every other pub in Scotland, the smoking ban had come into effect over ten years ago. However, unlike every other pub in Scotland, the decor in the White House had not been touched. The fabric on the back of the benches and seat pads were ingrained with every kind of tobacco; the smell of smoke, spilled beer and spirits hung thick, and would never go away; a bit like Mick and Willie.

Barney sipped his whisky but the answers weren't coming and the drink wasn't making him feel any better. He didn't want to go home. But he couldn't stay here either. Mulling over everything was only getting him down. He downed the rest, got off his stool and left the pub without so much as a goodbye.

"*Definitely* no like Barney," said Mick.

"No at all," agreed Doug.

"Who?" said Willie. "You got that r-r-roond in yet? Mine's a double."

Barney took a meandering route through the city by way of Duddingston and Holyrood Park. Arthur's seat was strangely quiet for September and he found himself walking the rocky track to the summit, something he hadn't done for years. At the top, a thin golden sunbeam sliced through the grey clouds, a brief ray of sunshine that was gone as quickly as it had appeared. Not unlike his life, or Stephen's, for that matter.

Barney began picking out obvious landmarks: Calton Hill, the Scott Monument, and the Castle, and was able to draw a line through all the places he knew or had run through during his training for fights or as a young tearaway, part of the Young Niddrie Terrors or YNT as they were more commonly known.

He remembered how, as kids, they used to jump on the number fourteen bus, getting off at Princes Street to hang about the shops and grab a Macky D's. Barney and his pals had run riot there; chased out of shops for stealing and fighting with kids from other places who'd *got wide* with them. They'd also met girls from exotic locations such as Penicuik and Glasgow, and tried to get their phone numbers or "bag off" somewhere discreet. They were streetwise and fearless. Nothing could stop them. Exciting times. Barney had left more than just memories on the streets of Edinburgh.

Barney, Tam and wee Euan were standing outside McDonald's dressed 'mod style' in their parka coats and drainpipe trousers. They'd been knocked back from seven pubs already. At only sixteen, none of them had enough facial hair to convince the bouncers they were of legal drinking age. As they loitered without intent, three punk rockers walked past. Big men, rough looking, with wild hair and hard faces. Tam had a notorious mouth on him but nothing to back it up with. Barney whispered through his teeth not to say a fucking word. Wee Euan pawed at Tam's arm like a scared puppy, urging him to keep quiet. Tam looked at him the way you might look at a bogey before flicking it off your finger. But he didn't say anything... not until they were about to turn the corner anyway.

"Shite bags! Away an throw shite at yerselves!" was what he came out with.

The punks stopped. Barney breathed in and held it. Wee Euan took a step back but to his relief, the punks didn't even turn around. Instead they walked on and around the corner. Tam started to laugh and looked to his pals as if to prove his point. Barney let out his air in a whistle. And then the men came charging around the corner at them, two with coshes and the other with a plank of wood with a nail in the end. Barney's first instinct had been to go straight for them, trusting his pals would do the same. But Tam and wee Euan were already bolting past Frasers at full pelt towards Shandwick Place and not looking back. While two of the men tried to catch them, the biggest one took a swing with the stick and caught Barney in the thigh. The nail went all the way in. Barney's leg spasmed and he fell to the ground. The punk put the boot in and Barney took a few kicks to the gut. With one of the wee cheeky bastards done, the punk bolted off after the others, leaving his tool behind. When Barney pulled it out, blood spurted over the pavement. By the time he'd got himself to the hospital his thigh had swelled to the size of a melon around the wound. The nurses cleaned the injury and wrapped it. Then he was given a tetanus and told not to play such silly games with his friends in future.

CHAPTER 4

REELING FROM THE PUNCH (PART 2)

Barney had started to cross the road halfway down Princes Street when a green blur shot past on two wheels and gave him a start. A cyclist in spandex turned back to shout, "Watch where yer going, ya cunt!"

He'd been daydreaming again. Walking without purpose or direction. He looked about him. Bus lanes, tram lines, cycle lanes... what the hell was this street coming to? He stepped onto the pavement and leaned against the railings overlooking the gardens and up to the castle. The old rock walls were even blacker than usual against the green of the hill and the leaden sky. A castle within a city, set upon an extinct volcano. The city he'd been born in. That distinctive and dramatic skyline was part of his life. His eyes ran along the battlements to the flags flicking up and down in the late summer winds. All this time and he'd never actually been inside. He started to cough. Just a little at first, a mere itch in the throat which might have gone away, except that it caught fire like kindle and grew into a violent fit that caused his eyes to water. He took some time to get his breath and then walked on in the direction of the mound.

The drone of bagpipes broke his thought pattern and filled the street as a piper clad in full military dress started a rendition of 'Scotland the Brave' near Waverley Station. That drone always gave him goosebumps. It was the music he'd often walked out to as a young amateur boxer representing his country. Barney watched some tourists drop in a few coins and stand beside the chubby, red-faced piper for a photo. The street was bustling as usual but with the festival finished there was a certain peace about the place, as if the city itself had just closed its front door and was sighing in relief after entertaining some guests who'd well overstayed their welcome.

Grey clouds pulled and stretched across the sky, tearing apart to reveal big gaps of pale blue. People of all ages passed with phones glued to their ears. Others sat in the tranquility of the colourful gardens, reading or just relaxing in groups. A few couples lay wrapped in each other's arms and legs. One pair must've been eighty if they were a day. The old boy was right into his petting in the park.

The doctor's question came back to him again. *Are you married?*

For the first time Barney noticed the tiny gap in his stomach. A little black hole that had started to grow. An emptiness he could not ignore. He had friends of course, and maybe he could've told them about his illness. But he didn't have someone to confide in. Someone you could tell anything and everything. Someone who knew your deepest darkest secrets. Was that the reason he'd focused so much on his businesses, working long hours and keeping busy? To make up for the fact he didn't have anyone? To fill the hole he'd done so well to cover up?

He cut up behind the National Gallery, through Cockburn Street to the Bridges. A maroon and white bus (the colour of Heart of Midlothian football club) struggled up the hill and stopped at the lights. Barney had never been too keen on football but his boxing skills meant no one had ever given him a hard time about it. When he was a kid, if you didn't like football, you were in serious danger of being thought of as gay and getting leathered. However, boxers were given equal respect. Maybe more so. The ability to be violent and tough was what proved you were a man where he grew up.

Most of Barney's friends were Hibernian supporters (the rival faction in the Burgh). A few, like his wee pal, Ben, an exceptional boxer, became involved in the hooligan side of things. They were called *The Capital City Service*. The *CCS* were well known for being a violent crew to come up against. Their deeds were legendary around Scotland. Mass brawls in the streets with rival fans, where not even the police would get involved; guys getting chucked over bridges and even out the top window of a double decker bus. Ben, AKA Southpaw, had been in the thick of it.

While Southpaw had made a big name for himself on the street, Barney had made a name in the ring. His professional record wasn't bad. Commonwealth champion had been as far as he went. A short career ended by niggling injuries and lack of decent promotion. But that was OK. Better to get out with your brains still intact than end up like so many of the old pros, scraping a living, drunk or dead.

Some time later he passed through Newington and Prestonfield, picking up some flowers on his way into Craigmillar Castle Park Cemetery; the final resting place of his family. Barney paused at the black iron gates to tuck in his shirt and put a comb through his hair. Then he walked along the path to find his family plot and the headstone he'd got specially carved in their memory. He'd been here five months ago for

Stephen's anniversary and it seemed unreal that he'd be joining him in only a matter of weeks. He'd never been able to picture his body in a coffin. There was something so claustrophobic about it. As a kid he'd always feared being put inside one. Just a silly childish fear. As if he'd ever be lying in a coffin if he wasn't already dead.

*Barney and Tam shouldn't have been up there. Their gang
had used wire cutters to break into a building site because
that's the kind of thing you got up to as a kid in Niddrie in the
evenings when there was nothing else to do. They climbed
ladders and explored the scaffolding but couldn't see in the
darkness where the contractor had neglected to fit a safety
barrier. Someone called out "Barney!" at the exact moment
he and Tam came to the edge of a level. Barney stopped to see
who'd shouted his name. Tam didn't, and fell two floors down
to break both legs.*

*Another time he'd been on his way to the harbour to join his
friends on a fishing trip. He was late and running fast when
he rolled over on some uneven ground and twisted his ankle.
He limped the rest of the way but took so long the other boys
left without him. It was the next morning he learned of the
accident. All three of his friends had drowned after their boat
capsized. It was the first time Barney would attend the funeral of anyone his own age.*

CHAPTER 5

A FORMIDABLE OPPONENT

It had been another one of those days where walking seemed the best thing to do. He'd arrived late at the doors of Edinburgh Castle and spent a few hours exploring. Might as well start ticking things off the bucket list. A bite to eat and a pint led him into an open mike night at Whistle Binkies pub. It'd been alright until some guy who called himself, 'Big James the Karaoke King,' got up and murdered, "My Way". Of all the songs he could've sung, he had to pick that one.

Barney started to cough and left without finishing his beer to go walking over the Bridges towards the New Town with the final lines, "And now I face, the final curtain..." being belted out by Big James for comfort.

The soles of his shoes had never touched so much pavement. Earlier he'd roved up and down the Cowgate and High street, browsing mystical shops and secondhand book stores until he ended up in the National Gallery, passing some time gazing at paintings and weird sculptures that some people called art. The same feeling of not knowing what to do or where to go guided him to the swanky George Street bar, a place neither Barney nor any of his mates would have chosen for a night out.

It was the kind of establishment that served fancy cocktails with umbrellas and sparklers, not real drinks. He was scrutinised by a pair of bouncers who looked more like male fashion models. Lucky they only had to deal with toffs and wannabes. Guys like that would be eaten alive by some of the clientele at the White House on a Saturday night.

Down the stairs and through some french doors, Barney entered a dimly lit basement level room. The interior might have been decorated by Jean Paul Gaultier. Pink spotted wallpaper and blue neon beams collided with soft fabrics and curving couches that ran the length of the walls. There were even private booths with curtains for privacy. What went on in there after midnight?

The people here seemed to be clones of each other. The guys all had the same gelled over hair style and were dressed in shiny shirts a size too small, tucked into neat fitting trousers and pointed leather shoes. The girls all wore tight dresses that only just covered their backsides. Cleavage was abundant and he could imagine Tesco Tam's eyes popping out if he ever made it past the doormen into the honey pot.

Everyone seemed to be staring at everyone else. A few were talking, but even then their concentration was more on the people around them. Barney brushed past a strong mix of cologne and perfume and pulled out a bar stool with a leopard skin seat. A mirror ran the full length of the bar. In fact there were mirrors everywhere. The clientele made good use of them.

Two seats down to his right sat a stunner in a black dress. Legs crossed. Nice legs, toned, with black high heels. Her auburn hair was swept back. A sophisticated woman if ever Barney had seen one. Out of his league, of course. Women like that didn't go for guys like Barney. They went for toffs and rich, smarmy guys who could buy them big cars and diamonds every week.

A barmaid who might have been a model, if she'd only been taller, handed him a menu.

"I'm no hungry, darling," said Barney.

The girl frowned. "It's a drinks menu," she said, opening it and pointing to the word *cocktails*.

"Do you serve beer?"

The girl rolled her eyes. "Yahha..."

"I'll have a pint then."

The barmaid gave a tut and walked down the bar to open a cabinet that seemed rarely used. She took out a tall, thin glass and proceeded to pull a pint with far too much froth at the top.

"Can I get some beer with that?" said Barney.

"Seven pounds twenty-five," the girl said, holding out her hand.

"I said one pint, hen, no two." The barmaid looked bored as Barney handed over the cash.

A female voice to Barney's right said, "They're not used to people with banter in this place." To his surprise, Barney turned to see the stunner with the auburn hair looking at him. She stirred her drink with a cocktail stick and then placed an olive in her mouth.

"Is that any good?" asked Barney.

"Not bad," she said, offering her hand to Barney. "I'm Grace."

"Pleased to meet you, Grace. I'm Barnabas Wild. Barney, to my friends." Barney gave Grace's slender hand a squeeze. Cool soft fingers responded with a good squeeze of their own.

"Barnabas Wild," Grace said, raising her eyebrows but not releasing her grip. "Unusual name." With a quick movement, she turned Barney's hand over, examining the front and back, running her finger over his knuckles and pinching at the fingernails.

"You're not a bunny boiler, are you?" Barney asked. "I've heard the more beautiful a woman is, the crazier she'll be."

Grace continued her examination and answered in a calm voice. "No, I'm actually a patron of the RSPCA."

Grace looked up into Barney's eyes. No, not *in* his eyes. *Around* his eyes. And then at his nose, squinting, scrutinising. "Uhu..." she said, and then slid off her stool and moved closer, fixating on Barney's chin. "Hmmm..." She put two fingers on his left cheekbone and turned his face to the side, "Interesting..."

Barney didn't object to her examination. "Is this what you do to everyone you meet?" he asked.

Grace ignored him as she lifted his hands once more and then flipped them over to run her thumb over his index and middle finger knuckles.

"Okay," she began, "first of all, you *used* to be a boxer. Though you're not anymore."

Barney's eyebrows shot up.

"So I'm right!" Grace reached back to collect her drink and sipped at her straw before continuing. "In terms of work, you've used your hands most of your life. I thought you might have been a chef, at some point, because of the scars on your finger tips."

Barney was about to tell her how far off the mark she was when Grace said, "Hold on, I only said, I thought you *might* have been. Because, when I considered it, your hands were too rough, dry, and weathered." She took his hands again, this time more delicately. "These hands have done manual work for a long time. Leathered palms built up through years of hard graft." She let her hands slip down his fingers and then let go. "My dad had hands like this," she said. "But I'm going to go with *carpets*."

"Are you a witch?" Barney asked.

"I've been called worse," said Grace. "I'm a lawyer."

"That makes sense."

"So, I'm right again?"

Barney took a sip of his beer and nodded. "I was a boxer first and then a carpet fitter. But how did you work all that out?"

Grace gave a sly look and tapped her nose with her finger.

"Okay, Miss Marple," said Barney, "just tell me how you knew about the boxing."

"Scar tissue around the eyebrows," said Grace, in a matter of fact way. "Thin cuts. Caused by gloves or a clash of heads. Your nose has been broken, not badly, but enough to notice, if you're looking carefully. Also, one of your ears is slightly cauliflowered. Together these suggest a fighter. Oh, and your left canine---"

"Aye, alright," said Barney stopping her. "I get the picture. Brad Pitt isn't going tae worry aboot me taking his handsomest man title this year."

Grace laughed. There was something of the cat about her. Her green eyes were calculating, clever, curious and playful.

"Your handsome enough, Barnabas Wild," she said, almost mocking him. "Oh, and the carpets deduction... I got that from the scars on your finger tips. Stanley knife. That had to be how you nicked them."

Barney smiled and played it cool. "But how'd you know so much about boxing? I mean, you'd have to know to look for those signs."

"My Granddad was a boxer when he was young. He used to tell me stories about his fights, and all the greats. By the time I was eight I knew everything about the sport. He taught me some moves and even took me to a few bouts in Edinburgh. My dad thought I was nuts. When my Granddad passed away, I told my dad I wanted to box. Of course, he said no. But I was persuasive. And persistent."

"I can see that," said Barney.

Grace lowered her eyebrows and tried to look serious. "Eventually my dad gave in and bought me some gloves. He taught me the stuff he knew from my Granddad. He'd get up early in the mornings just to train me and then work fifteen hour shifts so my sister and I could have a good education. The proudest moment of his life was when I graduated from Edinburgh Uni."

"Sounds like a good man," said Barney.

"He was," said Grace, "the best."

"Was?"

"He died last year. We thought for a while he was going to get through it, but then he just went downhill. Cancer."

The word caught Barney like a sneaky left hook to the liver. He took a quick sip of his pint, put his hand to his mouth and gave a slight cough. When he put his glass back on the counter, Grace was gazing deep into his eyes. Fearless and confronting; sure and unashamed of the slight watering that had come through to make the green iris glisten like emeralds tilted under a light.

"I'm sorry aboot your dad," said Barney.

Grace waved her hand and took another sip from her cocktail. Let's talk about something else," she said, coming back to life again. "Like, for instance, what is a guy like *you* doing in a place like *this*? And on a weekday too?"

"What d'you mean?" asked Barney waving his arm across the counter. "This is my local. They love me here."

The barmaid pouting into the mirror caught sight of Barney staring at her. She rolled her eyes and shook her head, moving away down the bar for privacy. Grace laughed.

"And what about you?" asked Barney. "Did you come here by yourself just to sit drinking cocktails all night?"

"Do you mean, am I single?" asked Grace.

"Aye. Suppose I do."

Grace sipped her drink and Barney watched as she pushed her fingers through her hair. She was gorgeous.

"I'm divorced," she said.

"Is that right?" said Barney, leaning forward on his stool.

"My friend is over there being courted by some guy with polished white teeth. And stop changing the subject. I asked you a question first."

Barney gave a wink. "Let's just say, I've been touring the city today," he said. "Seeing things from a new perspective."

Grace's eyes changed again, as she tried to figure him out. "Well I hope it's an improved perspective, now that you've met me, Mr. Wild."

Barney lifted his glass. Grace gave it a tap with her own and they both downed the last of their drinks. Grace's gaze momentarily moved to the dance floor where she caught sight of her friend leaving with the Colgate tooth model. The cheeky bitch hadn't even bothered to say goodbye; couldn't wait to get some action.

Grace turned back to Barney. "And on that note," she said, "do you fancy walking me home?"

As Grace leaned forward off the stool, Barney took in the uplifting view of her cleavage. "Aye, of course," he said.

Outside was nippy. Grace shivered and locked her arm around Barney's. They only walked about ten minutes to a posh Newtown house when Grace stopped and said, "This is me."

"Nice place," said Barney.

Grace stared back.

"I was wondering..." said Barney.

"Yes?" said Grace, quickly.

"If you'd like to meet up again sometime," said Barney.

Grace gave almost nothing away. "When?" she asked.

"Saturday," said Barney. "How about I arrange a taxi to pick you up at ten o'clock?"

"On a Saturday *morning*?"

"Aye."

"Where would you take me?"

"Destination's a secret."

"I like mysteries," Grace said. "And what if I *did* decide to take you up on your offer? What would I wear?"

"Gym gear. Running stuff," replied Barney.

"Okay," Grace said, slowly moving in, "I'll think about it."

"Will you now?" Barney put his arms around her and held her body to his own.

"Yeah, that's what I said. I'll think about it." She looked up, dark pupils pushing the green inside her eyes to the outer edges. Barney saw the opportunity and took it. Her lips were soft and she tasted like mint. Her hands moved onto his cheeks and then she pulled back with a smile.

"Goodnight Barnabas Wild," she said, walking up the outer steps and putting her keys in the door. "I'll see you at ten on Saturday."

Barney asked how you knew which person you were go-
ing to marry. It's just a feeling, his Granny said. Something
warm and familiar. They know you and you know them,
even if you've just met. You don't have to act or pretend. And
when they're sad, you're sad. And when they're happy, you're
happy. And you'll do anything for them. It's like when I met
your granddad. I couldn't stop looking at him. And he was the
same. Coming to see me everyday. Taking me to the dancing.
Sending me flowers and chocolates.

Do you miss him?

Granny had smiled at this and somehow she'd looked sad and
happy at the same time. She took a wee breath. Every day,
she said.

CHAPTER 6

A GENTLE SPAR

The taxi stopped outside an old church in a rough part of town. Barney was there waiting and opened the cab door, giving Grace a peck on the cheek and then telling her to close her eyes. He took her hand and put his arm around her back onto her hip, guiding her onto the pavement and through the doors of the converted church. "Skin tight lycra leggings definitely suit you," he said.

"Oh for God's sake!"

"Keep those eyes shut," Barney said, putting his hand over her eyes.

The taxi driver gave Barney a toot and a thumbs up.

When they were inside Barney told Grace to open her eyes. She let out a breath and said, "I don't believe it!" A boxing ring with blue ropes took centre stage in front of her. Punch bags and floor to ceiling balls lined the walls. Weights and gym equipment in the corners. Mirrors everywhere with racks full of gloves, head guards and skipping ropes. A couple of regulars were laying into the heavy bags and skipping in the corner.

"The other night you talked the talk..." Barney said, leading her to the ring.

"Oh don't you worry, Barnabas Wild," said Grace, climbing up and entering through the middle rope. "I walk the walk too." She shuffled her feet and put her hands into the air just like 'The Greatest'.

That evening, they went to the Witchery on the Royal Mile for dinner and then walked hand in hand along Princes Street. Barney's cough had not troubled him. The castle was lit up in amber floodlights and the red wine had made Grace more affectionate. "I love the castle at night," she said, taking his arm and leaning her head into Barney's shoulder.

"There's a better view of it from somewhere else," said Barney.

"Where?" asked Grace.

Barney only winked as they stopped at the foot of the Scott Monument. An old man was waiting outside. "Alright Barney," he said, opening the door.

"Thanks, Bill."

"I thought this shut at night?" said Grace.

"It does, but I ken Bill, the caretaker. Got him some boxing tickets a while back and asked if he'd do me a wee favour."

Grace's eyes glimmered. "You are full of surprises, Mr. Wild!"

The steep winding staircase eventually led them to a small plateau where they looked down on Princes Street and then to the castle.

"It *is* even better from up here!" said Grace. She turned to Barney. "Thank you." Barney smiled and gave her a hug. Grace's hands went to Barney's cheeks, her nails graced his stubble. She lifted her head to him and they kissed. Her lips were soft and cool from the night air, a taste of smooth strawberry lip gloss remained behind as she looked up at him. Barney's heart did the equivalent of an Ali shuffle and his Granny's words came back to him. This is what it felt like when you met the person you were going to spend the rest of your life with.

Just for a moment, Barney pretended everything was all right. Pretended he was well and had a future. It felt so good that, just for a moment, he believed it.

CHAPTER 7

ONLY ONE WAY OUT

Barney blinked the sleep out of his eyes and sat up on the bed. Grace had left a note telling him she had to go into work on some important case but that he could stay if he wanted.

He felt rough. But what a night they'd had. That click. That spark. It was like being a teenager again. As he sat up something caught in his throat, unleashing a deep, guttural convulsion through his chest. Barney swung his knees over the side of the bed and chose to ignore it. Just a hangover. That was all. He took a sip of water from the glass on the bedside table and then walked into an elegant bathroom, the type only a woman with money would have. Free-standing tub with candles, a large mirror set above a huge Moroccan tile basin. Polished brass

taps and a walk-in shower that could have accommodated four
people and their dog. Barney cupped his hands under the tap to
splash some cold water on his face and then came the coughing
fit which left him reeling. When he recovered he spat into the
sink like a boxer between rounds gasping for breath.

"What the hell are you doing, Barney?"

The face staring back at him looked no different than it had
a few days ago, but inside he knew. His body wasn't his own. A
microscopic intruder had broken in and waged a silent war on
the cells of his lungs. Subtle and stealthy. A secret infiltration
undiscovered until the campaign was almost over. An opponent
he couldn't beat. Not with all the precision punches and combi-
nations he knew. He decided not to stay any longer.

Grace called Barney's phone around lunch time but he didn't
answer. She left a message asking if he wanted to go out the
following evening. Maybe he could tell her. Warn her. Let her
decide. The thought gave him some hope. His fingers moved
to reply just as the next coughing fit started. This one made the
morning attack feel like a warm-up. Every time he thought it

had ended it would only start off another convulsion, building up into a crescendo of heaving and gasping. Barney keeled over and groaned, his stomach muscles contracting tight to the ribs as he finally brought up a deluge of unrecognisable fluid that burned his throat. He leaned over the kitchen sink and spat. His sides were sore and he suddenly felt cold. Bone cold. His hands were trembling. He recalled how the nurses in the cancer ward always had the temperature turned up because the patients complained of being cold. He touched his mouth and saw traces of blood on his finger tips. Sickness swelled into his mouth from his throat and he puked.

This was it then. The beginning of the end.

He couldn't have a life with Grace, no matter how much he wanted to. And no way would he allow her to see him rot away. Especially not after she'd nursed her father through it the year before. Barney was a fighter. He wasn't going to linger around like a bad fart just to endure the pain of a slow demise. No. Better to go quick and on his own terms. He'd done enough in his life to be proud of himself. There was no shame in it.

Barney was nothing if not practical. He had time to figure things out. He'd let Grace down as gently as he could and tie up the loose ends. He'd contact his accountant and lawyer the next day and sort his affairs out. Walking through to the living room, he picked up the Evening News which lay on the coffee table. Plastered on the front page was a picture of the brand new Queensferry Crossing.

'Over a hundred and fifty metres at its highest point,' it said.

So far no one had died working on it, unlike the railway and road bridges that had taken their toll of workmen, many killed by the fall into the cold waters of the Firth of Forth.

Another quick cough. Bits of saliva hit the newspaper but no blood this time. Barney put the paper down. The silence of the house pulsed inside his ear. He was far too aware of being alone.

CHAPTER 8

FORTH RAILWAY BRIDGE

He'd woken up in darkness at 4am feeling as lonely as any human being could. The anxious stirring inside his stomach made sleep impossible. It made life impossible too. He made up his mind then and there. No point in trying to eat breakfast. A cup of tea and then he left the house.

The old BMW rumbled towards the stretch of water known as the Firth of Forth and Barney noted the weather warning on the overhead signs.

HIGH WINDS - NO HGV's OR HIGH-SIDED
VEHICLES ALLOWED ON THE FORTH ROAD
BRIDGE.

To his right, he could see the old railway bridge. A few tiny silhouettes moving between the red girders confirmed the Southbound Walkway was still open. Nearly a week had gone by since the doctor's diagnosis and Barney's coughing had only gotten worse. He'd settled his affairs and felt in some small way that he was master of his fate again. Even if it was only how and when he'd meet the inevitable.

Barney parked the car and got out into what might have been the most miserably grey day there had ever been. Dreich. Dour. Depressing. He shoved his hands deep inside his coat pockets, dipped his chin and walked with short, quick steps onto the pedestrian access of the railway bridge. A blustering gale blew hard into his chest as if two hands were pushing against him. He leaned forward and turned his head to the side to breathe. Water streamed from his eyes as the bridge itself swayed from side to side in the wind. It didn't seem safe. But then again, what did that matter?

Barney stopped when he thought he was about half way across.

Don't think about it. It'll all be over before you know it.

The railing was high. He tried to lift his leg onto the bar three times before choosing to push up and get one leg over and then the other. Facing the track with his back to the sea, he heard a low rumbling that shook through the metal. The vibration grew in intensity until the approaching train whizzed by, not six feet from where he stood, rattling the structure with such ferocity that Barney clutched the bar and pulled himself tight to the metal. A surge of wind sucked into the rusty-red ribcage of the iron monster and Barney closed his eyes. The thought of slitting his wrists had just been too gruesome. He'd read that pills were slow, often excruciating in the stomach and not always guaranteed to work. The last thing he wanted was to be found by someone and then sectioned in the Royal Ed.

This was one of the highest bridges in Scotland and also one of the easiest to jump from. Not many barriers or people to stop you. A quick, painless death, he'd reasoned.

The wind calmed for a moment and Barney took a few quick breaths before attempting to turn around.

One move at a time.

Left foot first. Find the ledge. Good.

Now the left hand. Let go and reach to grip the bar again.

Now turn and face the sea. Don't look down whatever you do.

Barney attempted to keep his gaze locked on the highest point of the road bridge opposite, but the temptation was too great. Just a quick look to see how high he was. Why not? Might as well see what was below...

Holy fuck!

It was only a glimpse but the image of thick grey water rolling like mercury was branded into his mind. Barney shut his eyes but could not help imagining the grey mass rising up and making a grab for him. His legs lost all feeling and his knuckles turned white as his fingers tightened around the cold iron bar. Behind closed eyes everything was exaggerated as the bridge, the sea and Barney all swung from side to side in the howling wind.

He counted down from ten and pictured himself jumping.

When he got to five, he thought about what might happen if he didn't die from the fall. He imagined the impact of such a fall. Bones would break. He'd be stunned, possibly paralysed as an icy sea filled his clothes and shoes and then gradually numbed his limbs. He wasn't a good swimmer. He'd panic. Splash around, as the cold water of the forth forced him into taking his first gulp. Drowning was unthinkable. A terrible way to go.

Barney opened his eyes and shuffled centimetre by centimetre over to a pole placed just in front of the railing. He wrapped his arm around it, tight to the shoulder. But fear overcame him and he couldn't move. He closed his eyes again.

The bridge began to vibrate as another train approached. A few cold rain drops hit his cheeks.

Just let go. Head first. The fall will do the rest.

Against all his instincts, Barney let the fingers of his right hand release one by one. The left hand followed, pinky through to thumb. He took a slow deep breath and started to lean forwards. This was it. He could feel himself about to go...

A terrific gust suddenly shook the bridge and Barney was pressed back into the railing. Rain pelted from all sides and he felt sick in his stomach. He opened his eyes and the sea seemed to leap up at him. Barney flinched and his right shoe slipped on the slick wet ledge. He made a desperate grab for the pole shouting, "Fuck!" as he clung on, feet kicking the air to find a foothold. The tips of his fingers were all that kept him from the drop into the cold, grey sea. The mocking wind found every hollow and hole in the metal.

Heavy rain bounced off the girders making the old structure shriek and groan. Barney's finger nails clawed into the very paint of the bridge. Pure adrenaline and fear kept him holding on, as he swung from side to side, a human pendulum in the gale.

"Help!" he cried, hoping someone might be near. But no sensible person was out in the driving rain and winds. The pinky fingers betrayed him first. Then it was the ring fingers. Then the index's. Only the middle fingers kept on, as a final fuck you to the world. His last ounce of strength wained. The middle fingers came off one then the other. Barney gasped and fell.

A second later his arse hit a grated metal ledge, knocking the wind out of him. He lay on his back blinking up at an under-carriage ten foot below the railway line itself. The passing train roared overhead like thunder and Barney's body jarred each time the carriages hit a ridged section.

With a groan, he rolled onto his side. All notions of jumping had now deserted him as he lay stunned and utterly alone in the rain. He hit his fist off the metal grating and yelled. "FUCK IT!"

Despite himself, Barney welled up. His gran had often said that a good cry was sometimes exactly what was needed and so he lay there a while, shivering in the cold, wind and rain. A certain peace came over him. An acceptance. Or maybe just the adrenaline dump. Two weeks ago he'd been happy enough and running a marathon, this week he was trying to end his life do-ing a Peter Pan from the Forth Rail Bridge. What would his gran think of him now?

"This won't do," he heard her say. "Come on Barney, pick yourself up son." Even if it was only his imagination or memo-ry, the voice got Barney to his feet. He sighed, sniffing and wip-ing his eyes and nose. The cold and damp set off his cough. He checked his pockets and found his car keys were still there.

The kettle boiled and clicked, leaving a trail of steam running along the underside of the kitchen cupboards. Barney sighed and scrunched up the picture of the Queensferry Crossing. If he'd felt bad before, he felt worse now. A failed suicide attempt. Bottled it at the decisive moment.

He poured himself a cup of tea and popped some strong pain killers from the silver packet. Two capsules lay in his hand. Two. There was a bottle of whisky in the cupboard and enough left in the packet to do the job. He thought about it. Filling up his belly and drinking himself unconscious. He was going to die. There was no way out of it. The will was written. He'd made sure of everything. It was just the act of taking his own life. It went too much against the grain; like quitting during a fight. It didn't matter how much of a beating you were taking, pride or some warped sense of optimism kept you in there. So what choice did he have other than to grind it out and take the pain and humiliation? It didn't have to be in hospital. It could be here, in his own house, in his own bed.

He slurped his hot tea and started to think. Maybe there was another way? A way in which he wouldn't have to kill himself or succumb to cancer. A way in which he wouldn't know when or where his end was coming.

"Of course," he said, putting down his mug. "Roman Rock."

Roman Rock had invited "Salty" Mcguire, head of the infamous McGuire family, into his office to have a talk. McGuire's intention was to get Roman to respect his family's territory, built up over years of intimidation and violence. That side of Edinburgh belonged to them, he said. McGuire knew Roman was ruthless. That was his nickname. What McGuire didn't know was that Roman was also smart. He'd realised a long time ago that life was similar to chess. To be in control of things, you needed to be a few moves ahead of your opponent. He'd already paid off enough people to find out the McGuires' plans and their weaknesses. If McGuire had paid more attention to his surroundings, he'd have noticed Roman's extensive book collection, which included all sorts of philosophy from the East, including Sun Tzu's the Art of War. 'Know yourself and your enemy and you shall fight a hundred battles without defeat,' was one of Roman's favourite quotes. Roman presented a charming, reasonable facade and talked of peace between himself and the McGuires, offering a truce and a favourable share of wealth and business. More than McGuire had expected but not so much as to make him suspicious. He told McGuire he was branching out on an international scale

and a war on his home turf was bad for business. It would be better to have allies than enemies. Salty agreed. There were mutual interests and gains in working together, said Roman, who tapped out two lines of cocaine and said they would take one each to let bygones be bygones, in a new spirit of co-operation. After all, Edinburgh was surely big enough for both of them. When McGuire agreed, they shook hands and had their lines. The effects of the cocaine laced with cyanide went quickly into McGuire's brain and bloodstream. Red gushed down each nostril and he held his head and throat as if they were on fire. Roman watched him expire on the carpet. Fingers contorted into claws. Eyes bulging from their sockets. Salty's face a picture of agony. Dead in a matter of minutes. Roman's two-line cocaine trick was a secret known only to four people. Two of those people had died from knowing it first hand. The rest of the McGuires were killed off in what the police called gangland executions. Roman was suspected of ordering the hits but no one could prove anything. Where in the past the most powerful Kingpins and Drug Lords had hailed from Glasgow, Roman had now changed the players and the game, establishing himself as the most ruthless and feared Godfather in Scotland.

CHAPTER 9

SCOOBY DOO AND
THE TASMANIAN DEVIL

Dave and Marty received their instructions on a folded piece of paper. "Be there at one o'clock to collect the package," Hatchet told them. "That's one AM, not PM," he said, just to be clear.

It was still early when they got home, so Marty suggested they grab a bite to eat and then go on to the fancy dress party he'd found out about from some bird he knew.

"Why no?" Dave said. "Mind we've still got thay cracking costumes from the stag do a few years back?"

"Oh aye!" said Marty. "Perfect!"

The two men arrived dressed as Scoobie Doo and the Tasmanian Devil. Their costumes went down well. Pished by

midnight and chock full of party drugs, they'd only remembered about the package when Marty's watch started beeping
at twelve-thirty, a wise emergency measure that Dave insisted
they take.

They got a taxi to the house and rang the doorbell but there
was no answer.

"The boy must've gone tae his scratcher," said Dave. "Look,
there's a drainpipe, I'll gie ye a bunk up."

From across the street, Mrs. Baxter opened her curtains to
see Scooby Doo giving the Tasmanian Devil a leg-up onto the
drainpipe of the house opposite.

Using the pipe, Marty scrambled up to the porch roof and got
to his feet. From here, he was able to do a half pull-up whilst
jumping to tap the bedroom window. Dave was giving him the
thumbs up so Marty started dancing. Both started giggling. It
got so funny, they couldn't stop.

Suddenly, a light went on in the bedroom. Marty turned
and a woman screamed so loud he staggered back and fell off
the roof, landing on Dave and knocking them both out in the
process.

When they came to, there were blue flashing lights and two
police officers standing over them. "What are you two up tae?"
the first policeman asked, shining a torch in their eyes. The smell
of booze and cannabis on the two wasters was overpowering.

"Just calling in on a mate," said Dave, removing his Scooby-Doo costume head and encouraging Marty to do the same.

"What number?" asked the other policeman.

"Twenty-four," said Dave.

"Twenty-four's the hoose next door," said the first policeman.

"Ah, right, sorry aboot that."

"Hold on," said the second cop. "Why don't we all go around together just to check and see these two get in alright."

"Nah, nae need," said Dave, "honestly, we're fine."

"Aye," said Marty. "We're fine."

"We insist," said the second policeman.

The constables picked the men up and they all went to call in on the house next door.

"I'm sorry to bother you sir," said the first policeman, when the door opened. "It's just we've had some suspicious activity next door and wanted to make sure everything was in order. Could you identify the two characters standing behind me?"

"Aye," said the man, "Scooby Doo and the Tasmanian Devil."

The first policeman turned to see the two characters with their heads back on. The second officer never turned. He was smiling at the man standing in the door. Except his smile wasn't a nice one.

"Hello Jimmy!" he said.

"Eh?" said the man, suddenly looking worried.

"Constable Easton," said constable Taylor. "May I introduce you to none other than, *Jimmy the Deal*, infamous conman and low-life who skipped bail in Glasgow last year and has been missing ever since."

Constable Easton gave Jimmy a grin, showing a missing tooth he'd lost breaking up a fight a few weeks ago. "Isn't that a nice wee coincidence?" he said.

"They were all so worried about you in Strathclyde, Jimmy," said Constable Taylor. "Thought something *nasty* might have happened to you. Glad to see you're in good health."

Constable Easton radio'd in to say they'd just arrested two suspects whilst calling in on the notorious *Jimmy the Deal*.

"I've never seen these two cunts in ma life!" said Jimmy.

"Nonsense," said Constable Taylor. "You just positively identified them to me and constable Easton here! You're nicked pal!"

Dave and Marty sobered up in the cells, while Jimmy the Deal was questioned long enough for a search warrant to be made out. Some detectives returned with Jimmy to his address and found an interesting package all wrapped up like a birthday present. Upstairs they found a counterfeit note-printing machine and a specialised paper tray.

Jimmy went back to the station in cuffs just as Dave and Marty were let out with a caution. There was a bit of angry shouting from Jimmy.

"HE's going tae hear aboot this! HE's going tae kill you two fucking clowns!"

The police had a good idea of who HE was, though they knew Jimmy would never confirm it. It was more than his life was worth.

As for Dave and Marty, the officers knew the punishment they would receive from HIM was far worse than anything the police or crown could offer.

CHAPTER 10

THE GAME PLAN

The iron gates buzzed open and the deep bass voice on the telecom told Barney to come to the front door. He was aware he was being watched. CCTV cameras had been fitted all around Roman's plush Milton Road East mansion. Barney walked up the long curving sandstone driveway that most people would have called a road. On it was parked a silver Bentley with classic wood and cream leather interior, and a red Ferrari Testarossa sparkling with newly applied wax winking at him from the open garage.

Barney approached the tall greek pillars of the entrance where a sign read:

"BEWARE OF THE PARROT!"

The clang of five separate latches being drawn back one after the other on an impressive oak front door was followed by the sound of a large dog barking. Barney saw the sharp teeth and moist black nose of Roman's Alsatian, Floyd as the door opened by inches. Stooping down to hold him by the collar was Big Philip 'Boneheed' McCracken, all six-foot nine of him.

Floyd remembered Barney's smell and voice and was soon licking his hand and wagging his tail. Boneheed let Barney in, saying, "He's in his man cave."

McCracken had to stoop about a foot to avoid hitting his head as they entered Roman's private lift. A life-sized image of Pablo Escobar was plastered on the left wall. On the opposite wall was an equally sized black and white of Roman himself. Roman had told Barney years before that he and Escobar were similar men. The photos were unnerving. Like standing between a lion and a tiger. Barney felt sure this was another one of Roman's psychological ploys, intended to scare the shite out of any visitors.

Down one floor, the doors opened to reveal a large open plan lounge area. An extra long L-shaped white couch sat in front of a giant TV, which took up most of the square inches of the side wall. The football was on with the volume turned down. There was ample space for the antique snooker table and a bar stocked with all the best spirits and beers on tap. A couple of original Jack Vetriano paintings hung on the walls around what

Roman called 'The billiard room'. Barney recognised two more of Roman's goons, Hatchet the Halfwit and Billy Blow, having a drink and playing darts.

Billy Blow had got his name because of a massive cocaine habit which he'd somehow managed to kick a few years back. During his lowest spell, Billy had even asked a local heavyweight to break his nose to stop him from snorting. Hatchet the Halfwit was the kind of person who had just the right amount of intelligence to take everything literally. The 'Hatchet' part of his name came from when he'd once tried to hit Billy with an axe and accidentally swiped half his own ear off in the process.

Barney had been in the man cave before and was used to the extravagant decor and toys that furnished Roman's house. What he wasn't used to was the sight of two men stripped to their under pants with their arms tied behind their backs. One of the men was lying on the ground face up, holding a golf tee and ball between his teeth. The other one, about eight metres away, was tied to the frame of a golf net. This man had his pants down at his ankles and was bent over so that his arse was sticking out like a target.

Roman was standing over the guy on the ground, all tee'd up with the head of his Big Bertha resting on the guy's forehead. To look at Roman, you might misunderstand him. His curly black hair, curly black eyebrows and matching curly black moustache, together with his gold medallions and fat gold rings, gave him a short tempered but almost comic appearance. Except Roman was no joke. A big man with a hair-trigger temper that could get psychotic. 'Violent but fair,' he told people. And the sick thing was, he believed it.

"Now, listen up you cunts," Roman said. "I'm no the best golfer in the world, so..."

The man balancing the golf ball in his teeth started to speak, whereby the ball tipped out onto his eye and rolled across the floor. He groaned, spat out the tee, and then said, "Please Mr. Rock. We're sorry. It wasn't our fault. We---"

"Quiet David," said Roman. "You were warned. Nae mare outbursts like that or I'll have tae change tae ma pitching wedge. And I always take a *big* divot wae that club. If you would, McCracken..."

Boneheed placed the ball back on the tee and pushed it into Dave's mouth, giving him a friendly slap on the cheek.

"Now," said Roman, "if that ball falls oot again, I'm going tae take a practice shot intae the top of your skull." Dave gave a soft moan and stared at the ball with wide, concerned eyes but his breaths were quick and forced. "The mare still you are, David, the mare likely I am tae hit a nice, clean shot." Dave's breathing calmed noticeably.

"That's better," said Roman.

Roman composed himself, looked down the carpeted fair-way, wiggled the club, shook his hips and then swung. His connection was a little high on the ball which went low, taking a bounce straight through Marty's legs and into the net. Marty breathed a sigh of relief.

"Topped it," said Roman. "Thousands spent on golf lessons and still I top ma fucking drives. Now, where was I? Oh aye. David. Martin. You came tae me asking for work. I gave you a chance. A probationary period tae prove yourselves. I asked you tae complete one, simple, little task, and you cunts turned it intae the biggest fucking farce I've ever heard of, which not only lost me a new business but also put an associate of mine in the stardy. Jimmy the Deal looks like he'll be there a while. Luckily he's no grass. If he was, I might've been in some trouble. And then he'd have had tae commit suicide in prison. Which would've cost me a lot of money. Money you two cunts could-nae have raised in ten *fucking* years!"

Roman had shouted the last bit and his deep gravelled voice had gone through the very particles of the room and everybody in it, including Barney.

Silence as Roman composed himself. "So, David, Martin," he began again, "I dinnae care if we're here all night. 18 holes. 36

holes. 162 holes. Naebdy leaves till I get a hole in one! But, just to keep it interesting, what we'll dae is swap positions after every roond. That's fair, isn't it McCracken?"

Boneheed grinned. "Very fair, Mr. Rock."

Barney cleared his throat and came into view.

"Well, look who it is!" said Roman, changing instantly. "Ma wee pal, Barney! How're you keeping?" Roman immediately went over and shook Barney's hand up and down, almost wrenching it from his shoulder socket as he pulled his old friend into a manly hug and finished the ordeal with a firm slap on the back which sent Barney coughing.

"Oh dear, you'll need tae get some medicine for that, Barney. You sound like me in the mornings before I have ma coffee. I'll bet you've come for that two grand I owe you. Well, I have it ready for you, pal. I dinnae ken how you dae all thay marathons. I couldnae manage one mile never mind twenty-six. Cash is good, eh?"

"Actually Roman, I'm here for a different reason."

"Oh aye? What's that then?"

"Can we go somewhere more private. It's important."

Roman stopped and stared at Barney. He looked white. Bags under eyes that were red and tired looking. There was none of the usual spark. Barney was worried about something. But Roman kept it cool in front of the other men.

"Course we can. Right. McCracken, keep thay two cunts here. I'm no finished wae them yet. No by a long way."

Roman began walking to the lift doors. "Come wae me Barney, son, and we'll have a wee drink upstairs."

Roman poured them both a whisky from a crystal decanter and handed Barney a a glass. Floyd stood next to Barney, breathing happily with his mouth open as Roman tapped out two lines of cocaine onto a glass slate on his desk. "Want one?" he asked.

"No thanks. Your wee trick put me off it for life."

"Ah, you remember that?" said Roman with a grin, sniffing up one line, and then the other.

The African Grey parrot which stood on a perch next to Roman's antique desk squawked and then made a sound like someone sniffing. "You're ugly!" it said.

"Shut up, Monty!" growled Roman, wiping his nose. "Behave yersel."

"Get tae fuck!" replied the parrot. Then it said, "Sit Floyd!" in Roman's voice. Floyd sat back on his hind legs and looked to Roman with his ears pricked up.

"I hate when he messes wae Floyd," said Roman. "Poor wee dug. Go and lie doon, Floyd." Floyd waddled to the fireplace and lay down peacefully on the fur rug. Roman's office was kitted out old world style. He'd had some famous designer from London bring in genuine Edwardian furniture.

"So what's so important it cannae wait for me tae hit a golf ball up a man's arse?" Roman asked.

"I want you to put a hit on me," said Barney.

Roman never reacted the way you thought he would. That's one of the reasons he was so dangerous. He could go from charming to psychotic and back again as if a switch flicked in his brain. And it could happen over the smallest things. Right now, he sat in his leather chair behind his desk and took another sip of whisky. When he reclined, the expensive leather creaked and stretched. He drummed his fingers on the arm rests. "You're serious."

"Aye," said Barney.

Roman fixed his gaze on Barney. Many a man had crumbled under that examination, blurted out a bit too much, maybe made a few nervous movements; some had even broken down completely, crying for mercy or turning tail to flee. Roman had the presence and power to make you speak even if you didn't want to. Even for a man who knew he was dying, Roman's coolness was unnerving. Barney may have known him since childhood, been good friends all his life, but you never knew how people could change or forget things. Roman took drugs everyday. That had to effect your brain in some way.

"Barney," he said, "yer the only person in this world I trust. I've known ye since I was a bairn. Ye ken what made me the way I am. And ye stuck by me. Fought alongside me. And always told me the truth. Even when ye kent how I'd react." Roman stood up and moved into Barney's personal space. "We're night and day, you and me," he said. "But we're cut fae the same cloth. Different ends of the fabric, that's all. We've both got values that dinnae compromise. Your heart is on your sleeve and I ken *exactly* who ye are and what ye'll dae in any situation. Yer no ma friend, Barney. Yer ma brother. So why the *fuck* would I put a hit on ye?"

Barney took a breath. "I'm dying, Roman."

"Bullshit."

"Small cell lung cancer," said Barney. "Advanced stages. They say I've got six to eight weeks tops. Maybe less, because I'm not taking the treatment."

"Fuck off! Ye just did a marathon. Naebdy wae lung cancer could dae a marathon."

"I collapsed at the end."

"Heat exhaustion. Dehydration. It was a hot day."

Barney shook his head. "I'm starting to cough, Roman. Like downstairs there. Bad ones."

"Chest infection. Cold. Flu. Take some fucking paracetamol."

"I'm not going like Stephen did. I'm not going through that pain and humiliation. I'm no shitting myself everyday only for some poor nurse to clean me up. Even you understand that, Roman. I want it quick. I want tae go out while I'm still me."

"So top yersel if you feel that bad!"

"I can't."

"What d'ye mean, ye *can't*?"

"I tried."

Roman sat forward in his chair. "*What*? When?"

"Yesterday. On the Forth Rail Bridge. But I couldnae do it. I cannae kill myself, Roman."

"For fuck's sake! Ye tried tae kill yersel and ye didnae even have the decency tae come roond first and say goodbye?" Roman shook his head. "What aboot yer businesses? The boxing gym?"

"I've made my will. The gym mortgage gets paid off when the businesses are sold. The rest goes to charity."

Roman sighed. "Same old Barnabas Wild. Always thinking of others. Even when he's aboot to meet his fucking maker. What's that thing your gran used tae say? A Mcgee?"

"That's right," said Barney. "You remember that?"

"Course I fuckin' remember! Every cunt roond aboot loved your gran. Fine woman. Salt of the earth. Treated me like a son. Mare than ma own ma did."

"Me too," said Barney.

Roman put his head in his hands and ran his fingers through the thick shock of curly black hair peppered with tiny grey specs. He brought his hands down his cheeks to the point of his chin, and then flat onto the desktop. "I cannae fucking believe this."

Three veins had appeared on the centre of Roman's forehead. "I just *cannae... fucking... believe...*"

Roman downed his drink and poured another. He was a realist and a business man. It didn't take long for him to accept the facts. He inhaled through his nostrils and then looked up. "I ken the man tae dae it," he said in a cool voice. "It'll be quick. You willnae even ken it's happened. He's the best. But no cheap."

Barney pulled a large jiffy bag from inside his coat and dumped it on Roman's desk. "There's ten grand in there. It's all I have. The rest is in my businesses and property."

Roman didn't so much as look at it. "I'll make up the rest," he said. "For old times sake." He paused. "I wouldnae be coming to see ye rot in some stinking hospital anyway. Smelling of pish and shite."

Barney put out his hand. Roman stood up and grabbed it. That grip. The man could crush steel. He pulled Barney hard into his big chest and put his other arm around his back, slapping it hard three times. "I'll never forget what ye did for me, Barney. Never. Yer the only family I've ever had. You and yer gran."

Barney tapped Roman's back. "You're my pal, Roman. Always have been."

A low, growling sound rose up from Roman's chest into his throat but he shut his mouth before it came out. Then he pushed Barney away as if the affection had been too much for him. "Now fuck off oot ma sight before I start greetin' like a daft lassie."

Barney knew better than to linger. "Thanks," he said, as he opened the door.

Roman had his back to him, staring out the window at the view of the cold, grey sea. "Dinnae be thanking me for signing yer fucking death warrant!"

When Barney left, Roman downed the rest of his drink and took another deep breath in through his nostrils. His chin dropped to his chest and his shoulders shrugged up and down. Something was getting in the way of his eyes making them blurry. And then the rage came and he turned and threw his crystal glass at the fireplace. The fragments rained onto the hearth near

Floyd who cowered on the rug and whined. Roman picked up a baseball bat that stood by his bookshelf and with a roar, brought it down through a glass coffee table. That roar had done him some good, and so he filled his lungs and gave out another one. This time louder; a long, deep, gravelled baritone that went through the walls. Monty screeched and beat his wings, flying off his perch to take refuge in the high corner of the bookshelf.

When Roman stopped, it was like coming back to conscious-ness after being knocked out. He noticed sweat running down from his hair. His shirt was drenched under the armpits. Shards of glass everywhere. Furniture smashed to pieces. He tossed the baseball bat away and went to his leather couch by the fireplace. He stroked Floyd's head and gave a soothing word. "It's okay. Roman was just a bit annoyed at something. It's all over now."

Floyd looked up with unsure eyes.

"Looks like it's just you and me from now on, wee pal," Roman said.

"Fucking cunt!" squawked the parrot.

"Oh aye, and Monty too."

The men downstairs had all been silent, eyes moving up and down the ceiling to trace the breaking noises, roars, screams, pounding and heavy footsteps. Dave and Marty looked partic-ularly concerned.

And then they heard someone get in the lift.

And then the lift started to come down.

Down to the man cave.

CHAPTER 11

BACK TO THE HOSPITAL

Barney's phone jolted him awake from an unhappy, dreamless sleep. A hand came out from under the covers to fumble across the bedside table and cancel the call. The phone rang again and with a groan the hand re-emerged and brought the device back with it under the warm duvet.

"Hello?" he answered, his voice rough as a badger's arse.

"Is this Mr. Barnabas Wild?" a well spoken Edinburgh man asked.

"Speaking..."

"Mr. Wild, my name is Mr. Campbell. I'm a consultant from the hospital. I believe you spoke with a Dr. Noble a few days ago regarding your recent test results. We need you to come in immediately."

"I'm no taking the treatment," said Barney.

"I'm aware of that, Mr. Wild. However, this is something different."

"What's that?" asked Barney.

Mr. Campbell paused. "Unfortunately I'm not allowed to discuss the matter over the phone but what I can say is that we urgently need to take your tests again."

Barney sat up, throwing the covers from his chest. "What for?"

"I'm sorry Mr. Wild but I can't say anything else over the phone other than there may have been some errors in recent samples in our blood testing laboratory. Can you make it into the Western General this morning?"

"Aye," said Barney. "I'll be there in an hour."

"Good. Head to reception and they'll take care of you. Goodbye, Mr. Wild."

The specialist took a sample of Barney's blood and then he had to endure another painful biopsy. The samples were rushed through as priority and Barney was instructed to come back in two hours, whereby he was shown into Mr. Campbell's office.

"Please sit down, Mr. Wild. First of all, let me apologise for any inconvenience today. I must thank you for your patience, and for coming in on such short notice." Mr. Campbell inter-linked his fingers and leaned forward in his chair as if his voice might somehow carry through the walls into the corridor. "I'll get straight to the point, Mr. Wild. Unfortunately, there was a mix-up with some tests in our research laboratory which deals with analysing samples. Unfortunate indeed, yes. The bottom line is that your particular results were diagnosed incorrectly."

"What?"

"Yes, so it's good news. You do not have small cell lung can-cer. Or any cancer."

"*What*?"

"Yes. However, you do have chronic bronchitis, which will require a course of treatment." Mr. Campbell took out an inhal-er from his drawer and placed it in front of Barney. "This will make breathing much easier. Take two puffs immediately after or just before a coughing fit."

"Hold on, hold on! Wait a minute, here. You're saying, I *don't* have cancer?"

"That's correct."

"You've checked this oot? You're sure?"

"Positive."

"Then whose results did I get?"

"I'm not at liberty to say."

Barney took a moment to gather himself. This was very messed up.

"I've been reading your file," said Mr. Campbell. "I don't know how you managed to run a marathon in your condition. It must've been very difficult."

"No as difficult as the last few days," Barney said, with an acid tone. "Do you have any *idea* what I've been through?"

"I can only imagine," said the consultant, twiddling his thumbs.

"Aye right. I've got a good mind to speak to ma lawyer aboot this. This isnae right!"

Mr. Campbell's lips sucked against his teeth. "I can only apologise profoundly and ask that, on behalf of the hospital, you reconsider. Rest assured, we are going to review protocol to determine the causes and how something like this could be avoided in the future." Mr. Campbell smiled, showing small square teeth. His eyes contrasted with concern.

"So I've definitely *not* got cancer?"

"No, only Bronchitis."

"So, I'm not going to die?"

"Not from Bronchitis, no. By the way, we don't usually hand out these inhalers for Bronchitis," said Mr. Campbell, giving the cylindrical tube a tap. "However, in your case, we've made an exception."

Barney stared at the consultant, who returned a forced smile, blinking repeatedly before looking away.

CHAPTER 12

CANCEL THE HIT!

The first thing Barney did was call Roman Rock. Sod's law his phone was off. A desperate finger tapped the screen as Barney sent a text:

> *Call me ASAP! Major fuck up at hospital!!*
> *I don't have cancer!!! Cancel the arrangement*
> *immediately!!!! Barney.*

The next thing he did was call Grace. It rang twice and then went onto her voicemail. He left a message to say that there were things he wanted to tell her in person and that he'd like to take her to dinner to explain everything.

A few minutes later, a message came through from Grace. An emoji with a middle finger sticking up. And then another message:

I'm busy today. Maybe tomorrow.
I'll think about it.
G.

Barney smiled. Grace would speak to him, he knew. He could tell her everything. She'd understand. She might even have something to say about the mix-up at the hospital. But that didn't matter. The important thing was they could be together. His phone pinged: *Message to Roman undelivered.*

WHAT?

Barney whistled a taxi down and told the driver to take him to Milton Road East. And step on it.

Barney pushed the buzzer on the gate. He pressed it again. And again. And then he yelled Roman's name as loud as he could,

shook the gates and tapped the buzzer's camera in case someone was watching on the CCTV.

"It's me! Barney! I need to speak to Roman right now! It's
urgent!"

But there was no answer. The window shutters were all down
and the driveway was clear. No cars. The place was deserted.

OK. Think. Roman's not here. Who would know where he is?
Boneheed McCracken. Where would he be? The White House
pub? Maybe. Barney ran down the road all the way to the pub,
only stopping once to cough his lungs out and then try out a
blast of his new inhaler.

"Boneheed isn't here," said Doug. "No seen him in a few days,
come tae think of it. Can I help with anything?"

"Maybe," said Barney, out of breath. "I'm looking for Roman.
Or anyone who might ken where he is."

Willie and Mick, along with a few old degenerates, as much
a part of the pub as the wooden chairs and tables, were questioned. None had heard anything about Roman or his gang.
They'd keep an ear out though.

"Fuck!" said Barney to himself.

"You okay, Barney?" asked Doug. "Are you in some kind of
trouble, mate?"

Barney couldn't have been in more trouble had he been tossed into a dog pit with two starved rottweilers. "I just need tae find Roman," he said.

"I've got your number," said Doug. "I'll make a few calls. See if I can find oot anything."

"Thanks Doug. I appreciate that. There must be someone who kens where Roman is."

"Try the Ladbrokes Mafia," said Doug. "They're probably your best bet."

"Good idea," said Barney. "I'll head there now. If ye hear anything, gimme a bell."

"Will do, mate."

The Ladbrokes Mafia spent nearly all their time in the local bookies arguing with each other and recounting stories of days so far gone nobody else could honestly say they remembered, or even cared about. Sykes had been a professional shop lifter and thief. He still provided the crew with their Armani suits and brand name shirts all stolen from big department stores around the city. Freddie the Face had been a debt collector along with Basher, an ex-heavyweight contender who'd been stripped of his licence after accusations of rigged bouts. Of course, Freddie the Face had done all the talking. He'd been a sharp, good looking guy, and what he called 'a natural people person.' He still had a wicked way with the ladies. It was said that during his peak womanising years, he'd told his nine sons not to date any girls within a ten mile radius of their house, in case they ended up courting a sister they never knew about. Bob the bank robber would sit and dream about all the loot that had passed through his hands and the thrill of easy money. He'd spent more than twenty years in prison and read over two thousand books. He'd also done a degree in English literature while inside and was now writing a book about his life. He also kept the accounts. To an

outsider, it might have looked like four old codgers burning away their pensions on the Gee Gees. But that was all part of the façade. These guys still had some clout. People dropped by to talk on a daily basis. Packages were received and given out. They saw and heard things. Their fingers were in many dirty pies.

CHAPTER 13

THE LADBROKES MAFIA

The door to the bookies bleeped open as Barney stepped inside. All the heads of the Ladbrokes Mafia turned like meerkats to the latest person they could grill and banter with to pass the time and boredom of each other.

"Barney, son!" cried Freddie, getting to his feet. "How ye daein pal? No seen you in weeks! Are ye looking for a wee tip?" Freddie shook Barney's hand. Freddie always stood a bit closer to people than he knew was comfortable for them.

"Hello guys," Barney said, giving a nod to Sykes, Basher and Bob in turn. "No, I'm no here for the horses. I'm looking for Roman. Been up to his hoose but he's no there. Naebdy kens where he is."

Freddie's brown eyes lit up as he observed Barney's unusual nervous state. "You look a bit worried, pal. What's happened? Have ye got up tae some mischief with one of Roman's tarts?" Freddie was grinning, hoping it was true.

"Dinnae you worry, Barney," said Sykes, peeking up from his newspaper. "We'll sort that cunt oot for ye." Shifty Sykes, as he was known, had a face of granite carved with deep, straight lines. His greasy hair was combed back from his forehead and was of a darker grey than his skin, which made his yellow teeth stand out even more when he spoke. Sykes always looked cold no matter what time of year it was.

"No, it's nothing tae do with Roman's tarts," said Barney. "It's much worse than that."

"Hear that, Basher?" said Freddie. "Sounds like Barney's in the shite."

Basher looked up. He always had on a flat cap and tweed jacket that bulged around his broad shoulders and ape-thick arms. His flattened nose and thin, small lips, were out of proportion with his frying pan sized face. He was still an imposing man that even Boneheed McCracken wouldn't have been sure of beating in a square go. "Worse than Roman?" Basher said. "Who's after ye, pal? I'll sort them oot. You've always been good tae us Barney. Name the cunt."

"I can't," said Barney.

"How no?"

"It's complicated."

Bob pushed his glasses onto the edge of his nose to reveal watery blue eyes full of gin. "This is most intriguing..." he said.

Freddie flicked his head with a tut in Bob's general direction. "Listen tae him. Starts writing a book and all of a sudden he's William Cunt Shakespeare."

Basher and Sykes sniggered away as Freddie told Barney to sit down and explain everything over a cup of tea. He put his arm around Barney's shoulder and gave the rest of the crew a wink. "Look, pal," he said, "we're in the know. And if we're no, we soon can be. You tell Uncle Freddie all aboot it and guaranteed we'll figure something oot."

The four members of the Ladbrokes Mafia remained silent through Barney's entire account of his last few days, only letting out the odd exasperated, "For fuck's sake," or "Fucking disgrace," when he got to the part about the the mix-up with his test results.

When he finished, Freddie whistled through his false teeth. "Tricky situation," he said. "Though one thing is pretty clear. You'll have tae get right oot of here pronto. Cause if Roman *has* put a hit oot, you're as good as deid."

The others nodded in agreement.

"You'll have heard all about the McGuire family," said Bob. "Back when Roman was in his *expansion* phase. It was rumoured Roman brought in a special hitman to do the job. Never left a trace. Each one of the McGuires picked off within ten days."

"This isnae making me feel better," said Barney, putting his head in his hands.

"It's no meant tae," said Freddie. "This cunt might already be following you. Have ye thought of that?"

Barney raised his head, eyes wide and worried.

"Aye, better to be safe than sorry," said Sykes.

"What do you mean?"

"I think what Sykes is implying," said Bob, "is that you can't very well go out on the street as Barnabas Wild any longer."

"Here," said Sykes, "take ma overcoat. You can gie me it back when all this blows over. If no, I'll just go doon Jenners tae chore another."

Freddie's brown eyes lit up. You always helped out your mates and did your job well, that went without saying, but it was also important to make sure you had a bit of fun along the way. That was how he did business with Basher all those years ago. Tell some jokes. Make people feel safe. Then explain to them how it had to be. Make them feel like they were doing you a favour. It wasn't Roman's way. But then Roman wasn't the one out on the streets every day. Freddie made things easier to digest and then forget about. "Gie'im yer glasses, Bob," he said.

"My reading glasses?"

"Naw. That broken pair ye keep meaning tae take tae the oapticians."

"Oh yes, forgot about them," said Bob, reaching into his coat pocket. "Here you go, son. I've no use for them anyway."

"And there's a walking stick, perfect for the part," said Sykes, motioning to Basher, who pulled a battered wooden cane from the umbrella stand.

"Ye'll need this too," said Freddie, running his finger nails under his hair and lifting off his toupee. His bald scalp was speckled brown and the crew all laughed when they saw it. "Shut up ya cunts!"

"He's got a different wig for every day of the week," said Bob.

Barney frowned as Freddie handed him the toupee.

"It's clean," said Freddie. "Remember, this guy could be waiting ootside for ye right now." Freddie gave the other boys a quick wink as Barney gazed out the window and then patted the toupee onto his head. "That's it," continued Freddie, "Now let's have a look at ye."

Barney turned a circle in his new clothes looking unconvinced.

"Naw, naw, this'll never do!" said Sykes. "Ye cannae stand up so erect, lad."

"Aye," said Freddie. "It's like Sykes said, ye have tae play the part. Take a look at Bob there. Now there's a perfect example of a weathered old codger beaten doon by life. He's knocked his pan in for sixty years and all he's got tae show for it is a second rate open university degree done in Saughton jail during a twelve stretch. A sad story if ever I've heard one."

"Hold on a moment..."

"Wheesht Bob! I'm trying tae give Barney some direction here." Freddie began massaging Barney's shoulders. "That's it, hunch yer back a bit. Get stiff. Gie us a slow limp up and doon the shop. Much better, Barney! This guys' no fool mind. For all you ken, he's been scoping ye oot all day. This is yer chance tae gie'im the slip and buy yersel some time."

Basher bit his knuckles as Barney walked around the shop like an old man. Bob was taking notes, and giving little bits of advice on Barney's form.

"On ye go, pal," Freddie said, leading Barney to the door as if he was a genuine decrepit. "Straight oot and on yer way. We'll gie ye a shout when we hear fae Roman. And mind tae keep in character. Yer a coffin dodger noo!"

The Ladbrokes Mafia held in their laughter as Barney trembled out the door with a noticeable limp and crook of the neck. Up the street they watched him go, tapping his walking stick along the pavement and turning the corner in the direction of Tesco's.

Barney eyed each person he passed with extreme suspicion. If Freddie was right, any one of them could be the hitman. He continued at his geriatric pace to the only person he could think of who might know where Roman had gone, Rab "Crazy Horse" Lawrie. However, going into the infamous Coffee House of Niddrie was not something he wanted to do.

In fact, up until then, he'd always managed to avoid it.

CHAPTER 14

THE TARGET

He'd been lucky. On his way to the target's house, he'd caught sight of a male in an agitated state exiting the White House pub. The face was the same one he'd been committing to memory the past few days. He checked the photos and description again to make sure. Barnabas Wild. A positive match.

He followed the target from the pub to the local bookmakers, and remained in his car, watching, with a newspaper and the occasional check of his phone, so as not to arouse suspicion. Not that he needed to be so cautious. He had a way of blending into the background of life. A body type of average proportions helped, of course, but it was more than that. A kind of human camouflage developed through years of not wanting to be noticed. People wouldn't remember his face. Or the colour of his eyes. Or his voice. Everything about him was so spectacularly *normal*.

Hunter, he wrote, filling in a line on his crossword.

Two hours went by as local men between the ages of twenty and ninety years of age, went in and out, some with their newspapers and racing guides rolled up in their back pockets. Others sneaking in bottles wrapped in brown paper. But Barnabas Wild never exited.

The hitman knew from experience it wasn't uncommon for men like this to spend hours in the betting shop. However, something akin to a sixth sense urged him to investigate. He got out the car and slipped into the bookies behind two other men around his age. There were eleven men inside talking and watching the screens. He moved to the counter which ran along three of the walls and picked out a slip. Making a pretence of being interested in the next races, he gazed up at the numerous screens planted under the ceiling, and then checked his watch, clocking the punters as he did so. None of the faces inside was the target.

The hitman turned back to the counter, clicked his pen and filled out a betting slip. He took his slip to the counter and handed over a five pound note. The young man never so much as looked at him as he returned a pink receipt. The hitman placed the receipt into his coat pocket and then left the bookies. No one had paid him any attention. No one ever did.

When he got back in his car, he sniffed and frowned. Puzzles and problem solving were hobbies of his. Various scenarios played through his mind and were then eliminated, leaving only two plausible explanations:

One: Barnabas had left the building by another exit, possibly a back door for staff.

Two: Barnabas had somehow exited the building via the front door without him knowing.

Either of these meant it was probable the target knew, or at least suspected, he was being followed. It was possible Barnabas Wild was running from someone else, which might explain his agitated state earlier when leaving the pub. If someone else *was* after him, it could complicate matters.

The hitman started up the car's engine and decided to go back to his initial method of locating a person. More often than not, targets would return home at some point, even if they suspected they were being followed. He'd have to conduct a reconnaissance on the house, in case someone else *was* trying to find Barnabas Wild.

After that, he'd use his *particular* skills to get inside and wait. Waiting was part of the business, and he could use the time to finish his crossword and then the job. In that order.

Earning the nickname "Crazy Horse" in a place with as many bampots as Niddrie, was akin to being tagged the team's best footballer when you played for Real Madrid. Back in Primary six, Barney and his classmates had been at the Commie Pool having swimming lessons when someone dared Rab Lawrie a pack of pickled onion Space Invaders to do a backflip off the top platform of the diving pool, a mere ten metres high. Rab was up there in a second, toes peeping over the ledge as his classmates, some wee fatties, others so skinny it was a miracle their trunks stayed up, shouted encouragement from below. "Come on Rab! Dae it Rab! Jump ya radge!" The lifeguard blew his whistle indicating the area was clear for the top diver. Rab turned around and then flipped backwards off the ledge, landing on his back with a slap that made his classmates groan and laugh. Up he came, clawing, gasping and gulping. Tam, his best friend waved to the lifeguard, who sat up in his chair and asked what the matter was. "He cannae swim!" was Tam's reply.

Tesco Tam's only ever job had been in his local Tesco store. He'd managed a good stint of six months but was sacked when the management discovered he'd got creative on the price gun, replacing the bar codes on bottles of champagne with what he called, 'cheap shite sparkling wine'. With the top-notch Champers flying out the shop faster than a contestant on 'Supermarket Sweep', it didn't take long for his bosses to check the CCTV and then show Tam the door.

CHAPTER 15

THE COFFEE HOUSE

It was said, Rab and Tam's Coffee House was named after a similar establishment located on the eastern side of Jamaica, famous for serving excellent coffee and snacks, along with Marijuana in many forms. Their Niddrie version wasn't set in an idyllic beachfront location, nor was it blessed with tropical sunshine. And it didn't sell coffee, or tea either. As for snacks, the proprietors, if you could call them that, usually had a bowl full of Tunnock's Tea Cakes, Caramel Logs, Wafers and Snowballs on the coffee table; though if they caught you choring one of those you'd be made to pay fifty pence on the spot or get marked down if you didn't have the coin on you.

However, people who frequented the Coffee House didn't actually come for any of those things. They came for the best and most reliable supply of cannabis you could get in Scotland.

Rab was the brains behind the operation. His mysterious supplier would produce week in week out, rain or shine. Not even Tam knew his identity. According to Rab, this secret was what kept everything running so smoothly. To Tam, Rab was smart. Possibly a genius. He'd been one of the few of their circle to get Standard Grades. And the only person Tam knew who'd been allowed to sit Higher exams. Rab was able to think and see things in a way Tam could not.

From the outset, business had been good. Too good, said Rab. Far too easy to join in the with the peaceable cannabis crew and sit talking philosophical pish about the universe whilst listening to Pink Floyd or Bob Marley. Before you knew it, a week had passed, nothing had got done, and quite a few folk owed you money.

Locals would tell you that until recently the Coffee House had been *thee* place to chill out with like minded folk; a gathering spot for the young unemployed, unemployable and stoners seeking banter in any form. *Sex Pistol* posters lined the walls along with *The Damned* and other punk bands. There was even a games room with a genuine pinball machine from the seventies and original pac-man and space invaders games to waste away the hours and countless fifty-pence pieces. Rab had a competition going to keep the clients playing whereby the top score every week got some free weed. This little sideline covered their electric and water bills, with enough left over for other expenses.

For the more discerning clients, Rab had sourced a chess set, draughts and dominos, and of course, there was a play-station-three with eight controllers and a multi-connector for day-long tournaments of FIFA. A pot of Tetley was always on the go, as were the Tunnocks tea cakes and caramel logs. *Crazy Horse* and *Tesco Tam* were considered top dudes, and many's a time a visitor had floated in after a long night to smoke themselves down off harder drugs.

However, the clientele had become too familiar. Dishes piled up. Tea cups were never washed. Pizza boxes twenty stories high had been made into a kind of artwork squashed between the floor and the ceiling of the hallway. Spillages on the carpets and general loose behaviour had forced Rab to draw up some ground rules. The clientele complained. The place had lost its soul, they said. It was more of a take-away joint than a Coffee House.

But Crazy Horse didn't care. A letter had come through from environmental health. He'd cleaned up his act and pulled Tam along with him, enforcing strict codes regarding who was allowed in and how long they could stay. The toilet, in particular, was strictly off limits. Too many drain blocking turds, and smells that burned the hairs in your nostrils, had seen to that. Fucking youth of today. No respect. And not one of them had ever thought to bring a bog roll round. Not one.

The police had stopped busting the Coffee House years ago. Unofficially it was deemed a waste of police time. There were only ever small amounts of class C's to be seized and it was too easy for the clientele to argue personal use. Besides, these were all low-end stoners, smoked out and going nowhere. Better they were hanging around in there and out of trouble's way.

Crazy had gone the whole hog with his new plans and arranged for an old dear to come in every Wednesday and clean the place. On that day, the Coffee House was shut for business. Today happened to be a Wednesday, so when Barney chapped the door, a voice called out from inside saying, "We're shut Wednesday's! Read the notice on the door!" The notice also read: *No Paedo's or Grasses!*

Barney peeked through the letter box into a kitchen. Looking right, down a hallway and through an open living room door, he saw two pairs of feet in slippers resting on a table in front of a TV.

"Pssst! Rab!" Barney hissed. "Open the door! It's me, Barney!"

Two heads leaned forward into view. "Who?" they both said.

"Just hurry up!"

Rab stubbed out what remained of his cigarette and went to tell whoever it was to personally *get tae fuck*. When he opened the door he saw Barney all dressed up like an old codger. He gave a slight raise of his eyebrows. "It's a bit early for *Trick or Treating*, is it no, mate?"

"Shhhh!" Barney said, stepping in and motioning Rab to shut the door. "Keep your voice down."

"Tam!" said Rab, pretending not to know who it was. "Help me oot! Some old codger's just let himsel into the hoose!"

Tam came running into the kitchen. "What the fuck?" said Tam, "Get oot a' here ye old cunt!"

Barney took off the wig and glasses. "It's me!" he said.

"Fuck me!" said Tam. "It's Barney! What the fuck are ye dressed up like some old cunt fur?"

Barney brushed past Tam into the lounge, hugging the wall and then sidestepping to the window. Tam watched, captivated, as Barney lowered the blind .

"What's up?" said Rab. "Your acting like ye've been shagging one of Roman's tarts!"

"Aye, I've already heard that one today," said Barney, taking a seat.

Rab noted the sweat running down Barney's face as he stared at a poster on the wall which read: *Alcohol. Helping ugly people to have sex since 1862.*

Rab and Tam sat down on the chairs beside him. "This isnae like you, mate," said Rab.

"Dae ye want a spliff to chill ye oot, like?" asked Tam.

"No," said Barney, "I've got Bronchitis."

"Is that some sort of STD?"

"It's a lung condition, ya muppet," said Rab. "Go and dae summit useful and make us a cup o' tea."

Tam trudged into the kitchen to fill the kettle, his green Adidas tracksuit bottoms half way down his arse. When he came back, Barney told them the same story he'd told the Ladbrokes Mafia not half an hour earlier.

"Holy shit!" said Tam. "That's some fucking yarn, like. Gives me the Heebie-jeebies."

Rab was more logical. "This is bad, mate. I've heard of this guy. He'll find ye. I mean, yer hardly inconspicuous. Everyone kens ye roond here."

"Aye," said Tam, "you're like one of thay upstanding pillars of the community cunts, ken? Like Jimmy Saville, or something."

"What?" said Barney, almost spitting out his tea.

"Before he went bad, I mean."

"I think Uncle Jimmy was always bad," said Rab, lighting another fag and contemplating Barney's situation.

"What should I do?" asked Barney. "No one kens where Roman is. And I can't wait around till he turns up."

"Nope," said Rab, puffing out on the letter P.

"Hide!" said Tam.

"Where?" asked Barney. "From what folk are saying, I might have the fucking Terminator after me."

Tam scratched his head and then put his hand down his trousers and scratched there too, looking confused.

"Listen Barney," said Rab. "I've got an idea. Mind Junior? Ma wee bro?"

Barney nodded. Though he hadn't heard anything about Junior since he joined the army ten years before. Rab went on, "Naebdy kens this, but Junior's oot the army right now, recovering. He was in a vehicle that drove over an IED in Afghanistan. He's got some bad facial scarring. Doesnae want tae be aroond folk."

"Fuck. Why didn't you tell me before?" said Barney. "I could've visited him. I used to coach him, remember?"

"I ken, but he's no the same guy. He needs time tae work it all oot. And he telt me no to tell anyone. Listen, what I'm saying is, maybe ye could go stay wae him. He's living remote. Off the radar. In fact, I'm the only one who kens where he is."

Just then, someone gave the door a slow knock three times. Tam's hand shot onto Barney's shoulder. "It's HIM!" he said. "He's found you!"

Barney jumped up.

"Hold on, hold on," said Rab, as a newspaper grew out of the letter box and then landed on the floor, "it's just the paper boy." Rab gave Tam a look, throwing his eyes towards Barney who was still fixated on the door. "I forgot tae pay him last week. Isn't that right, Tesco?"

Tam scrunched up his face. "Eh?"

"The paper boy!" said Rab.

Tam's confusion dropped away in stages. "Oh, aye, aye, that's right! Aye! Daft cunt forgot to gie the boy his money, eh! Aye."

Rab went down the hallway to answer the door. "How ye daein Archie?"

Archie was a deprived looking urchin with a three week grown-in crew cut and small hazel eyes that couldn't settle on any one thing for more than a split second. He stepped inside, clocking Barney and Tam, but then slipped out of sight as Rab beckoned him into the kitchen with a gesture of his finger.

Archie pulled out twenty editions of the Evening News from his luminous yellow paper bag and laid them on the worktop. Into each newspaper, Rab placed a small, tightly wrapped, see-through bag of cannabis stuck down with sellotape. Archie separated the *loaded* newspapers into the front half of his bag, dividing them with a blue folder so they wouldn't get mixed up. Rab then pulled out a twenty pound note from his wallet and handed it to Archie, who folded it once and placed it in the inside zip pocket of his tracksuit top.

"Cheers," he said, in a low hoarse whisper.

Rab looked him dead in the eye. "Mind what we always mind?"

Archie lifted his chin as he zipped his top all the way up the neck. "Aye."

Barney settled back into his chair, though he was far from at ease. "So," said Tam, "Have you seen any decent films lately?"

"Eh?" replied Barney.

"Films," said Tam, "seen any decent ones lately?"

"No," said Barney, staring out the window at a man who was walking down the street with his dog.

Tam sat forward, keen as a puppy with someone new in the house. "Funnily enough," he said, "I was watching a film the other day aboot a hitman. This cunt didn't just *kill* his victims. He tortured them. Cut off their ears and fingers and put them in a freezer, but he stitched them up so they were still alive, like, cause he used tae be a surgeon. Then he did the same with their hands and feet. And then their arms up tae the shoulders---"

"What the fuck?" said Barney interrupting him.

Tam gave a confused look.

"I dinnae really want to hear that sort of thing right now, given my current situation."

"Oh aye, sorry mate..."

Tam piped down, looking sheepish as Rab came into the room to take his seat. "Where were we?" he asked.

"You were telling me aboot Junior," said Barney, not wanting to waste any more time. "How he's holed up somewhere remote."

"Aye," said Rab, "that's right. He's off the radar. And I reckon that's exactly where you need tae be."

CHAPTER 16

OPPORTUNITY KNOCKS

Barney's unexpected visit had given Rab something to think about, and Tam a meaning to his day.

"Mind what I said, it's got nae tax, so dinnae stop if the cops try tae pull ye over."

"What?" said Barney.

Rab's cigarette hung out the corner of his mouth and some ash dropped onto the kitchen floor. "You've nae choice, mate."

"I'll need tae pack a few things," said Barney.

Tam almost spat out his tea. "Are you oaf yer nut? It's like the boy in the film! Ye cannae go hame. He could be there waiting tae chop ye up!"

"He's right," said Rab. Ye cannae go back to your place if Roman's called the hit in."

"Nae danger!" said Tam, nodding with excitement.

"What about my car?" asked Barney.

Rab gave a tut. "Barney, mate, get it into yer heid, you're being *hunted*. You've got tae think like an ootlaw. Dinnae go anywhere ye normally would."

"Aye," echoed Tam. "Dinnae go anywhere you normally would. Dinnae do anything *normal* at all."

"I'll call Junior tae let'im ken what's happening. Dinnae worry aboot the inconvenience of taking ma car. Just fill the tank and bring me back a bag fae Junior's. I left it there last time I was up."

"Thanks, mate," said Barney.

"The Audi's up at Tesco car park," added Rab. "I dinnae trust parking it ootside with all they wee bastards aboot. I ken the security guard at Tesco. He's into his weed, so he lets me leave it there as long as he gets his freebies. I'll chum ye up."

Barney picked up his walking stick and stuffed Freddie's wig and the glasses into his coat pocket.

It was only a half a mile or so up the road to the local Tesco store. The car park was half-full.

"Car's over there," said Rab, motioning with his chin as he handed Barney the keys. "I'm just popping in for some groceries. Let the engine run a bit first. I'll meet you ootside in five."

Barney walked through the car park, passing a young dad who was half in the rear door of a ford fiesta strapping a toddler into a child seat while at the same time talking on the phone. A couple of old dears with tan tights and inch thick spectacles waddled by pulling granny bags.

"That new caller at the Gala's a right handsome man," said one of them.

"Did you no get a full hoose last night?" said the other.

"No, no me. That was Jackie."

Barney smiled. Hitman or not. Cancer or not. Life in Niddrie went on as usual. He might've been slightly spooked earlier in the bookies by the Ladbrokes Mafia, and worse by that scaremonger, Tam, but now that he was by himself again, Barney began to wonder if he wasn't getting a bit worked up over nothing. It'd only been five days since he'd seen Roman. Was it even possible for a hit to be arranged so soon?

The hitman had pulled into the car park to eat his packed lunch and continue his crossword when Barnabas Wild walked past for the second time in as many hours. He stopped midchew. Not taking his eyes from the apparition in front of him, he put the rest of his half-eaten Ploughman's back into the plastic tupperware box next to an apple and a digestive biscuit.

The opportunity was there. The car park empty. It was never his way to rush a job but it seemed almost as if fate wanted Barnabas Wild done quickly. He fitted the silencer to his pistol, put on his balaclava and got out the car. A slight gust of wind pushed the door shut with a little more force than he intended. He ducked and watched through a car window as Barnabas glanced behind and then walked on. The hitman stood up and followed, his soft soled shoes custom-made for quietness.

Barney frowned as he found the Audi; an old low-set rectangular black block with alloys to match. The kind of thing you associated with some dodgy Eastern European types. Various scrapes and dents stood out like scars on an old fighter; a bash on the driver's door, a broken wing mirror and rusted wheel arches, to name but a few. He cooled the side of his hand on the tinted driver's side window and put his face to the glass. Half a dozen empty tins of Tennent's lay strewn on the seats on top of pages of old newspapers and decaying bottles of Lucozade. Sweetie papers were scattered like confetti.

As he put the key in the door, Barney caught a slight movement in the reflection of the darkened glass. No sounds or footsteps. Just a movement. Normally he wouldn't have bothered, but today he turned around to see a man in a black balaclava walking towards him. The man was so calm that Barney thought Rab or Tam must be playing a sick joke. The man reached inside his coat and pulled out a gun. A pistol. Still he walked at the same measured pace. The man had gloves on. Black leather gloves. There was no one else around. Barney blinked. But didn't move. Couldn't move.

The hitman had seen that reaction before. Someone who couldn't believe their eyes. In psychological terms, Barnabas was in a heightened state of denial. The hitman raised his pistol and saw the look of horror creeping over Barnabas Wild's face as it dawned on him what was about to happen.

The thud on the hitman's wrist was shocking and strong enough to bring his hand straight down to his side. The next swing of the handbag caught him full in the face and stunned him.

"Dinnae you dare!" shrieked an old woman who'd appeared from nowhere. "Leave oor Barney alane, ya bastard!"

Old Betty was a Niddrie diehard. She set about the hitman with her shopping bag, screaming and cursing in a voice that could've been heard in the city centre. People came out of the shop and faces were already looking over from the street. The man had no choice but to abandon the hit.

Barney watched him slip between cars and then dip out of sight. An engine revved and then a car pulled out in a quick but controlled way to exit the car park. The other cars made it difficult to see what model it was and Barney could only really say it was medium sized and greyish in colour.

"Dinnae you worry, Barney," said Betty, coming over to see him. "He'll no be back in a hurry. Coward that he is! How are you anyway, son? Are you keeping well? Wee Ricky's really enjoying his boxing. Won't be long before all ma grandchildren are world champions eh?"

Barney was breathing deeply. His heart was being worked on by some tiny boxer inside his chest. Rapid punches in a steady rhythm. "Aye, good," he managed to say, eyes fixed on the point where the hitman's car had disappeared down the road. "World Champions."

Rab's voice sounded from somewhere behind. "Mate, I telt ye tae meet me oot front. Oh, hello Betty. How you daein?"

"No bad," said Betty. "Say Rab, are you still able tae get the Sky TV channels for free?"

"Maybe. I'll speak tae a guy I ken. Could probably arrange something though."

"Oh, that's grand. I'll pop roond later in the week tae see ye aboot it. Ciao for now, son."

"Bye Betty." Rab reached into his plastic shopping bag and took a bite out of a warm croissant. "Bet she was a go-er in her day, eh mate?" he said, ejecting flakes of pastry from his mouth. "Barney?" Rab waved a hand in front of Barney's face. "Are you okay, mate? Barney? Hello?"

"Aye, good," said Barney, still staring down the road where the car had disappeared. "World champions."

CHAPTER 17

NASH!

"Nash oot of here! Pronto!" Rab told him, when Barney described the attempted hit. "I'll tell Junior what's happened. Ye'll be alright up there."

Three hours later the black Audi was rattling along the A86 with whistling wheels and one headlight. Barney took a right at Spean Bridge, and then it was North West all the way to Loch Duich.

Rab had written down the route on a piece of paper, along with a crude diagram. Take a right into Glen Affric, and then a left at a fork, onto a private road, which soon became a bumpy track. Mind the potholes and look out for a wooden sign for Dorusdain. That's when you'd ken you were close. Junior's place lay in the glen behind some trees and Rab had warned him you could easily miss it if you weren't careful.

Barney ran his hand down his cheek and across his mouth. The shock of almost getting shot in the car park was only now beginning to wear off.

Fuck. What a mess. Where the hell was Roman?

Recently promoted Detective Inspector Souter had been called in after the arrest of Jimmy the Deal, who'd been caught with a money printing machine and a large wad of forged notes in his residence courtesy of those bumbling bampots, Dave and Marty. With his previous record he was looking at ten years inside. For Jimmy, at forty-five years of age, the thought of spending the last decent bit of his life without the prospect of drink or a whore was just too much to take. Added to the equation were a few 'old friends' who'd be only too ready to give him a warm welcome if he returned to Saughton Jail. Jimmy decided the witness protection scheme suddenly looked pretty good. He wanted a deal. But what could he offer the police? Roman Rock was the answer. Souter told Jimmy he only had to testify to that effect in court and Souter would do the rest. And so Jimmy made the decision to break the first commandment of the underworld.

'Jimmy the Deal' had now become 'Jimmy the Grass.'

CHAPTER 18

SOUTER VS ROMAN

Souter and his officers arrived early in two cars. Eight of them in total. Enough to outnumber but not enough to overwhelm, tempting Roman and his goons to resist arrest, which would only add to the list of charges when they got to court. It'd also give Souter and his men a bit of action. An opportunity to get the batons out and go old-school on the bastards.

They'd been all set to bust into Roman's property when they saw him and his gang leaving the house and getting into Roman's Bentley.

"That's Hatchet, Billy Blow and Boneheed McCracken," said Harrison, one of Souter's detectives.

"A right little party," said Souter. "Wait until they're out the gate," he said, over the radio. Harrison started the engine. "Hold on a second," said Souter. "I don't want them seeing us before that bloody gate opens."

The radio crackled. "Gate's opening now, sir," said one of the officers from the other car.

"Wait for my order," replied Souter. "That's it... OK... Standby... Go! Go! Go!"

The two unmarked cars sped towards the gate, screeching and skidding to a halt, blocking in the silver Bentley. Souter and his men jumped out and surrounded the car. Hatchet opened his door and was immediately pulled from his seat onto the ground. A knee pressed into his spine and he tensed up. "Fucking cunts!" he screamed, as his arms were wrenched behind his back and cuffed. A boot kicked him in the ribs and he groaned.

Billy Blow, Boneheed and Roman were cuffed without much of a struggle.

"No need for me to read you your rights," said Souter. "You've all heard them so many times you must know them off by heart."

"I hope you've got a fucking good reason for this," said Roman.

Souter smiled. "I'd say counterfeiting and money laundering are reasons enough, wouldn't you, Roman? Here's the warrant if you'd like to read it."

Roman spat on the piece of paper Souter held an inch from his face. His hands were behind his back but he shook away the officer holding him. "Get yer paws off me," he said.

Souter nodded at his man and Roman was allowed to stand unmolested.

"Boss," said Buchanan, one of the detectives, who'd been examining the inside of the car. "Found this under the driver's seat." Buchanan was holding up a pistol with his pen through the trigger guard.

"Never seen that before in ma life," said Roman, looking away.

"Got one here too, Boss," said detective Harrison. "Under the passenger seat."

Souter smiled again. "Doesn't look too good for you Roman," he said. "Counterfeiting, possession of firearms. Nope, not good at all. Is there anything else you'd like to confess to while we're here?"

Just then, there came a thud from inside the car. "What was that?" asked Souter.

Boneheed McCracken grimaced. Hatchet and Billy Blow sighed in unison.

"Open the boot," said Souter, gazing at Roman who refused to meet his eye. Detective Buchanan put the keys in the boot and opened it.

Souter stepped round to have a look. "Oh dear, dear, dear," he said, unable to hold back his glee. "What have we hear? Two naked men bound and gagged, wriggling like a pair of worms in your boot, Roman."

The men stopped wriggling and twisted their bodies round to stare at Souter, who cocked his head slightly. "Is that a golf ball?" he asked.

Boneheed, Hatchet and Blow started sniggering as Detective Buchanan donned some latex gloves and prised the man's arse cheeks apart. "Yes, sir," he said. "That is indeed a golf ball."

CHAPTER 19

RECOVER BETWEEN ROUNDS

The hitman pulled into the quiet lay-by and opened the boot of his car. Inside were two black hold-alls and a hard case. He unzipped one of the hold-alls and took out two standard issue number plates. One yellow, one white. Using his screwdriver, he replaced the plates on the front and back of the car with the ones from the bag and then used a shovel to bury the old plates in the ground. When he was done, he got back into his car and finished his lunch, pondering over the irregular start to the job.

The target, Barnabas Wild, appears right in front of him outside the White House Pub, then he mysteriously disappears from the bookmakers, only to reappear again a couple of hours later at the local Tesco.

The fiasco in the car park meant he'd have to forgo visiting Barnabas Wild's residence in case the police had been called and now had people waiting. How had he not noticed the old woman? It was only her that had stopped an easy hit. Never before had he made a mistake like that. Being so spontaneous was unprofessional, no matter how good the opportunity. What had happened earlier could, of course, be put down to bad luck. But having luck in the equation was the result of poor planning.

The hitman sniffed and opened his laptop.

It was important to keep up to date with the more creative aspects of modern technology, as much for his own protection as for his work. The simplest way into people's lives was through the internet. Acquiring certain hardware and software from the Dark Web allowed him to tap into the life of almost anyone he wanted. Cameras, email accounts, phones, even TV's could all be hacked and information gained. IP addresses could be used to triangulate locations of internet use, meaning most of the population could be found in minutes and then tracked on a sophisticated GPS mapping system designed by the CIA.

Barnabas had made things even easier by leaving a map application open on his phone. The exact co-ordinates were pinpointed as a green dot on the hitman's laptop screen. He clicked onto street view and saw a line of terraced houses less than half a mile from the bookies where he'd lost contact the day before.

Of course, locating was only half the work. You still needed to be on the ground and able to get 'eyes on' to make sure. Out of sight, he liked to watch and learn a target's particular habits and routines. If they were interesting, he might take his time. It was similar to reading a good book. Sometimes you didn't want it to end. He enjoyed being outside looking in, much as a nature enthusiast would observe the silent world of insects from the perspective of a god. Once satisfied, he'd use his data to pick the exact moment when the target was most vulnerable and he was least likely to be compromised.

CHAPTER 20

GET THOSE HANDS UP!

The sun slipped down behind a big hill to the north west as Barney pulled up outside what appeared to be half a cottage. Hidden behind a group of tall fir trees, the traditional Highland abode was, in an architectural sense, terminally ill. The roof had caved in on one side and long grass protruded from a broken first floor window. The grey stone of the exterior walls showed large patches of damp and other areas looked blackened by smoke.

Barney put on Freddie's wig and glasses as a precaution, and then got out of the car. The absolute silence of the Highlands pulsed inside his ears. The grounds were in keeping with the general mess of the house. Moss-ridden roof tiles lay like broken pottery in the garden. A small, rusted tractor sat abandoned under a sheet metal covering, while a weather-beaten caravan from the sixties with no wheels and closed curtains stood propped up on bricks to deteriorate with the steady passing of time.

Following a trampled down grassy path, Barney made his way past wild flowers and waist high thistles to the front door, the top hinges of which had come away from the frame so the door rested askew with gaps where the cold and weather could penetrate. He could see a fireplace in the caved-in room but feathers, broken bricks and other debris showed it hadn't been used in a long time.

This ramshackle abode had nothing to do with the disciplined and eager kid Barney had once trained in his boxing gym. Junior had been in the army too, no doubt subjected to rigorous standards of cleanliness. Surely this couldn't be where he now lived. He looked at Rab's instructions again. And then a voice said his name and Barney turned on the spot to see a man with a shotgun in the garden.

CHAPTER 21

JUNIOR

Barney's arms went up in some useless natural defence and he sucked in a short, quick breath. The man opposite cradled his shotgun in his arms; stock in his shoulder and barrel pointing down just in front of Barney's feet. His face was turned slightly inside his hood. There was a poise about the man. Something deliberate and trained. When Junior had decided to go into the army at sixteen years old, he was a skinny lightweight at best. This man was a light-heavyweight and thick around the neck and shoulders.

"I'm looking for Junior," said Barney, unsure if he was in the right place.

The man looked Barney over, and then scanned the house and garden, as if searching for someone else who might be concealed. The long grass quivered around his knees in a breeze that came and went as a whisper.

"Who are you?" the man asked, in a voice that could have been Junior's, except it was deeper, and the words came out slower than Barney remembered.

"A friend of Junior's," said Barney, taking a step forward. "Is that you, mate?"

The man raised his rifle and Barney stopped. "How do you know my name?"

Barney removed his wig and glasses. "It's me," said Barney.

Junior relaxed his posture, allowing the rifle to dip to the ground. "Rab said some psycho was after you. You looked a bit different in that disguise, mate. Better safe than sorry."

Barney laughed as he came forward to greet his old protege. "You had me worried for a minute there! How you daein?"

Junior pulled back his hood and stopped Barney mid step. The side of his face had been burned off. Melted skin hung over his right eye and the corner of his lip pulled down as if the muscles were ruined. Only patches of hair remained around an ear that had been formed out of silicon and sewn onto his head. Junior noted the look Barney was giving him. He'd seen it all too often since the operations. "Rab probably told you about what happened. This is the result."

"Jesus. I'm sorry, mate." Barney offered Junior his hand. Junior took it in a firm grip, his confronting eyes holding Barney's gaze. "Well, it's good tae see you again, pal," Barney said. "How long's it been?"

"Ten years," said Junior.

"I didnae even ken you were oot the army until Rab told me today."

"Medically discharged," said Junior, without emotion.

Barney nodded. He didn't know what to say to that.

CHAPTER 22

SHIT STIR

"What the fuck?" said Tam, wiggling in his seat. "Have ye got a vibrator in the couch?"

"What-are-you talking aboot?" asked Rab.

"Something's buzzing doon here!"

"Where?"

"Under ma arse!" Tam sprung up and lifted the cushion. "A phone!" he said, as if it was treasure. "Some bird called Grace is calling. Hey, she's no bad! No bad at all, like! Look!"

Tam held out the screen to Rab who examined the caller ID and image as the phone rang out."Grace the Lawyer. Tidy. Wait a sec, that's Barney's phone."

"Fuck!" said Tam. "It must've fell oot'is pocket when he was here. That's how it's ended up doon the couch!"

Rab shook his head. "You've missed your calling, mate."

"What d'ye mean?"

"You should've been a detective."

"Ken, eh! Ma ma said that when I was a bairn, before I got a criminal record, like. We should probably turn his phone off though, in case that hitman cunt is tracking it."

"Aye right!" said Rab.

"It's nae joke. It's scary what they can dae. I saw a programme where the FBI were following some cunt using the cunts' ane phone, listening in and watching through his camera."

A text message came through from Grace telling Barney she would be at a certain bar near her work at eight o'clock if he still wanted to see her. Tam glanced at Rab who'd gone back to watching TV. His shit-stirring nature couldn't resist a reply. 'I'll be there, cupcakes!' he typed. And then as an afterthought, 'Put on the red panties!' Tam pressed send and then turned the phone off.

The tracking signal gave co-ordinates which translated to a specific address in Niddrie, Edinburgh. The hitman typed this address into the car's GPS. Suddenly the signal disappeared from the Dark Web tracing programme.

A leather gloved finger tapped the gearstick twice. A signal would only disappear if the phone was turned off, or destroyed, or if the target had anti-tracking surveillance devices that detected an intrusion.

The hitman sniffed, logged out and then started up the car.

CHAPTER 23

MALTESERS

Young Kenny, Tam's nephew, had been hanging around like a stale fart, hoping to score some free weed, which Tam was not going to give him.

"I gave ye some last week, ya cunt!"

"I ken but it's gone and I dinnae get ma joab-seekers till next Tuesday."

"Tough tits! Get a fucking joab and ye'll have plenty of money tae buy weed."

Kenny sighed and gazed out the front window.

"And get yer hands oot your pants, numb nuts!" said Tam. "What'll the neighbours think, you standing there scratching yer baws in full view of the street?"

Kenny mumbled something and moved over to the mantlepiece, looking for scraps or residue he might scavenge into a tiny smoke but there was none, only a small wooden sculpture of Buddha and an unopened box of Maltesers, the latter of which took his fancy. He stood with his back to Tam and quietly tore the serrated cardboard seal with his thumbs, millimetre by millimetre. Sneaking a look over his shoulder, he observed uncle Tam still engrossed in daytime TV, and so he opened the lid, stuffing Maltesers into his mouth until his cheeks bulged. A few loud crunches aroused in Tam some internal alarm that broke the spell of Jeremy Kyle on the TV.

"Hey! Is that ma Maltesers? Get tae fuck ya sneaky bastard!"

Before Tam could get up from the couch, Kenny had bolted out the living room and then out the house.

"Ya wee cunt!" cried Tam. "An dinnae bother coming back!"

"What's all the commotion?" asked Rab, coming in and settling into his favourite armchair.

"Cheeky cunt was helping himself tae ma Maltesers, eh! Scarpered when I caught him."

"What was he daein here anyway?" asked Rab.

"Trying tae score some free weed, of course. Stingy wee bastard."

"Says Shylock himself!"

"What are ye talking aboot?"

"Tam, you're so tight ye think a vodka and red bull is two drinks."

"Oh, let's no have this argument *again*! That wee cunt kens I have diabetes. I keep them Maltesers for emergencies, in case I get hypo... hypo..."

"Hypochondria?" suggested Rab.

"Aye, that's it," said Tam.

The Maltesers lid was lying open and so Tam got up to close it, picking out a few treats and popping them into his mouth. He allowed the milk chocolate to melt on his tongue before crunching into the honeycomb centre. He turned to Rab with a triumphant grin before his face contorted and he began to gag. Coughing and retching, he dropped to his knees and spat the chocolate biscuit mix onto the floor.

"Urgh, ya clarty bastard!" said Rab.

With his eyes watering, Tam scraped a finger nail down the back of his throat and pulled a single thread from his tongue. He gagged once more, and then squinted at the curly ginger culprit stuck to his finger that still had tiny bits of biscuit on it. Confusion gave way to horror. Tam resisted the urge to be sick but made a peculiar sound; an ape-like cry of fury and disgust.

"What is it?" asked Rab.

"Baw hair!" cried Tam. "Fucking baw hair! That cunt Kenny had his hands doon his troosers, then he got right into ma Maltesers. Dirty wee bastard! I'll kill him!"

CHAPTER 24

TRACKING

Through his binoculars, the hitman was able to determine that there were at least three people in the house. One adolescent male of around eighteen and two males of around forty years of age. There was some sort of altarcation, after which the younger male left the house.

The hitman's data told him the man in the kitchen was likely to be Robert Lawrie, owner of the property. Mr. Lawrie's passport ID and photo came up on the screen. When the man checked through his binoculars, he could positively identify Mr. Lawrie as the one now laughing hysterically on the couch in the living room, while the other man - who was definitely not Barnabas Wild - gesticulated, waving his arms and shouting something that couldn't be heard through the double glazing.

The hitman checked his data but there was still no signal from the phone or any sign of recent internet use on any device. He'd already tapped into Barnabas Wild's bank and credit cards and found no transactions had been made in the past thirty-six hours.

The man sniffed and put his finger to his mouth. For all intents and purposes, Barnabas Wild had disappeared.

CHAPTER 25

WELCOME TO THE HIGHLANDS

Junior showed Barney into the rustic house, through to an old kitchen with wooden cupboards and a dark wood floor which must've been an original feature. At the far end, a couple of ancient green arm chairs faced a small fireplace. A bucket of coal, a poker, tongs and a stack of old newspapers lay on the slate tile hearth. There was no television, only a small transistor radio on the worktop. A large bookcase with nine shelves crammed to the edges lined one of the walls. Tidy, solitary living for a male seeking to escape society.

Junior boiled water in a pan to make some tea. He didn't say more than a few words before handing Barney his cup and going to sit at the other end of the room on a deep window ledge.

Barney pulled a chair from the kitchen table and tried some small talk but Junior seemed content to stare outside, only giving short, one word answers.

Sitting still wasn't something Barney was good at. He sipped his tea and longed for a biscuit. Through the long sash window, his eyes wandered out across a wild country of purple heather, moorland and fir trees, all enclosed within a cauldron of Scottish hills that seemed to close in on the cottage as the light became less and the sky turned a brilliant pink. Barney became aware of water trickling over rocks nearby and the chirping birdsong of sunset. "It's like a scene oot a whisky advert," he said, as much to himself as Junior.

As if to impress the newcomer, a young, brown deer appeared out of the tall trees that concealed the house from the road. It wondered into the expanse of grass that might be called a garden, munching away on saplings, small shoots and flowers.

"Look at that!" said Barney, as the fawn decimated a collection of autumn flowers Junior had planted in the Spring. "I dinnae think I've ever been anywhere so quiet. Nature. Really is something, eh? Back tae basics. This is exactly what I need."

"You hungry?" asked Junior, lifting the latch and opening the window to view the fawn. "I could fix up some dinner, if you want?"

"That'd be great," said Barney, who was still watching the wee creature when a shot burst the silence of the room and the animal dropped down dead. "Holy shit!"

"Venison alright?" asked Junior, holding the smoking barrel out the window.

CHAPTER 26

WHO KILLED BAMBI?

Barney sat with his mouth gaping, unable to do much more than blink at Junior, and then back at the poor wee deer, and then back at Junior again. The words *medically discharged* took on a whole new meaning. Was Junior actually cracked? Barney looked for a reaction, some manic grin or evil laugh, but Junior simply got up from the window ledge and placed his rifle against the wall, next to the back door, as if it were an umbrella. Then he went outside to pick up the fawn.

Barney put down his mug, trying to keep calm. It was important not to set off an unstable mind. He knew that much. God knows what might happen if Junior got worked up. He had at least one rifle in the house. Barney felt he had to do or say something. Something that might help him work out if Junior was dangerous. He went outside to see his old protege crouched over the dead fawn. What the hell should he say to someone who'd been through what Junior had? The first thing that came to mind was, "Aren't you supposed to have a licence to dae that?"

Junior lifted the fawn onto his shoulders, pulling it's legs together in front of his chest. "For shooting deer?" he said. "They're fair game."

"What does that mean?"

"It means if they come onto your land, you can shoot them. They're not owned by anyone. Also, they're seen as a pest around here. They eat ma plants and saplings before they can grow into trees. Problem is there's no natural predator."

"Predator?" said Barney. "Then what are you?"

Junior stopped. The vehemence in Barney's voice, along with the redness in his cheeks and rapid breathing, told him Barney had been shocked by the kill. Some people had never seen an animal killed before, let alone a human being. "Even if I killed a hundred deer every month, it still wouldnae make a dent in the population," he said. "That's why people are campaigning to bring back wolves."

"*Wolves*? Who the hell'd want wolves back?"

Junior kept walking. "Lot's of people. The eco-system is com-plicated. You take one factor out, you create an imbalance. When wolves disappeared in Scotland, the deer population multiplied. Bring back wolves and deer numbers will fall."

"Is that right?" said Barney, who began slapping his neck in response to a sudden attack by midges.

"Aye. There's also a theory that because of the same lack of a natural predator, at some level, the midges who are now eating the shite out of your neck were allowed to multiply to the extent they are now."

"You're joking?"

"It's a theory," said Junior.

Junior had grown up in Niddrie, just like Barney, but he was talking more like a university graduate. Ten years. Clearly the army had taught him more than just how to shoot.

"I take it you've been reading a lot of books," said Barney.

"Not much else to do around here," said Junior.

Junior asked if Barney wanted to learn how to skin and prepare the deer. Barney could hardly look at the poor creature whose sad brown eyes seemed to be watching him. However, he felt the only way to ease the uncomfortable silences was to get to know Junior better. Get him talking about something he was interested in, like that eco-system pish. It might open him up more. Who knows? Maybe he would find some of the old Junior in there somewhere.

Junior carried the animal into an outbuilding around the back of the house where he strung it up by the hind legs on some hooks hanging form the rafters. "Are you sure you dinnae want to wait outside until I'm finished?"

"Thanks," said Barney, "But I'll watch. I've seen the wee thing get killed, I might as well see how you skin it."

"Up to you," said Junior.

Using a Bowie knife, Junior made a few precise cuts around the hooves, along the legs, and around various places on the animal. Then with vigorous pulls, and some more cuts, he ripped the fur clean off to the neck, revealing a grey and burgundy body with a sleek membrane. Lurid cream cartilage, fascia, tendons, ligaments and dark red muscle had not long ago been a bonnie wee deer running around the wild. Junior cut the fur around the neck and opened the deer up from the belly. Internal organs splattered onto the ground along with a strong smelling gush of dark red. Barney jumped back, put his hands over his mouth and ran outside to be sick.

Junior continued preparing the rest of the carcass. Hind legs, ribs, rump, neck and back, keeping two large steaks for dinner. The rest was cut and wrapped in butcher's paper for the freezer. When he emerged from the outhouse, Barney was sitting on a tree stump wiping his mouth and looking pale. "You alright?" asked Junior.

"Never seen that sort of thing before. Pretty grim."

"Aye, if folk had tae kill and prepare their own meat, most of the population would be vegetarians."

"Who taught you to do all that?"

"One of the guys in my troop was into hunting. Went poaching in the Highlands wae'im. Took me out a few times in Afghanistan too."

"What kind of things did ye hunt out *there*?" asked Barney.

"Taliban," said Junior, "though they're harder to skin than deer." There was a pause before Junior spoke again. "No need to look at me like that, mate. I'm just winding you up."

Junior offered a hand and pulled his old boxing coach to his feet. "These steaks'll be a good feed," said Junior. Barney's less than enthusiastic response amused him. "At least you ken where the animal's been. It's had a good life. Not like some pig or cow pumped full of steroids and treated like shite every day. You ken they kill the animals on a conveyor belt in front of each other? Folk don't see it. All they see is their nice juicy rashers or steaks ready for the frying pan. People are blind because they want to be. But it's hard to look at something *gruesome*, isn't it?"

Barney was staring at Junior with two thirds confusion, one third intrigue. He knew what Junior meant. And so he kept his eye contact. "You *have* been reading a lot," he said, with a bit more of himself and the toughness they both knew from boxing and growing up in Niddrie.

After dinner, Barney and Junior sat by the fire with a beer. Junior insisted the lights be turned off, and took the right-hand chair. Barney gave a satisfied groan as he removed his socks and placed his feet on a stool in front of the open flames. The chairs were of a soft corduroy fabric that warmed with the fire and seemed to mould around Barney's body. A few embers sparked and crackled against the fireguard. Shadows flickered on the walls and Barney snuggled into his seat with a satisfied yawn. He could hardly move after dinner. The venison had been better than his steak at the Witchery with Grace.

"Great scran!" he said, rubbing his hand over his stomach and congratulating Junior, who'd served it up with potatoes, peas and carrots he'd pulled from the garden. "You're quite the chef!"

"Aye. All home grown."

"*More* books?" Barney wiggled his toes. "Tell you what though, I could get used to this. Good food, drink and a cosy fire..."

"And what about the poor wee deer?" asked Junior. "The look on your face when it went down was priceless."

"Aye, well, I wasn't expecting it, was I? There was wee Bambi out prancing at sunset and the next moment BOOM! Fucking rifle goes off and there's Bambi deid on the groond wae its legs sticking up."

"Just like that Sex Pistols song," said Junior.

"Aye, *Who Killed Bambi.* I ken who killed Bambi alright."

Junior laughed. "Maybe we can go hunting while you're here. It's no a bad idea you learning to use a rifle given your situation."

"Aye, we'll see," said Barney. "I'm still no so sure aboot that. I'm more of an eater than a shooter. As you say, one of those folk who like to be blind..."

"Nah, you've done pretty well. So what dae ye think of it?"

"Aye, it's no a bad wee hoose."

"I was talking about my face," said Junior, trying to take Barney by surprise again.

But Barney was now at home and the beer and a good meal had settled his nerves. "Well," he said. "You'll no be walking doon any catwalks. But I've seen worse."

"You lying bastard."

"You're still better looking than Tesco Tam."

"Fuck, I could be deid six months and still look better than that ugly cunt. How is he anyway?"

"Like a car wae one gear."

"Eh?"

"Never changes. Anyway, scarring is on the ootside. Naebdy can change what's inside. The things you've done and been through. Your accomplishments. That stuff cannae be taken away from you. And you cannae buy it either. Ye've done more in yer twenty-six years than most people dae in a lifetime. The ootside changes all the time, mate. We get old. We get scars. We look different from ten years ago. That's life. Ye never had yer nose broken did ye?"

"My nose? No. Why?"

"Cause, first time I did, I went into shock. Changed my whole appearance, or so I thought. Until I realised most folk didnae even notice. When you're an old bastard, dae ye think you'll even care aboot how ye look? Course not. Aye, okay, it's fucked up. But you're still the same person inside."

"Aye, well...," said Junior who reached over to a small wooden table where he had his papers and tobacco. He opened a small tin and rolled what looked like quite a big cigarette. When he lit up, even Barney knew the unmistakable smell.

"Are you smoking *weed*?" he asked, the surprise in his voice was almost that of a father.

"I am," said Junior, who's answer conveyed the disdain of a teenage son. "In ma own hoose. And for medicinal purposes, due to the fact I've chronic fucking pain in ma face all day, every day."

Barney wound in his neck. "I didnae mean it like that. I just... well, I suppose part of me sees you as the wee laddie in the boxing gym."

"I was just a kid back then, and anyway, it helps me relax. Numbs the pain." Junior let the smoke out of his lungs in one long breath. "Sometimes I wish I could go back to those days in the gym. Everything was simpler then." Junior took a long draw. "But you're wrong about one thing, Barney. I'm not the same person. Too much has happened."

The two men gazed into the warm glow of the flames before Junior spoke again.

"Did Rab tell you why I'm up here?" he asked.

"Just said you were recovering. But I'm no as daft as I look, pal. I might be on the run, but I'd say *you* were daein as much hiding as I am. What happened oot there in Afghanistan?"

Junior's eyes were lost in the fire. He took another puff and then stubbed out the rest of the joint. "Uch, nothing much," he said, standing up. "I'm going to ma bed. Dinnae bother aboot the dishes. I'll dae them in the morning. Your room is first on the left up the stairs. It's been good to see you again, mate. Goodnight."

CHAPTER.27

GRACE IS STOOD UP

Grace checked her phone. Barney was fifteen minutes late and hadn't replied to her last message. What the hell was his game? On their first meeting he'd been so decent. Charming and funny. A gentleman in every way. The next day had been even better. Exciting. And at the same time... familiar. She felt she knew Barney. And he was easy to read. Honest and straight to the point. The type of person who couldn't lie.

That night in her bed had been more exciting than any time with her ex-husband in their ten years of marriage. But then this sudden cool off. And 'cupcakes'? What the hell was 'cup-cakes' and 'red panties'? She couldn't imagine Barney saying that. In fact, she couldn't imagine him being late for her either. And if he was, he'd have at least given her a message, especially after his voicemail. 'Something I have to tell you in person...' and all the rest.

She checked the conversation thread and saw her last messages hadn't been delivered. Curious. Curiosity was one of her weaknesses. Competing against her pride, it won out easily and she decided to call him. His phone was turned off and the little drop in her stomach told her he wasn't coming. However, the old feelings of being let down time and again by Martin, her ex, didn't resurface. She was over that. And there was something fishy about this whole situation. She began to run it over in her mind from the time he'd first walked into the bar. Too many things didn't make sense. Over the years, she'd become an excellent judge of character. She'd known Martin hadn't been the one for her but she'd also been young and ambitious, and foolish enough to think she could change him. She treated this situation more like a case. A client. A mystery. She loved mysteries. Detective novels lined her bookshelves and she was able to get involved in real life cases in her role as a criminal lawyer. Many times she'd worked out a case well before those clueless policemen like the narcissistic Detective Ross Souter, who was always trying to take her out to dinner.

She bit her lip and tapped a pencil against her notepad. Barney was one of the rare good guys. But something wasn't right. Maybe he was in trouble. He'd wanted to tell her something.

Something important. Besides, he'd got under her skin now. Not to mention *into* her bed. She had a right to know what was going on. She looked up her contacts and selected Clare Scott, alias Miss White.

"I'll find out what you're not telling me, Barnabas Wild," she said. "I always do, in the end."

CHAPTER 28

PHONE CALL TO MISS WHITE

"**W**ell *hello* Grace Farquhar!"

"Hello Clare..."

"It's Miss White! How many times, woman?"

"Oh yes, sorry."

"What can I do you for at so *late* an hour?"

"Oh, sorry. Is it that late? I need a background check on someone."

"Ooh, another dodgy client, eh?"

"I hope not."

"What's the name?"

"Barnabas Wild. Wild with an I."

"B-Wild. Cool name. Age?"

"Hmmm... around forty-five, I'd say." Grace heard the tapping of keys in the background.

"Address?"

"I don't have one," said Grace.

"So he's *not* your client..."

"You'd make a good lawyer with all your leading questions, Miss White."

"Ha! Or a good detective. Any other information?"

"He used to be a boxer. Runs a boxing gym in Niddrie."

"Tough guy, huh?" Clare said, in a kind of old fashioned American accent. "I know what to do with tough guys!"

"What?"

"Oh, it's from a James Cagney film I saw the other night. Never mind. Okay, I've got a Barnabas Wild that fits the profile. I'll do a bit of digging and see what I can come up with. It'll take a couple of days, though."

"That's fine."

"And you know my rates for a background check..."

"Yes. I'll meet you at the usual place."

"See you there then."

"Thanks, Clare."

"It's MISS WHITE!"

"Oh yes, sorry."

CHAPTER 29

THE NEWS REPORT

It'd been a long day. Grace poured herself a large glass of wine and turned on the TV. Curling up on the couch, she flicked off her shoes and squeezed the tension out of her feet. On the TV, a reporter was grilling a medical consultant named Mr. Campbell, regarding a mix-up with cancer test results. Members of the public were furious after being wrongly diagnosed with cancer. Some of them given only weeks to live had since found out they were perfectly healthy. Mr. Campbell was attempting to play down the incident but you could see the strain in his face from the way he kept blinking and fidgeting. A man trying to keep his head above water in a rising swell.

"That's at least one lawsuit coming your way, Mr. Campbell," Grace said, sipping her silky Chateaux-Neuf-du-Pape.

A video appeared of the person who was, according to Mr. Campbell, 'directly responsible for the mix-up', a twenty-five year old man named Callum Hunter; white skinned and baby faced, he was the scapegoat who'd been suspended and was now under investigation for alleged substance abuse. Callum and his adolescent spots and baby fluff hurried down the police station steps as the vultures chased him with cameras and microphones, looking for something to put in their papers.

Meanwhile in Niddrie, Rab and Tam were watching the same news flash.

"Holy shit!" said Rab, "Is that no that Callum boy you gave the *special* joint tae?"

Tam squinted at the TV. "Fuck me! What's he done?"

"Some scandal at the hospital. A mix-up wae results. They're saying he's an addict. That's him coming oot the polis station the noo!"

"Check oot'is face," said Tam, putting his hands on his head and laughing in a high pitched voice. "Fuckin bawbag! He's in the shite!"

"Big time!" said Rab. "And ye'd better hope he doesnae land you in it either."

"What d'ye mean?"

"Eh, who's the cunt that gives him his stuff on a regular basis?"

"Fuck! I never thought of that!"

"Arsehole. Let's get this place cleaned up in case they come roond. This could be bad for business."

CHAPTER 30

RUNAWAY TRAIN

Barney had remained in his chair, content to stare into the warm, glowing embers of the dying fire until the last crackle and flicker of flame. As the heat ebbed away from his feet, he spread out the blanket Junior had given him and snuggled down a few inches.

In the silence of the room, the day's events jumped like a flick-book through his mind. Half dreaming, he pictured a runaway train with the consultant Mr. Campbell as the driver. He got on at the hospital, gaining speed and momentum through the White House Pub and Niddrie. Doug the barman waved from a platform as he flew past. Freddie and the Ladbrokes Mafia passed through the carriage and then in came Tam and Crazy Horse to collect tickets. The train began to slow into Junior's station and there was the man in the balaclava walking through the turn-stiles towards his carriage. Barney jolted awake to see the fire had burned to cinders and ash. What a thing to happen. Hard to believe it was all real.

"You can look at almost anything in a positive way if you want to," his gran used to say.

Barney closed his eyes and soon the train began moving again. He was alone in the compartment watching a green countryside go whizzing by. *Destination Unknown* was writ-ten on the panel above the door at the front of the carriage. He tried to think of the positives in his current predicament. All he'd been through the past week. What good had come of it? Grace, of course. She appeared suddenly beside him, her green eyes asking questions. Suddenly the train entered a tunnel and all went dark. When it came out Grace was gone.

Grace. The one shining light in an otherwise seriously fucked up situation. Take the positives. He'd never have met her had all this not happened. But was it all worth it for a woman? His gran's voice came over the train driver's speakers.

"Not just any woman," it said. "The woman you are going to marry."

CHAPTER 31

THE FALLS OF GLOMACH

Barney lay on his side watching golden speckles of dust revolve and dance inside a streak of sunlight that streamed through the gap in his curtains. The gentle bubbling of the burn nearby seemed to soothe away any thoughts of Edinburgh, and he was in no hurry to start the day. His eyes wandered around the room, taking in the old tea-stained floral wallpaper. The carpet had the kind of dull pattern you only saw when viewing a house that was on the market because the former resident had died of extreme old age. A good paint job and some IKEA flooring wouldn't go amiss. Maybe he and Junior could work on it together before this whole affair got sorted out and Barney went home again.

When he did eventually get dressed and head downstairs, he saw the dishes from last night had been washed and were now dry on the rack. He yawned and turned on the stove, bringing the water to boil and making a cup of tea and some toast. The stillness of the house was mesmerising. Barney stood in the silence, daydreaming out the window, watching Junior sprinkling some feed for the chickens. The birds were kept in a large run protected by a wire mesh that Junior had built himself.

On finishing his toast, Barney went outside to a battered up picnic bench to enjoy the rest of his tea in the pleasant September morning sunshine. His cough hadn't really affected him since arriving and his lungs felt better in the fresh Highland air. Junior gave him a wave. "Morning," said Barney.

"Sleep well?" asked Junior.

"Like a baby."

"I'll say. You've missed half the day already."

"It's only nine o'clock," said Barney, checking his watch.

"Aye. What do you say we go for a wee stroll and I'll show you the neighbourhood?"

"Why not?" said Barney.

Two hours later, Junior's 'wee stroll' had taken them through the valley and plantation forest, across ankle turning heather, up and down hills, and eventually onto a stalker's path. The din of rushing water began to build as the path thinned and climbed up to higher ground. The hills either side became sheer and Barney did his best to keep his eyes focused on Junior's boots striding in front of him.

Soon they came to a sign which advised walkers it was dangerous to proceed further, but Junior picked a careful route down and told Barney it was safe to follow. The rock was damp and it was no easy thing to lower himself down. His heart had a healthy beat by the time they rounded the side of another hill and the roar of cascading water rushed to meet them.

"The Falls of Glomach," said Junior.

Barney swooned as white water tumbled over a high cliff, bouncing half way down onto soaking black rock and then spouting in all directions into a dark pool enclosed by walls of granite and lush green vegetation. A flashback to the Forth Railway Bridge caused him to stiffen up. He took a step back, his hand went up and Junior caught him by the wrist. "Easy mate."

"I'm no too good wae heights," Barney said. Junior offered him a drink from his water bottle and Barney took a swig with trembling hands.

The two men sat down in silence, looking into the falls as the constant roar swallowed up all other sounds. It was Barney who broke the mesmerising spell of the waterfall.

"Look mate, aboot last night. I had nae right tae ask aboot that stuff."

Junior sniffed. "It wasn't that," he said. "It just stirred up a lot of old memories." Junior picked up a rock and tossed it over the cliff into oblivion. "You wanted to ken what happened oot there. Well, I'll tell you..."

Junior is in the military land rover with three oppos when the wheel hits the mine. A boom and wave of energy rises up through the vehicle. The noise of metal being torn apart is deafening. Junior hears it in slow motion. He feels the jeep lifting up and then smoke fills his lungs. Scalding heat. Fire at his feet. The vehicle is rolling over. It stops but he can't get out. A smell of bbq meat. Burning alive. Pitch black and choking. Screaming and kicking. Glass breaks and he finds a gap to scramble out of. Crawling away on fire, he rolls and rubs sand on his face to douse the flames. He looks over at the burning vehicle but then passes out.

"I wake up sweating, and for a moment I dinnae ken where the fuck I am," Junior said. "My three oppos were all killed. One guy had just got married six months before. His wife had a baby on the way. What must their families be going through? So yeah, I'm hiding up here. Same as you."

"And that's why you got a medical discharge?" asked Barney.

"Not exactly. I was discharged for the physical injuries. Psychiatrist told me I had PTSD and advised my unit I'd have to go through a series of *mental examinations*. I ken what that meant, so I didn't bother telling them about the flashbacks. Truth is, I'm not sure I'd want to go back, even if I could. Sometimes I'm just out walking in the hills and I hear the explosion. I'm back in the vehicle. Breaking glass. Smoke. Smell of burning skin. My face stings to buggery. I'll come to and check ma watch and there's five or ten minutes gone by. I've been oot the game." Junior paused and then said, "You're the only person apart fae Rab that I've told that tae."

"That's heavy," said Barney. "But what aboot all your old mates? Surely we could have helped."

Junior shook his head. "I dinnae want people tae see me like this. A few days back in the army rehabilitation centre down south was enough for me. Went out walking in civvy street, but people's reaction to my *new face* made that a no go. Instant horror. And then pretending they havnae seen you as they walk past, eyes dead ahead as if I don't exist. Except I can feel them and they can sure as fuck feel me. Bairns pointing and embarrassed parents pulling doon their arms and telling them off for it. Nah. Fuck that. It's one thing you coming up here. It's another thing me trying to live back there."

"Is there nothing they can give ye for the nightmares or flashbacks?"

"I've got pills and shit," said Junior. "All they really wanted was tae ask questions and run tests. And if I failed their tests? Then what? The looney bin? Nae danger."

"Wait," said Barney. "So you're on the run?"

"No. It's not difficult to know what to say to appear normal tae a shrink. But that didn't help me. I spoke to the Commanding Officer. A good guy. Said I was having trouble sleeping. He suggested I be temporarily discharged for physical injuries. So, I came up here. It was our Granddad's place a long time ago but naebdy's been up for years, except Rab. I'm doing a bit of work on it... and stuff."

When they got back to the house Junior prepared omelettes, beans and bread, pouring out some tea to wash it down with. "I was thinking, it might not be a bad idea for us to do a bit of range work. Get you comfortable with a firearm. We could head out on the hills and I'll show you a few things. Rab told me a bit about this hitman who's after you."

"It'll be fine," said Barney, scooping up some beans with his spoon. "Roman must be somewhere. He'll take the hit off. And no one kens where we are except Rab."

"No offence, mate. But dinnae be so naive. If you have to face that cunt, he'll make short work of you. It'll be like me and that deer last night. Except you're the deer. Better to have a chance. What else you gonnae do up here?"

Barney had stopped chewing. "This is grim talk for the dinner table, mate."

Junior got up and opened a hidden door in the wooden panel wall.

"Holy shit!" said Barney. "What have you got in there?"

"One Browning 9mm pistol; one Walther P38 from the second world war; one AK-47 assault rifle; and an antique double barrel shotgun. That was my Grandfather's. It's worth a mint."

Barney's nose was in the door, eyes going from left to right like a kid in a sweetie shop. "Where the hell did you get all these?"

"Ask me no questions..." said Junior, taking out the Browning 9mm. "Let me show you this one first, then we'll go ootside and see what you're like with a pistol at ten paces."

CHAPTER 32

_____

BREAKING AND ENTERING

Using anti-surveillance programmes to check for police communication frequencies, the hitman ran an online check on Barnabas Wild's house. When he was satisfied there was no one in the vicinity, he drove by the house with his scanners activated, searching for signals that might indicate a presence nearby. The place looked clean and Barnabas's car was parked outside.

The hitman parked in a residential street. The data uploaded to his laptop showed no activity detected outside Barnabas Wild's house and so he waited until dark for a quiet time to pick the lock and enter.

The house produced little in the way of clues. All personal belongings seemed to be in place and there were no signs of a rushed exit or packing of clothes. He certainly hadn't been home in the last twenty-four hours.

Going through personal items, the hitman built up a picture of Barnabas, analysing the artefacts of his life, furniture, photographs, clothes, books, even the way he kept his cutlery. He found Barnabas Wild's passport in his bedside drawer.

If he'd decided to flee the country, he wasn't going by the usual methods.

CHAPTER 33

TARGET PRACTICE

The outline of a man had been painted in red onto a huge eight-foot rotting tree stump in Junior's garden. Barney had hit the target six times, none of which had been a kill, though one had been in the nuts.

"You've got tae learn tae control your breathing," said Junior. "Relax. Dinnae rush or squeeze too hard."

Barney's final shot hit the target in the shoulder, the crack from the pistol instantly met by the thud of dead wood as tiny splinters from the tree went flying into the air. "It's no as easy as it looks in the movies," he said.

"Aye, and harder still when it's moving, or firing back."

Junior took the weapon from Barney, clipped out the magazine, pointed the pistol to the sky and squeezed the trigger so the mechanism clicked. He then slotted the empty magazine back in, switched the safety catch and holstered the weapon. "Why don't we try the rifle?" he said. "Longer range. You can lie down if you want."

"Let's dae it," said Barney, rubbing his hands together. "You know, I could get right intae this sort of thing if I lived up here. It's like being a bairn again, running aroond wae pellet guns."

Just as with the pistol, Junior made Barney watch as he stripped the rifle and re-assembled it, naming the component parts and making Barney repeat them to remember. Then it was Barney's turn to do it himself. Only then would Junior allow him to go out and shoot.

Junior loaded the bullets into the clip, thumbing them down one by one until they made a satisfying click. "You need to un-derstand the entire weapon," he said, "not just the end result. What you don't want is a stoppage in a fire-fight because you're weapon's dirty. Court martial for a rusty weapon."

"Ma weapon's never been rusty, ta very much," said Barney, as Junior pushed the magazine into the hunting rifle and handed it to him. Barney pointed the barrel down the make-shift range and gazed through the sights which bobbed up and down, on and around the target.

CHAPTER 34

JUNIOR'S SECRET SIDELINE

Barney turned the old brass faucet in the shower. A deep rumble from ancient pipes somewhere within the heart of the house was followed a few seconds later by a forceful blast of freezing water which struck the tiles and bounced back, soaking Barney's arms and a bit of his top. A couple of rotations set the other tap for a balance between hot and cold.

Barney pulled the shower curtain over and then lifted the toilet seat to take a pee, humming some old Neil Diamond song. After flushing, he put his hand under the shower water, which was about right. "Sweet Caroline... oh oh oh... good times never seemed so good..." Only when he was undressed did he remember his towel was still in the bedroom. Sod's law.

He went into his room to collect it. On the way back to the bathroom, he noticed a wooden ladder leading up to an open loft at the end of the hallway. That was strange. Junior had said he was going to go and feed the chickens. He was about to call out when he thought better of it. Maybe he was still unsure about Junior, or maybe he was just a nosy bastard, but he decided to take a peek, going up the steps, one by one, doing his best not to make them creak.

That smell again.

Pungent and becoming thicker as he got higher on the ladder. He sniffed once and then twice in quick succession. Cannabis. Maybe Junior had taken to smoking up there instead of in the lounge. He climbed two more steps and stuck his head up to see an indoor plantation in Junior's loft. A den stuffed with green cannabis plants. Every bit of floor space was taken up with hot lamps and foil, reflecting heat and light, making the atmosphere a jungle.

While Barney was having his shower, Junior had come up to check on Rab's stock. It would only take a few minutes and Barney would be none the wiser. The temperature gauge was correct, the lamps were all working well, and the plants looked good.

When he turned around to go back down, he saw a head popping up. A head without a body. Barney's head. It scanned the entire loft, a look of confusion and then surprise as it locked onto Junior. "For medicinal purposes, is it?" Barney said. "Now I ken why you two are so secretive aboot everything. And that sneaky bastard Rab wanted me tae bring a bag back for him. What would've been in that, eh? Enough tae get me sent doon for a few years, that's for fucking sure! Cheeky cunts."

"Look," said Junior, "this isnae something I'd have got intae but I'm only on half pay with the army now. It's just a temporary sideline tae pay ma groceries. I'm in the middle of naywhere up here. I've got tae dae something for cash."

"How long have you and Rab been at this?"

Junior squatted down onto his heels because the low roof was giving him a tight back. "A few months," he said. "Rab started it a few years ago. He had some Spanish hippie living up here with his Missus but they went hame and Rab needed someone else tae take over. Got me involved when I wouldnae come back tae Edinburgh. It's quite a science, getting the most oot the crop. The male and female plants. Temperatures. Lighting. There's all sorts of theories and methods."

"Aye, I'm sure there is," said Barney. "But as far as I ken, this is just a *normal* Highland cottage, owned by some *normal* weed smoking, ex-army sniper who gives names to his chickens and shoots small deer in his garden for dinner. Now if you'll excuse me, I'm going doon tae have ma shower."

Barney lay in bed staring at the stars and milky way through the old, single pane, sash window. His breath rose up from the two thick blankets and sheepskin throw. The other parts of the bed were like ice. When he closed his eyes, he thought of Grace. Her green eyes and her scent. Was it possible to remember smells in your mind? Barney thought so. That night they'd shared. So brief but so good. He wished he could send her a message to explain things.

"She'll be there when you get back, Barney," he imagined his gran saying. He looked forward to that moment. He'd waited his whole life. He could wait a while longer. A week wouldn't hurt and it'd make seeing her again all the sweeter. That's how his gran would have said it anyway.

If only Roman would show up. Where the hell could he have got to? Rab had promised to call Junior the moment he got word. But what if something had happened to Roman? Forget it. There was no point thinking like that. He'd show up. Probably went on one of his deep sea fishing expeditions or some dodgy business trip. Maybe he'd gone abroad to organise the hit. Fuck.

He hadn't thought of that. Maybe that was the reason nobody had seen him. He might have turned it into a holiday, killing two birds with the one stone. That was a fine way of putting it.

Barney pulled the covers up to his chin and rolled onto his side. It didn't do any good over-thinking things. Positives. He was with Junior, an old buddy and an ex-army marksman. No one could find them here. It was a good place to relax. All he had to do was stay low and enjoy his time in the Highlands. Treat it like a short break. After the past few days, he needed one.

CHAPTER 35

SPY IN THE CAMP

"So what've you got for me, *Miss* White?" asked Grace. Clare slid a brown A4 envelope across the cafe table. "Okay, so... Barnabas Wild, also known as Barney, isn't exactly inconspicuous. Ex-pro boxer, held a commonwealth title at middleweight, retired early after some injuries, none serious but kept him out for long spells. Both his parents are deceased. His younger brother died at twenty-seven from cancer."

"Really?" said Grace.

"Yep. Barney owns the boxing gym you talked about. He's brought through a few national champions and he's well liked in the local community. Pays his taxes and runs a carpet business which employs a handful of people. He's had other businesses in the past, a couple of building firms, which he sold, and a few commercial properties which he leases out, so his money is well spread. Financially he's doing well. Might even be up there with your law firm when you consider everything..."

"Character background?" asked Grace, not taking the bait.

"Here's where it gets interesting," said Clare. "On the surface Barney appears to be, how would you say it in court, a *regular upstanding pillar of the community*? He's done a fair bit for charity, running seven marathons, no less. He puts on amateur fight nights at his gym with all ticket sales going to charities. He's been in all the local papers too. See?"

Clare pulled out an article with a photo showing Barney with a big smile on his face, holding an oversized cheque written out to Sick Kids for twenty thousand pounds. "He raised that on his last marathon. So it seems he's completely legit..."

"I'm sensing a big *but* coming up," said Grace.

"*I sense big butts and I cannot lie! You other brothers can't deny!*" sang Clare, giving an impromptu version of the song and wiggling in her chair. "Whoop whoop!"

Grace remained impassive and so Clare switched back to business mode. "Anyway," she continued, "the answer is yes *and* no. It's not Barney who's dodgy, it's more the people he knows. But I suppose the boxing world is like that. It's rough, isn't it? You don't get posh private school boys becoming pro-boxers. It's a working class sport."

"Hey!" said Grace. "My Granddad was a boxer, thank you very much."

"Ooh, is that why you're so feisty?"

Grace gave an authoritative, school-teacher glare, and Clare shrank in her seat.

"Are we talking gangsters?" Grace asked.

"Have you ever heard of a guy called Roman Rock?" asked Clare, lowering her voice.

Grace sighed and rolled her eyes.

"I thought you might. Well it seems Mr. Rock and Barney have been friends since primary school in Niddrie. And there are a few other dodgy characters who frequent a place called the White House Pub, Barney's local. He definitely mixes with them, but it seems he keeps away from any of their dastardly deeds. Now here's where things get a bit strange." Clare pulled back her hair and sucked at the straw of her Green Highlander juice. "Delicious. Really has a kick to it. It's the ginger."

"Can we get back to the matter in hand?" asked Grace.

"Yeah sure. Well, Barney hasn't been active in nearly a week. By that I mean his phone is off. Not trackable. So I have no idea where he currently is. He's not used social media or the internet, which is unusual, as normally he makes a lot of updates for the gym. The last few texts he sent were to none other than Roman Rock. Before that he hadn't text Roman in so long I wasn't able to acquire records. And that's not all. Here's the show stopper. Roman Rock was arrested hours before Barney sent those messages. He's currently being held by serious crime squad and not being given bail, as yet. Finding that out was risky, but I've decided to do it for free, seeing as though you're buying lunch."

"I am?" said Grace.

"You are," said Clare. "And if you want me to find out more about Roman Rock, it'll be a lot fancier than the usual grub. It's risky hacking into police files. Especially when it's someone as dodgy as him."

Grace nodded, looking concerned. "Anything else?" she asked.

"Yes. Something s-s-s-sinister..." Clare leaned closer and looked around the cafe before she spoke. "Someone *else* has been hacking into Barney's data. Phone records, emails, credit card account etc. And it's not the police. At least, not officially. I couldn't get a trace on them, so I reckon they know what they're doing."

Grace frowned. "Interesting," she said.

"That's everything so far. It's all in that envelope. On paper, Barney looks fine, but I guess you never know."

"Great. Thanks Clare."

Clare's eyes widened and she held out her palms.

"Oh," said Grace. "I meant, Miss White."

CHAPTER 36

PHILIP ROBERTSON QC

Grace passed through the open door into the police station and heard the words, "Unreasonable. Totally unreasonable!" The articulated arrogance caused an involuntary cringe as she registered the voice of her own personal nemesis, Philip Robertson QC, the most corrupt barrister in Scotland. The man would sell his soul to any sort of disreputable cause if there was money to be made. No morals. No ethics. The go-to-guy for Roman Rock and a host of other undesirables. She'd had to endure his tactful commiserations on three separate occasions after Roman slipped the net of her prosecution through various underhanded means. None of it could be proved, of course. That was what left such a bad taste in the mouth.

The law was open to interpretation, her mentor had told her. The law was *all* interpretation, she'd learned.

"What does he expect?" said Robertson, standing at the reception desk with his back to Grace. "Miracles? I'm a QC, not a magician."

"Is Roman not paying you enough blood money this time, Mr. Faust?" said Grace, approaching from behind.

The policeman at the desk gave a wry smile. Philip Robertson turned his entire upper body as if the muscles in his neck didn't function. "Just when I thought my day couldn't turn any more sour..."

"Save the sardonic crap for the courtroom," said Grace. "Tell me, have you ever won a case without bribing jury members or having your clients sabotage evidence?"

Philip Robertson QC raised his head as if catching a foul smell in the air. His thinning, grey hair was fashioned into a middle parting, and two bird-like eyes peered down through small spectacles that rested on the tip of a very pointed nose. "I do hope you have sufficient evidence to back up such allegations Miss Farquhar... unlike the last time we met."

A trace of a grin grew out from the corner of Robertson's thin, rosy lips. Observing Grace's eyes blaze in green only spurred him on. "In my opinion, your closing speeches lack a certain, how should I say, *conviction*?" This time Philip Robertson allowed himself a chuckle.

"If you'll just sign here," said the officer on duty, passing the QC a piece of paper. Robertson turned to sign, placing his briefcase on the floor.

"You're a disgrace to the profession," said Grace. "It's no wonder your only clients are scum. From what I hear, there's no way even your legal slithering will get Roman Rock out this time. I hope you go down with him. Now that would be justice."

Mr. Robertson emitted a low sigh. "Oh, dear, dear. You never were very well informed as to the proper facts. That was one of your failures too, if I remember. It might interest you to know, I no longer represent Mr. Rock."

Philip Robertson dipped his knees to pick up his briefcase and then strode out of the building without further conversation, his chin raised and one hand holding the lapels of his over coat; the epitome of the grand barrister.

"Don't you mind him, Miss Farquhar," said the officer. "Everyone knows he's a first class prick. Best not to trade words with a creature like that. He'll get his comeuppance one day. You mark my words."

"And none too soon," said Grace, still fuming.

"Who is it you're representing today?"

"No one," said Grace. "I'm actually here to see Detective Sergeant Ross Souter."

"It's Detective *Inspector* Souter, these days, Miss Farquhar. His office is down the hallway, last door on the left."

CHAPTER 37

STAG HUNTING

They moved behind the hill in order to get upwind of the stag they'd been tracking for the past half hour. Junior spoke in a low voice, telling Barney to, "get to ground." They crawled around the brae over heather and the odd well placed rock before Junior stopped and lifted his chin a few inches to see through the long grass. He waved Barney up to join him, putting his finger to his lips and mouthing to, 'move slowly.' When Barney came alongside, Junior pointed to the stag which was not two hundred yards away. The big beast was surrounded by grazing females and some fawns. Junior passed Barney the rifle and whispered, "Take a look."

Barney got the stock tight in his shoulder and wriggled into a comfortable position in lee of the hill just below Junior. He bent his right leg at the knee to cater for the uneven slope. Two days before, he'd managed to place a surprising number of shots into a target at three hundred yards from this same position. Junior had even complimented him on his grouping, saying he had the makings of a rifleman or sniper, though he was clearly no pistoleer.

Barney leaned his head to the side and gazed down the hunting scope to view the herd close up under x50 magnification. Sweeping his field of view among the females and fawns, he eventually centred the crosshairs on the impressive stag that displayed some sort of sixth sense by raising its head and looking around, as if sniffing danger.

"Take the shot," whispered Junior, through his teeth.

Barney pulled his eyes away from the sights. "Why?"

"Why do you think? You could have his heid up above the door if you wanted."

"I don't want. It's done nothing to me. And there's about two weeks of meat still in the freezer from Bambi."

"Could you dae it though?" Junior asked, and there was a challenge in his voice.

Barney pulled back from the scope and met Junior with a steely blue gaze. A warning. He put his eye back to the sight. The proud stag raised his head and called out, his antlers tall and strong. Barney took a slow breath in and then let the air out over a longer time. On the pause between breaths came a stillness that seemed to stop the world. He squeezed the trigger. The rifle had not been cocked but it didn't matter.

"Aye," said Barney, calm and poised as the hunter. "I could dae it."

Junior nodded.

And then they crawled back out of sight.

CHAPTER 38

ROSS SOUTER AND GRACE - ROUND 1

Ross offered Grace a seat at his desk and sat opposite, eager to know why she had come.

"I need to see Roman Rock," she said.

Ross Souter laughed and leaned back, tapping the desk three times with his palms.

"I'm serious," said Grace.

The change in Souter's face was almost comic. "What makes you think he's even here?"

"I passed his brief in the hallway on the way in. You might be interested to know they've parted company."

"What?" said Souter, sitting forward. "You're joking?"

"Nope, Philip Robertson told me himself."

Ross took a moment to digest the information. "So why do you want to see Roman?"

"I'm looking for someone," said Grace. "I think Roman may know where that person is."

"Who are you looking for?"

"A client who's gone missing."

"You could file a missing person's report," said Souter. "What's the name?"

"Barnabas Wild," said Grace.

"The boxer?" asked Souter, interested.

"You've heard of him?"

"Aye, he was pretty good. How do you know *him*?"

"I can't say. Client confidentiality. But it'd really mean a lot to me if you let me speak to Roman. From what I know, he could be able to help. It's got nothing to do with the charges against him."

Ross Souter was unconvinced. "Sorry Grace, but I can't. Roman's not seeing anyone. No calls. Only his brief. I don't want any leaks. The case we have against him is watertight."

"Do me a favour," said Grace. "All the years we've known each other. I want to see Roman sent down as much as you do."

Ross sighed and then pushed back into his new expensive office chair.

"Have I ever asked you for anything in the past?" Grace asked.

"Yes!" answered Ross.

"Okay, let me re-phrase that. Have I ever asked for anything that's got you into trouble or been bad for your career?"

"Well, not exactly..."

"Have I ever refused to give my professional opinion when you've asked? Or said NO to looking into things for you?"

"No, Grace, but- - -"

"On the contrary, I've pointed you in the right direction more than a few times *and* provided you with certain *information* you might not have been able to acquire within the constraints of your professional capacity."

Ross sighed. "You're talking like a lawyer now."

"Come on, Ross," said Grace. "It's me. We worked to together to build the last case against Roman. I need this favour. It's important."

Ross drummed his fingers on the edge of his desk. "Alright," he said. "Fifteen minutes before he goes back to the cells. That's all you're getting. And it'll be in interview room one, so I can see and hear everything."

CHAPTER 39

GRACE AND ROMAN

Roman Rock had been moved to an interrogation room and was awaiting his next pointless meeting with Ross Souter when Grace entered instead. An officer remained inside the room, stone faced and impassive, gazing ahead into the wall.

"What have we here?" said Roman. "They said someone wanted tae talk tae me. If I'd known it was you, I'd have got them tae bring a wee bottle of champagne."

"Mr. Rock," said Grace, cordially. "How are you today?"

Roman didn't get up but flicked the air with the back of his hand. His shirt sleeves were rolled up and his collar undone, exposing a very hairy chest and bullish neck. "I'm enjoying a brief stay at her majesty's pleasure. Not that I gie a fuck about that inbred man-cunt."

"Looks like you may be here a bit longer than you think," said Grace. "I just passed Philip Robertson QC at reception. He says he's not representing you this time."

"Aye, well there's plenty more where he came from," said Roman. "Lift up a stone and there they all are, crawling aboot ready to jump the moment you flash some cash."

"I'd say that was a fairly honest appraisal of your former brief," said Grace. "Anyway, let's get started."

Roman smiled. "You ken how much I like tae help the police with their inquiries..."

"I don't represent the police," said Grace. "I'm here on a private matter."

"Are you noo? And what would that be?"

"I'm looking for someone."

"Oh aye, and only I can tell you, eh?" Roman beamed. "My brief does a runner and two minutes later you're in here on a *private matter* looking for information. Darling, dae I look like I was born yesterday?" Roman leaned forward on his elbows, "You ken, I remember a few times in court, I caught you looking over at me. I kent what you were thinking. Men like me attract women like you. Pure animal magnetism. I'm the king of the jungle. I dae whatever I want in this life. Posh girls like you dream of having a *real* man like me show you who's boss. A bit of rough with balls the size of coconuts."

"Aye, and just as hairy," said Grace. "Now let's get down to business, Mr. Rock."

"Ah," said Roman, sitting up straighter, "now we're talking."

Grace returned Roman's gaze, considering the best way to illicit the information she needed. The trouble was, beneath Roman's neanderthal exterior was a sharp mind. He'd risen to the top of the underworld by making strong plays and out-smarting opponents. Any hint she was trying to trick or manip-ulate him would shut him up like a clam.

"I want you to know this is strictly off the record," said Grace.

"Is that so? And I suppose that arsehole Ross Souter isnae be-hind the glass over there with his cock oot?"

Roman and Grace looked at their reflections in the interview room mirror.

"Bastard!" whispered Souter, from behind the glass.

"If he is, or he isn't, it doesn't matter," said Grace. "I'm not here on police business. And I reckon you owe me a favour."

Roman laughed. "And how's that?"

"Three times I've had watertight cases against you. Three times you've got off by playing the system. Witnesses refusing to testify, others disappearing, evidence going missing before trial. You were a blot on an otherwise perfect copy book."

Roman stared back at this firecracker of a woman sitting opposite. She might have looked good enough to eat but she had some fucking balls about her, and a brain to go with it. He opened his palms, elbows still on the table. "What is it you want to know?"

"I want to know where someone is."

"Who?"

She decided to lay her cards on the table. "Barnabas Wild."

Roman leaned back and folded his arms, a perceptible veil drawing over his eyes. He took a breath that filled his big chest and didn't let out until Grace spoke again.

"I know you and Barney go back a long way," she said.

"Barney is it now? So you ken him personally?"

"I do."

"Obviously no well enough," said Roman.

"What's that supposed to mean?"

"It means, if Barney wanted you to ken where he was, he'd have telt you."

"He *did* want to tell me something. Something important. We arranged to meet two days ago and he didn't show. His phone's been off ever since and I'm concerned." Grace noticed Roman's eyebrows dip a smidgen. "I think you know something," said Grace. "Listen to this and tell me if you still don't believe me." Grace put her phone on the table, opened her voicemail and selected speaker phone. Barney's voice came over loud and clear.

"Grace, I'm sorry for the way I acted. It's been a crazy week but I've just had some news that changes everything. I'll need tae explain in person. It's all good though! Let's meet for dinner. You choose. Anywhere you like. See you soon, love."

"I texted Barney to say I'd meet him on Wednesday night at a bar in town," said Grace. "He texted me back saying he'd be there. Since then, his phone's been off and he hasn't been seen. Not at the gym, not at his work, not anywhere."

Roman's eyes swept in a diagonally upward gaze across the table and up to the ceiling. He was working something out.

"Roman," said Grace, "I came for Barney's sake, nothing else. I may not have known him as long as you but I know enough to care what happens to him. If he's in some sort of trouble, I'll help him. I've got contacts. I know Barney's your friend so- - -"

"It couldnae have happened already," said Roman.

"What couldn't?" asked Grace.

But Roman was deep in his own head. "It's too soon."

"What's too soon? Roman!"

Roman looked up but there was none of the bravado he'd ex-uded earlier. "What did he mean by, *it's all good?*" he asked.

"I don't know," said Grace. "He sounds relieved about something, happy even." Grace lowered her voice and said, "I had someone look into his phone records. He made a call to you the same day you were arrested. In fact, after you were arrested. He also sent you texts. Did you talk to him? Was he worried about something?"

Roman ran his fingers through his hair. "This isnae good."

"What isn't?" asked Grace. "What's happened to Barney?"

"I need tae make a phone call," said Roman, with all his hardness and force.

"Only your brief can get you that," said Grace.

"Ma brief's done a runner," said Roman, suddenly changing to cool and dangerous. "But I'll tell ye something, darlin', if I dinnae get that phone call, Barney'll be done for. If he's no been done already..."

Grace could see Roman was serious. And not even he would pull a stunt like this for a phone call. Barney was obviously in some real danger, and so Grace did something she didn't ever do. She made a snap decision without considering the consequences. "I'll represent you," she said, hardly able to believe the words as she said them.

Roman's face relaxed into a deranged smile, and then he brought his hand down hard onto the desk. Grace jumped. "Now we're talking, Miss Farquhar!" he said.

CHAPTER 40

ROSS SOUTER AND GRACE - ROUND 2

Ross Souter slammed the door of of his office and was already shouting before he turned back to Grace. "What the *hell* do you think you're playing at?"

Grace sighed. "I know this seems strange---"

"Strange? You representing Roman Rock *strange*? Oh no, that's not strange. Not strange at all..." Ross stopped mid rant and blinked as if a message had just been downloaded from one part of his brain into another. "Wait a minute! Is this why you came to see me earlier? So you could get the lowdown on the Rock and then use it to try and get him off the hook?"

"No," said Grace. "Don't' be silly. I had no intention of repre-senting Roman. I told you, I needed information about someone he knows."

"This Barnabas Wild you spoke to him about?"

"Yes."

Ross put both hands flat down onto the desk and leaned over his elbows as if Grace were a suspect he was grilling. "Go on..." he said.

Grace scratched her temple. "Barney and I were... seeing each other." Grace's words were like a quick one-two into the soft spots of Souter's pride and vanity. All those times they'd spent together and even after a couple of drinks and some banter she'd never wanted anything to do with him. He took a moment to recover. "What's all this got to do with Roman?" he asked, trying not to sound bitter.

"He knows something," said Grace. "You saw how he reacted. Barney's his friend from childhood."

"The Rock doesn't have any friends. Men like him only have enemies... and lap dogs, like Boneheed McCracken."

"He seems to care about Barney," said Grace. "When I played him that voicemail he changed completely. There's something going on, Ross. Roman knows more than he's saying, and I'll get it out of him as my client."

"Client confidentiality," said Souter, shaking his head.

"It's the only way he knows he's safe. Trust me, Ross, do you think I'd do something like this if it wasn't serious?"

"How serious?"

"From Roman's reaction, I'd say, *very*."

"Life or death serious?"

Grace nodded.

Souter took a deep breath in through his nose. His hands went onto his hips, pulling back his jacket. "Right," he said. " I want to know what Roman knows about Barnabas Wild. And don't give me any of that client confidentiality crap either. If this is as serious as you think, then it's your duty to tell me."

"I'll do what I can," said Grace, picking up her bag. "But my first priority is Barney."

CHAPTER 41

RAYMOND AND BURNSEY

Roman waited for the door to shut before speaking. "I've called some people," he said. You were right. Barney was looking for me. According to ma sources he was pretty woond up. That was the Monday, like you said, and he's no been seen since." Roman paused and then said, "I need oot."

Grace blew air from her lips. "Roman, give me something to argue with. With your history and the seriousness of the charges against you, they aren't going to let you out on bail in case you flee the country."

"Flee the country? I live here. Ma hoose is in Milton Road East. I dinnae run fae anybody."

"What is it your not telling me?"

"I cannae say here."

"Roman---"

"Are you sure there's nay recording devices in here?"

"They can't record what's said between a client and their lawyer. It would not only be inadmissible in court, it would also be breaking the law."

"I dinnae trust that Ross Souter. He's a sly wee bastard."

"Roman, I need to know what's happened to Barney."

"I dinnae ken anyone by that name," said Roman.

"What?" said Grace.

Roman leaned closer, lowering his voice. "Though I do ken someone called *Burnsey*," he said, with a wink. "So listen carefully, Miss Farquhar. *Burnsey* was a good pal of a guy I knew, whom we'll call, *Raymond*. Raymond was a hard bastard. A proper Big Man. Violent but fair. And a right good looking guy. Curly black hair and moustache..."

"Go on," said Grace.

"Bursney and Raymond kent each other since school. Back then, Raymond wasn't the exactly man he is today. He was shy and quiet. A wee kid who got bullied and walked alone aroond the playground at lunchtime. No friends except a few stray animals. Raymond had the shite beat oot of him on a daily basis by his stepfather who was a drunken alcoholic bastard. The type of scumbag who pressed the stop button on the bus with his middle finger, just in case he could piss someone off for free. A cunt. With a capital fucking kicking K."

Three heavy veins appeared on the centre of Roman's forehead in the shape of a trident. Grace asked if he wanted some water. Roman shook his head. There was an internal venom about him. Some deep mental trauma had been roused and he was suddenly a different animal. Grace couldn't take her eyes from him.

"One day," continued Roman, "young Raymond was getting a proper leathering by three boys after they called his mum a whoore and he told them to go fuck themselves. They had him on the groond and were playing football with him when in comes this wee ginger haired whirlwind that fights them off. Fists flying at a hundred miles an 'oor like some fucking cartoon character. When one of the boys' older brothers comes jumping in, Burnsey knocks him oot with a punch that breaks the boy's jaw. Burnsey picks Raymond up and asks if he's okay. And that was that. Raymond and Burnsey would always be pals. They lived near tae each other and Burnsey showed Raymond a bit of boxing so he could take care of himself. When Raymond got older, he filled out, big and strong. And he had a rage that could take him through any cunt alive. One day he comes hame to hear screaming in the hoose. He opens the living room door to see his stepdad strangling his mother. She was blue in the face and on her last breath. Raymond couldnae remember what happened next. Only that when he came to, his stepdad was deid. Beaten to a pulp. And his mother was barely alive. He phoned the ambulance and called Burnsey who told Raymond tae say it was self defence. Raymond's stepdad had a history of beating up women and so the police believed it. After that, Raymond got a reputation. People feared him. And he saw that when people feared him, he could dae whatever he wanted. Raymond loved that power."

A shiver ran up Grace's spine. Roman's eyes were alight with violence. But then they changed again. "Cut a long story short," he said, "one day, not long ago, Bursney comes tae Raymond and says he's got weeks to live. Same cancer as what killed his wee brother. And Burnsey's feared of cancer. He cannae handle the thought of wasting away in a hospital. But he cannae kill himself either. That's no him. So what does he dae? He goes to Raymond and asks him tae put a hit on him."

Grace's eyes widened. "And does he?"

"Course he fucking does. It's his best pal in the world. The only person who's ever done anything good for him. But then Raymond gets nicked and Burnsey somehow finds out he's- - -"

"The hospital report!" said Grace. "It was on the news the other night."

"What?"

"Some cancer test results got mixed up at the Western General. There was an investigation. Oh my god. It couldn't be..."

"But if it was..." said Roman.

Grace finished his thought train. "*Burnsey* goes to see *Raymond* but Raymond isn't there. So Burnsey would have no choice but to run and hide until Raymond came back."

Roman nodded. "Aye. But he'd need tae tell someone of his plans so they could reach him once Raymond did get back."

"Who?" asked Grace.

"I dinnae ken."

"But Raymond *needs* to take the hit off, right now!"

"Easier said than done, Miss Farquhar. Raymond has most likely contacted a hitman in a way that only *he* could. He'd have tae get his computer back tae do it. And even then, it's no a sure thing. This hitman might not dae take-backs. It's not like returning a fucking jumper to Marks and Spark's. So Raymond's lawyer had better come up wae *something* soon, otherwise *Burnsey* is going tae be hunted doon. And mark ma words, he *will* be hunted doon. No matter how long it takes. This is a professional we're talking aboot. A cold, calculating, psychopathic cunt."

CHAPTER 42

ROSS SOUTER AND GRACE - ROUND 3

Ross Souter sat forward at his desk, hands and fingers locked together, eager and at the same time, defensive. Grace began to recount the same coded story Roman had told her. Hearing Roman call someone else psychopathic was worrying to both of them. She assured Ross that Roman would give his word and not try to escape. All he needed to do was go back to his house and send word to the hitman to call off the hit. Then they could take him back. He'd even agreed to be handcuffed the whole time, if necessary.

Ross seemed unable to stop his head from shaking. He even laughed at one point. "Can I remind you a man's life is at stake?" said Grace.

In a cynical pursing of his lips, Grace saw there was no way Souter would release Roman. His prize. The man he'd been trying to nail for ten years. The devil himself, Ross called him.

"The Rock's not going anywhere, except hell. And before that he's doing life inside. It'll be Monday before he has the bail hearing. And even if he gets it, and that's a big *if*, he'll be on a tag and his passport'll be confiscated. And I'll personally make sure there's surveillance on him round the clock. Nothing short of a heart attack would get Roman out of that cell."

And that's when Grace had an idea as spontaneous as her offer to represent Roman. It came as all great ideas do, with a spark that brings clarity and utter conviction. She re-visited Roman to tell him of Ross's refusal to let him out, and described to Roman a plan to save Barney. Roman nodded his head in approval. A proud smile made him seem almost human.

"You're even better than Philip Robertson QC," he said, enjoying seeing Grace dip her toes into the mirky waters where he'd dwelled most of his life.

CHAPTER 43

SEARCHING FOR MR. WILD

The hitman's investigation into Barnabas Wild's whereabouts had turned up nothing. He'd scoped out Rab Lawrie's place for two days but Barnabas had not shown himself either inside or outside of the house, and the habits of the two residents were not in keeping with harbouring a guest or a kidnap victim.

Lead after lead had proved useless. The hitman had done jobs similar to this in the past and simply waited them out until the target resurfaced, which they usually always did. However, something here was different. Barnabas's phone signal cutting out in the house of Rab Lawrie could mean it had been stolen and then turned off to be unlocked, wiped and sold on.

Another more sinister possibility presented itself. Barnabas might have been killed and dumped, his belongings salvaged in the process.

He pondered over the facts again, considering Barnabas's behaviour that first day when leaving the White House pub. He'd been agitated. Nervous. Was it conceivable Barnabas could have known a hit had been called on him? The hitman sniffed. It might be wise to keep an open mind and return to Rab Lawrie's house again. A listening device planted discretely should give a better insight into the situation.

CHAPTER 44

TOILET PAPER

Rab reached for the bog roll but his fingers touched only a cardboard cylinder empty of paper. He sighed and leaned forwards to open the bathroom door. "Tam! Are you there? Tam!"

The living room door was shut and the TV blaring. That tight-fisted bastard bought fuck all for the house. At least when he was in Tesco he came in with the odd pack of unsellable crushed toilet rolls or a few tins of Tennent's he'd scanned for five pence each.

Rab looked down the corridor into the kitchen, where a roll of paper towel stood teasing him on the worktop. There was nothing else for it. He got up and waddled down the hallway with trousers and pants at his ankles.

Unbeknownst to Rab, he was being observed by a man peeking through the letter box. The man recoiled as he got an eyeful of Rab's mucky arsehole.

Rab picked up the paper towel but didn't notice the tiny listening device that had just been planted inside the letter box as he passed the front door on his way back into the bathroom.

CHAPTER 45

PISH TALK AND DORUSDUAIN

The hitman's listening device was relayed by satellite back to his laptop, allowing him to listen in whilst driving as he looked for a suitable hotel. He paid cash, providing a false ID, and was given a room overlooking Princes Street and the Gardens. Dragging a high-backed armchair over to the tall Georgian window, he settled his gaze on the busy street as the sunset turned the sky a deep purple and navy blue. Then he put on his headphones. The lights of slow moving traffic were hypnotic and helped drop his brainwaves into the alpha state he found ideal for processing in audible data.

From the conversation taking place in the terraced house of Robert Lawrie, the hitman knew Rab and his housemate had been drinking. They appeared to be watching a local football

match on television. Their voices slowed as the match pro-
gressed and the conversation became slurred and meaningless
at times.

"Any news fae Barney?" asked Tam, during a boring spell
of play where Celtic played keep-the-ball from Hibernian's
forwards.

"He left his phone here, mind?"

"Oh, aye," said Tam.

"Let's hope that hitman doesnae *track* it and come here looking for him," said Rab, sarcastically.

"Aye," said Tam, not catching on. "Tell you what though, if he
did come roond, I'd kick his cunt in."

"Fuck off! You'd shite yer pants and tell him where Barney
was before he even touched ye! He'd never get it fae me though.
He could stick needles in ma eyes and I'd no tell him where
Barney was."

"Aye right!" said Tam. "I was a Young Niddrie Terror. I've got
way mare stamina for torture than you. That cunt could water-
board me and I'd still no grass."

"Half the folk roond here were YNT! Me included. That cunt
could fuckin' surfboard us and we'd still no talk!"

"Aye! Nae danger would we gee up Barney!"

The two pals laughed and banged their cans together.

"What aboot Junior," asked Tam. "Has he no called?"

"Nah. But it takes near five 'oors tae get there."

"Get where? Where is Junior?"

"Up near Dorusduain," said Rab.

"Dorris what?"

"Dorusduain."

"Where's that, like?

"Yae ken Dorusduain."

"Dae I?"

"Course ye dae! You were there once, d'ye no mind?"

Tam stared into the carpet, a haze of weed smoke clouding his mind.

"A few miles up fae Loch Duich," said Rab, observing Tam's confusion. "That wee hoose oor Grandda left us."

Tam opened his mouth, the memory like an itch in the nostril that didn't quite materialise into a sneeze.

"Tam, ye've a mind like a goldfish. Ye've smoked too much shite. Yer memory's fucked."

"I remember something..."

"Up by Dorusduain, before the waterfall at Glomach. The only hoose up that way. Has a wee forest and the broken doon roof."

Click! The image suddenly appeared in Tam's memory banks. "Oh aye! That year we all went up! Man, that was a barry wee place!"

"Aye! Mind that summer? Must've been twelve of us in three cars. Camping, swimming, skinny dipping in the loch? Beer, girls, weed, LSD and good music."

"I cannae remember much actually..." said Tam.

"I'm no surprised. When ye weren't pished and stoned oot yer nut, ye were nose deep in Paula McFeely's tits!"

"Paula McFeely!" cried Tam. "Jesus! Whatever happened tae her?"

"Married. Five kids and a junkie husband," said Rab.

"But what a pair, eh?"

"Aye, ya jammy bastard. Many's a night I dreamed of diving headfirst into that melon rack. She must've been oot her face tae bag off with you."

But Tam was swimming in a distant happy memory, an easy smile plastered across his drunken face.

"May I propose a toast..." said Rab, raising his can of special brew. "To Paula Mcfeely's tits!"

Crazy and Tam hit their cans together, downing them in a frothy oner just as the Hibees scored an equaliser one minute from time. The microphone distorted and the hitman had to remove the headphones as the two subjects started screaming, singing and dancing round the room.

The hitman scribbled the important information onto his notepad. There was no rush. He'd spend the night in the hotel and breakfast early before planning his route to Junior's cottage in Dorusdain the next morning.

CHAPTER 46

ROMAN'S HOUDINI

Ross Souter got the call that ruined his year at four-thirty am. He answered still half asleep. The parts of his brain that registered voices were not yet functioning.

"Guv, it's Andy," said the voice in the speaker.

"Huh?"

"Sergeant Hume, officer on night watch."

Souter sprung up into a seated position. He knew even before a thing was said it was something to do with the Rock.

"I've got some bad news," said Sergeant Hume, in his naturally blunt way. "Roman Rock's escaped."

Souter's brain received the human equivalent of a jump start. "Is this a fucking joke?" he said.

"I'm afraid not, Guv."

"How?" Souter asked. "He was in a locked *fucking* cell!"

"Aye, but he had a heart attack, or at least we thought he did. It was about two am. There was a big ruckus outside the station just before it happened; a gang of youths started smashing up a car with baseball bats. Then they set fire to it and were rocking another one, trying to tip it over as I came out."

"There were six of you on duty!"

"Constables Taylor and Watt were called out about fifteen minutes earlier to a burglary nearby."

"How fucking convenient," said Souter.

"Aye, turned out it was a hoax," said Sergeant Hume. "Constables Lynch and Burns came out with me to tackle the gang, which left only young constable Arthur guarding the cells."

"You didn't think all this happening in the space of fifteen minutes was a bit fucking suspicious?"

"Not at the time, Guv," said Sergeant Hume.

Souter squeezed the bridge of his nose and winced in mental pain. "Go on, Sergeant."

"Well, while we were outside, constable Arthur heard Roman banging on his cell door. He went to look and saw the Rock on the ground struggling to breathe and holding his chest. Face like a beetroot, he said."

"Farquhar," said Souter.

"What's that, Guv?"

"Nothing. What happened?"

"Arthur called the ambulance and did the best he could for the Rock. The ambulance arrived and the paramedics loaded him onto a stretcher. They said he'd had a heart attack and needed to be taken in immediately. Arthur shouted over to us but we were still battling with those wee bastards outside. He told the paramedics to wait, so he could go with Roman but when he raced over to tell me they shut the door and drove off. And then those wee bastards all scarpered."

"And?"

"Well, here's the thing, Guv, just as they turned down the street, another ambulance arrived."

"You better not tell me what I think you're going to tell me," said Souter.

"I'm afraid so, Guv. We called the hospital but that was the only ambulance they'd sent. Apparently they'd reported another one stolen a few hours earlier. We found it abandoned a few streets down from the station."

"How soon did the ambulance come after Arthur called it?" asked Souter.

"About two to three minutes, he said."

"And he didn't think it was a bit fucking fast to get the whole way across town?"

"He's only a young lad, Guv. And he's no the sharpest tool. It all happened a bit quick, and what with the commotion outside..."

"You stupid bloody bastards!" shouted Souter. "I'll have your fucking stripes for this! I'm coming down there right now!"

CHAPTER 47

SOUTER SEARCHES

Souter organised a large scale manhunt scouring every shithole in Edinburgh with detectives and uniformed officers grilling anybody they could think of, threatening and making deals in equal measure, anything to get the Rock.

They visited Roman's house four times in two days but Roman was nowhere to be found. Boneheed McCracken had taken up residence in his absence and the big man was enjoying every minute of Souter's grief as they turned Roman's house upside down.

Souter's endeavours produced nothing and the papers had gone to town on it. Roman was now the gangland boss turned Houdini, and Ross Souter was the muppet cop who'd been duped by an elaborate plan worthy of a Hollywood film. One reporter in particular, a Mr. Warren Bailey, seemed to relish rolling Souter around in the proverbial shite, portraying him as totally incompetent and about as effective as Watson would be without the great Sherlock Holmes.

Souter finished Mr. Bailey's latest piece and threw the newspaper at the wall. "Bastard!" he shouted.

CHAPTER 48

KING OF THE JUNGLE

Roman checked his laptop and breathed a sigh of relief. There had been no message to say the job had been done, which meant Barney was safe and probably in hiding, just like himself. At no small risk, Roman had sent a clear and direct communication to the hitman ordering him to cancel the hit on Barnabas Wild.

He closed his laptop and poured a drink. The counterfeiting charge he could beat. They only had the one witness. And that grassing bastard scum, Jimmy the Deal, could be got at well before trial. In fact, once he heard back from the hitman, he would set him onto Jimmy. It made perfect sense. A simple change of target. It'd cost a bit extra for a target under protection, but so what? Life was good.

The kidnapping charge only rested on the two daft cunts, Dave and Marty, who would now tell the cops they'd made a mistake and were only involved in a game that was made to look like a kidnapping. Either that or they'd disappear along with Jimmy. The firearms would be blamed on his loyal pups, Hatchet and Billy. They'd do some time, of course, but not much. And he'd see they were rewarded. Roman always rewarded loyalty. It was the one of the best ways to impress him. The jail was like a second home for those two idiots anyway. They'd live the good life because everyone would know, from cons to screws, they were part of the Rock's firm. Top dogs in the big house. Drugs, drink, women, anything they wanted.

Even Roman's escape from the cells could be changed to put him in a favourable light. His picture was on the front pages of every paper. The public were enamoured with his antics. He was more famous now than ever. He imagined the interview with the reporters, telling them firstly how the officers in the station had, in all likelihood, spiked his food in an attempt to comatose him; and then secondly, how, after collapsing in the cells, he was kidnapped by paramedics he believed to be government agents or ex-cops sent to kill him. However, like the lion of a man he was, he fought them off, surviving and escaping by jumping from a moving ambulance and rolling on the tarmac at speed.

Of course, as anyone with half a brain would see, it was far too risky to go back to the police, and so he'd kept hidden until the truth came out and he was sure his life was no longer in danger. The public would know if anything happened to him now. His persecution by the authorities was out in the open. That was the beauty of it. And Philip Robertson QC would be only too happy to come crawling back out of the woodwork to play his part with all his eloquence and dramatic courtroom bullshit.

Souter would be implicated and then suspended from duty. A big black mark against his name. Possibly even sacked for malpractice. He'd see the turncoat Robertson did his best to even the score.

Roman put his feet onto the table, sipped his Old Puntey and smiled. "King of the Jungle, Miss Farquhar," he said, toasting her health.

CHAPTER 49

HATCHET THE HALFWIT AND BILLY BLOW

Hatchet and Billy's orders were to gain information on the whereabouts of Barney. Roman had spoken to them on the phone and left some petty cash with Boneheed McCracken to help with the less communicative characters. Failing that, they were to get it by whatever means they saw fit.

Their first port of call, Roman told them, should be the Ladbrokes Mafia. Rumour control, as they were known, usually got wind of anything that went on around Niddrie and the wider Edinburgh area. They might know something about this.

"Where *is* Roman?" asked Billy.

"Dinnae ken," said McCracken. "Just calls when he needs tae. Ma orders are tae watch the hoose, and feed Floyd and Monty."

Hatchet nodded. He and Billy jumped in Billy's motor and drove away. A few minutes later they came to a T-junction. Billy couldn't see past the stocky wee Hatchet and the van signalling left. "Any cars coming?" he asked.

Hatchet turned his head. "Nope."

Billy pulled out to go right and immediately heard the screeching of tires and the deep bellowing horn of a large vehicle. He slammed on the breaks as a double decker bus swerved out in front of him, bumping up the kerb onto the pavement and then rolling into a ditch. The bus tilted dangerously on the embankment.

"You said there was nowt coming, ye fuckin halfwit!" cried Billy.

"You asked if there were any *cars* coming," said Hatchet. "*That* is a bus." Hatchet was calm and undisturbed by the near death situation. Billy shook his head and watched as passengers rubbed their necks. Some were already trying to open the emergency door at the rear. Those upstairs were quickly coming down in case the bus tipped over. The overweight driver screamed at Billy from his window whilst struggling to undo his seatbelt.

"What's his fuckin' problem?" said Hatchet. "I'll sort that cunt oot!"

"We need tae fuck off fae here!" said Billy, turning the key and putting the car into gear. He pulled hard right on the wheel to miss the bus and then sped down the road before anyone could clock their number plate.

"You crack me up, Hatchet!" said Billy, with a laugh. "I asked, are there any *cars* coming? Surely to *fuck* that means buses or vans and any other traffic as well!"

Hatchet shook his head. His reasoning as simple as he was. "You said cars. That was a bus. No ma fault."

The bell chimed as the door to the bookies was pushed open, and the two henchmen entered. Freddie met them in his congenial but confronting way.

"What can I dae for you two boys?" he asked.

"We're looking for Barney Wild," said Billy.

All four members of the mafia looked up. "Oh aye?" said Freddie. "What for?"

"For the Rock," said Hatchet.

"For Houdini himself, eh? That's funny. We might know something aboot that. But then again, we might no. Where's the Rock been these past few days?"

"None of yer business," said Hatchet.

"Well, I reckon if the Rock's got you two oot looking for Barney, he'll like as no have given ye a wee wad of notes tae get tongues wagging. I'll tell ye something aboot Barney, but it'll cost two hundred."

"A hundred and that's all," said Hatchet stepping forward into Freddie's face, or rather, his chest. Freddie was six-feet tall, Hatchet only five and a half feet wearing heeled shoes.

Basher cleared his throat in an obvious way and the two goons turned around to see him smile at them. It wasn't what you would call a nice smile. More the smile of someone who enjoys their sport. He was as tall as Hatchet even though he was sitting. "Freddie said two hundred," said Basher, in a quiet, husky voice.

Billy Blow pulled out some notes, folding them in half and passing them into Freddie's hand. Freddie gave Hatchet a wink. Hatchet, he knew, was a bully. Roman's personal dog for hire who wouldn't bat an eyelid at hurting anyone, women and kids included. Freddie told them about Barney's visit, the cancer test results and leaving in his disguise.

The door chimed again and in stepped Archie, the paper-boy, to deliver Bob his daily edition of the news. Billy figured a paperboy got around the area and might have seen Barney. He asked Archie if he knew who Barney was. Archie didn't answer, not knowing why all six men were staring at him, and what he should or shouldn't say.

"Don't worry, lad," said Freddie, "ye can talk freely."

Archie nodded. "Aye, I ken who Barney is."

"And have you seen him lately, son?" asked Billy.

"Maybe. What's it worth?"

Freddie laughed aloud. "Good lad!"

Hatchet grabbed Archie by the collar and twisted it in his fist to bring Archie onto his tip toes. Basher immediately put his hand on Hatchet's wrist and gave a squeeze. Hatchet's face tightened in stages before he let go his grip on Archie. Basher brought Hatchet's arm down to his side and smiled at him again. "Boy asked you a question," he said.

"It's worth twenty," said Billy Blow, handing over a note, which Archie put into the inside of his tracksuit top.

"I saw him in the Coffee Hoose on Wednesday afternoon," said Archie.

"Rab and Tam's place?"

Archie nodded.

"What time was that?"

"Three thirty-seven," said Archie. "I always get tae Rab at that time on a Wednesday."

"I can vouch for the boy's punctuality," said Bob, lifting his eyes over his newspaper. "Good to see it in the youth of today. That's an hour after Barney left here. And I know my timings."

"Well, that'll be all," said Freddie, ushering the goons out. "Give oor regards tae Roman when you see him. And do let us ken when you hear fae Barney."

Hatchet gave Basher a stare down on the way out.

"I'll dae that big fucker one of these days," he told Billy, as they got into the car. "I'll stick ma hatchet in that thick nut o' his. I swear, I hope his next shite's a hedgehog."

The previous night had been rocking at the Coffee House. Hibs had not only got an equaliser, they'd pressed forward from the restart with some do-or-die football and got another goal four minutes into injury time to win the game. Tam had stuck The Proclaimers on full volume to celebrate and the beer started flowing. And then the spirits. And then the cocaine appeared. Some local stoners took it to mean the Coffee House was relaxing its policies again. They knocked on the door and were offered a beer by a jovial Tam. A few texts and phone calls later, and a full-on house party had kicked off. Rab had pulled some local tart and it was Tam who ended up chucking everyone out at four am.

In the morning, Rab called in the cleaner and told her to bring backup. The three old dears were handed sixty-five in cash and asked to be thorough. They were as good as their word, cleaning walls, floors, couches and carpets; wiping cocaine residue from the coffee tables and work tops, and unblocking the sink and toilet. One of the old dears removed a strange little plastic disc stuck to the inside of the letter box. All was taken out to the wheelie bin, which was being tipped into the garbage truck by the council's finest just as Hatchet and Billy Blow pulled up outside.

CHAPTER 50

HATCHET VS CRAZY HORSE

A red-eyed Rab greeted them at the door, steaming coffee mug in hand.

"Rough night, Crazy Horse?" asked Billy.

Rab groaned a response and poured some of the brown stuff down his neck.

"We're oot on Roman's behalf," said Billy.

"Roman?" said Rab, suddenly awake. "Where the hell's he been? I've been trying tae reach him for days!"

"In the stardy," said Hatchet. "D'ye no read the papers?"

"Aye but where's he now?"

"In hiding! Where d'ye think, ya dafty!"

Billy gave Hatchet a look. And Hatchet stopped talking.

"Listen," said Billy to Rab, "The Rock's looking for Barney. It's important. Rumour is Barney visited you Wednesday afternoon."

"Aye, he did."

"So where is he noo?"

"I'd rather talk to Roman," said Rab. "Where is he?"

"Roman's undergroond," replied Billy. "Just tell us whit ye ken and we'll pass it on."

"No offence boys, but this is a sensitive situation."

"Ye'll talk to us, ya cunt," said Hatchet, standing right in front of Rab and looking up into his face. "And *we'll* tell Roman. Got that, fuck nuts?" Hatchet pushed the end of his finger into Rab's chest to emphasise the point.

Crazy Horse took a sip of his coffee and then smashed the mug across Hatchet's face. Hatchet went down and so Billy threw a hook which cracked Rab on the jaw and put him to sleep.

Rab awoke to shouting and angry voices as hard heeled shoes and trainers jumped and stepped on the slabs around his head.

A dull pain made itself known in the right hand side of his jaw. He opened his eyes. Tam was threatening Hatchet and Billy with a baseball bat, dancing back and forth as if about to strike and then pulling back as the two goons tried to crowd him. "Come on then!" cried Tam. "YNT ya fannies!"

Rab staggered to his feet and told them all to calm the fuck down.

"Get tae fuck," said Hatchet, blood pouring from a gash on his temple. "You're getting your face smashed in!"

Rab touched his jaw. "I think I already have."

Just then, Billy Blow's phone rang. "Hold on," he said, raising a defensive arm to Tam. "Fuck, it's Roman!"

The four men all stopped what they were doing and looked at each other.

"Boss?" said Billy, answering. "Aye Boss. We did. Last seen at the Coffee Hoose. Aye, Crazy Horse. He's here noo. Gave us a bit of shite. Says he won't speak to anyone except you. Will do, Boss." Billy held out his phone to Rab. "Boss wants a word."

CHAPTER 51

BARNEY IN THE SIGHTS

Barney slumped into the corner stool. Sweat poured down his face and he was breathing hard. George appeared in front, blocking out everything except the ropes either side.

"What round is it?" Barney asked.

George stuck two fingers and a thumb into Barney's mouth and pulled out his guard. "Roond seven," he said, forcing the plastic straw between Barney's lips. Barney took in some water.

"No too much, son," George said, pulling it out again.

It was Rab who held out the bucket for Barney to spit. He was looking worried.

George wiped vaseline over Barney's eyebrows. "Watch oot for his jab."

Barney nodded and spat again.

The bell sounded and George gave Barney a tap on the cheek. Barney sprung to his feet and strode into centre ring. The man in the balaclava was waiting in the opposite corner with his pistol raised.

BANG!

Barney awoke with a start, the sound of the pistol still ringing in his mind. He wiped his face and blinked into the absolute darkness of the room. The stream outside tumbled over rocks, reminding him of where he was. He lay back and sighed. His heart took a long time to slow down.

Barney chewed on some toast and marmalade and turned a page of National Geographic. There must've been about a hundred magazines piled up on the floors in blocks around the house.

"I'm just popping into the village tae get some supplies," said Junior. "I'll be aboot an 'oor."

"Aye, nae bother," said Barney. "Could ye pick me up some crisps and a few cans of beer while yer oot? D'ye need some cash?"

"Dinnae be silly, mate. Though if you dinnae mind, you could feed the chickens for me. Just scatter one bowl of grain into the run."

Junior's mud-covered 4x4 grumbled down the pot holed track as Barney started filling the kitchen sink to do the dishes. When he was done, he went outside to feed the chickens. "Come on then, girls," he said. "And you Randy..." Randy the rooster came bolting over to get his fill, pecking at the ground and flapping his wings when any of the chickens got too close. He found a worm and began pulling it out the earth with his beak.

The hitman had been watching from his observation post, dug into the hill on the other side of the road. Through binoculars and webbed netting, he'd observed a man with a badly disfigured face get into a Land Rover and drive down the track in the direction of the A87 and Shiel bridge. That man, he deduced, must be Junior Lawrie; Robert Lawrie's brother. He was able to find out quite a good amount of info on Junior. He was registered to the Royal Scots, though some of his files were hidden and only showed military service and dates rather than a unit. Medically discharged after serving some long stints in Afghanistan and Iraq. Some of the dates didn't add up. The Scots had never been in the region where Junior's accident was reported to have taken place.

He'd have liked to watch the target a while longer but it was likely Junior would return soon, and hitting Barnabas with him in the vicinity might escalate into something unprofessional. Collateral damage was akin to failure, and a duel with a professional soldier, though stimulating, was not what he was being paid for.

He clicked open his hard-shell case, containing the four separate parts that would clip, screw and lock into a high-powered, custom made sniper rifle. Gazing through the scope and cross-hairs, he made a positive identification of the target and proceeded to pull back the bolt handle and slot in a .338 Lapua Magnum bullet.

As a ritual, he took out a small titanium tube and tapped out a line of cocaine onto a short slate tile he carried with him. It was a fine thing to snort a line after a target had been eliminated. A little reward that heightened the natural exhilaration. He pushed the bolt handle forwards and locked it down. Three deep breaths.

The hitman peered down the sights to observe a calamity in the garden. Chickens were running around everywhere, flapping their wings for short bursts of flight. Barnabas was chasing and waving his arms, presumably to get them back into the run. The cross-hairs followed him as he tried to catch one chicken in particular.

And then he saw Barnabas stop and gaze into the ground near his feet, body rigid and a blank look on his face. What was he doing? The hitman considered catatonia, a condition he'd studied in the past. It might've been brought on by boxing. He took his finger off the trigger. Perhaps Barnabas Wild had suffered a brain injury during his career.

The hitman clicked twice on his sight to zoom closer. Still Barnabas remained, as if turned to stone. His eyes blank. A catatonic fit. Riveting. It also offered an easy way to finish the job. The hitman put his finger back on the trigger and centred the crosshairs on Barnabas's head. He breathed in once more and then let out the air in a controlled manner. At the calm between breaths, he squeezed the trigger.

CHAPTER 52

CHICKEN RUN

Since watching the first Rocky film at the age of nine, Barney had always wanted to try and catch a chicken. Just to see if he could. Junior wouldn't mind if he let one out and had a go. Why not? A wee bit of fun up here wouldn't do him any harm. The chickens seemed preoccupied with the feed and he wondered if any would even bother coming out. He turned the latch and opened the wire mesh door. A rush of chickens! As if they'd been waiting for this moment all their lives in some epic escape plan. Barney covered his face as wings and feathers, beaks and rubber feet went by him in a blur of cluck-cluck's and cock-a-doodle-doo's to scatter around the garden finding worms and beetles to feast on.

"Back in!" said Barney, with his arms wide, trying to encourage them into the run, "Come on! In ye go!" Junior would have a fit if he came back and saw this. Barney bent down to catch one but it jinked past his flailing hands away down the garden. Nifty wee buggers.

After a few failed attempts, Barney changed tactics. He got within a few steps of a chicken and then froze. He'd learned from Junior how animals could sense when they were being watched.

This particular chicken had a white streak on its back and was the one Junior called, Bertie. Bertie pecked at the ground, not bothered by Barney's presence. She wandered a little closer. Barney didn't move a muscle, except for his eyes. Now she was just below his feet. Still Barney remained a statue, waiting for her to get just a tiny bit closer. Waiting, waiting, waiting, until she was pecking at his shoes... and then with a quick dip of the knees, he bent down to snatch her up in both arms. "Got ye!" he cried.

At the same moment, he heard a sharp ping and a crack of brickwork. He turned to see an explosion of feathers and goo, which was splattered red all over the grass. Bertie clucked as Barney held her up with straight arms.

Something weird had just happened. Not to Bertie but to another bird. There was blood all over the outhouse wall. The head of a chicken was lying on the ground. That sound was familiar too, a bit like the thud of the tree at target practice. A bullet. Barney glanced at the damage to the wall, and then over the road where a slight puff of grey smoke rose from halfway up the hill opposite. Junior had said that to spot a sniper you often had to wait for a shot. A sniper. A shot. The penny dropped.

"Oh fuck! Holy fuck! Fuck me!" Barney said, as he bolted across the garden to the house, tripping up and rolling over on his shoulder he somehow staggered inside and fell again, kicking the door shut as he got to ground with Bertie snuggled up in his armpit.

CHAPTER 53

BARNEY'S ESCAPE

Belly to the floor, Barney slithered from the kitchen to the hallway and through to the drying room where Junior kept his outdoor gear and smelly boots. Bertie followed him, giving a curious tilt of her neck and a short cluck as Barney kicked the room door shut, got up, grabbed the car keys from the hook on the wall and lifted the trapdoor. A blinding light and heat rose up to greet him. Barney shielded his eyes with his forearm. What the fuck? That smell again! He lowered his arm. Cannabis. The whole fucking cellar was stuffed with plants, lamps and tinfoil. It looked like the inside of some hippie'd up alien spaceship.

"Fuck me!" Barney said, lowering himself into the heat pit. "No, Bertie! You cannae come doon here. Shoo! Fuck off!"

Junior had given him explicit instructions on what to do if this unlikely scenario unfolded. He was to go through the cellar and foundations of the house, along what was basically a corridor to the eastern exit trapdoor, which would bring him out at the end of the garden among the trees beside Rab's car. The old Audi had been hidden under netting and leaves to conceal it from prying eyes.

"As far as anyone knows, I live here alone," Junior had said. "If your hitman sees two cars in the driveway, he'll ken someone else is aboot."

Barney grabbed and pulled at the camouflage netting which snagged on the passenger side wing mirror. He ran around the car to free it. "Fuck! Fuck!" He threw the remainder of loose material over the roof and then ran back around to the driver's door to get inside and start the engine. His heart was pumping into his throat. Water rushed across the rocks in the stream. Birds called out around the house and chickens were running everywhere. Peace transformed into chaos, as if someone had shaken up a miniature glass snow globe of the cottage and garden.

Junior had told him this was a last resort. "You cannae outrun or outsmart this guy. And you definitely *cannot* duel him. Not with your shooting skills. It'd be like taking on Tyson in a boxing match. Ye'll have the jump on him this way. He won't expect it."

Barney put the car into gear, swallowed, and then put his foot down, going hell for leather down the track and keeping low in the seat; gritting his teeth, he weaved and swerved, waiting, expecting, knowing any moment would come the second shot through the window.

CHAPTER 54

THE BIG MISS

The hitman lifted his head from the rifle scope. For the first time in his life, he'd missed the target. Not only had he missed, he'd killed a chicken. Collateral damage. A chicken. A human. To the hitman, it didn't matter.

His disbelief had given Barnabas Wild time enough to get inside the house. The question now was what to do about it. Go to the house and finish it or wait to take out Junior Lawrie first. Wild could already be using a phone to call him or the police.

The decision was taken out of his hands when a car started up nearby. The sound of the motor carried through the glen and then a black Audi suddenly appeared, careening down the potholed track, bumping up and down as it got closer to the cottage, the engine gunning and tyres churning up loose stones and gravel which sent clouds of dust rising into the air. The car skidded. Wheels spun and the motor complained in high revs as it took a corner at its limit.

In the soft foam packing of the rifle case were four more bullets. The hitman's fingers fumbled to pluck one out. The car was almost at the cottage. His breathing was not controlled. The bullet wouldn't go into the chamber. The bolt handle was still forwards from the first shot. He grasped it as the car screamed past the cottage in line with his position. He pulled the bolt back and took his eyes off the car to slot the bullet into place. Then he slammed forward the bolt handle and locked it to load the round. In less than a second he was gazing down the scope, picking up the brown dirt track and sweeping through falling dust, his cross hairs found the back of the car and homed in on the tinted rear windscreen and then to the rear passenger window and then there was just a purple blur as the car rounded the hill and his sights were blocked by a clutch of heather.

The hitman blinked twice involuntarily; the only outward sign of the catastrophe that has just occurred. There was nothing more to do, and so with meticulous care, he unscrewed the silencer and took the rifle apart piece by piece, placing each component into its particular slot of foam packing within the hard case.

Undeserving of his treat, he tried to tip the line of cocaine back into the container but his hands were not quite themselves and the white powder fell mostly into the damp earth and heather. A tremor went through him and his special titanium cocaine tube that he'd had crafted and engraved with the words *Hunter*, somehow dropped from his hand to roll in the earth. He stopped. There was dirt on it. Dirt. The hitman blinked twice again. He licked the tip of his gloved finger and then wiped away the peaty black soil. But it wasn't clean enough. And so he took out his handkerchief and rubbed vigorously until all the fragments were gone and it gleamed again. He swallowed away something like emotion and then put both items into his inside pocket, picked up his case and made his way back to his car.

CHAPTER 55

CHECKING IN

The fuel gauge pinged and lit up about two and a half hours drive South from Junior's place. It'd been pedal to the metal the whole way down with some dodgy overtaking and fast cornering. The old Audi had more than proven it's worth, though there had been some worrying rattles and groans from the undercarriage.

The initial adrenaline rush that had brought him flying out of the glen had given way to a more focused state of concentration and driving precision. He still couldn't believe a second shot hadn't been fired. Or if it had, it'd missed and he'd been too het-up to hear the crack of the rifle.

The neon red rim of the garage up ahead came not a moment too soon as the motor gurgled and chugged on its last drops of diesel, rolling into the empty courtyard on fumes and momentum alone. Barney sighed and held his face after bringing her to a stop by the pump.

A young man in attendance looked over as Barney put the pump nozzle into the tank. After filling up, he checked the tyres and undercarriage. There seemed to be no obvious damage. The exhaust was still there and the tyres were all inflated. On a spur he checked for bullet holes but found nothing. He gave the Audi a grateful tap on the bonnet, noticing the phone booth on his way to the entrance. It wasn't an easy decision to make. The hitman might be close behind. But he needed information. Where should he go? Who could he call? Rab seemed the best bet.

"Aye?"

"Rab, it's me, Barney."

"Barney! Fuck! You're okay!"

"Aye. I've stopped at a garage."

"Junior said he got back and the hoose was empty, except for a chicken."

"Aye, long story. Short version is someone took a shot at me and I scarpered. I'm heading back to the burgh."

"Holy Fuck! Don't come here."

"Thanks a lot, pal."

"I dinnae mean it like that. It's an obvious place to go is all."

"Any news of Roman?"

"Aye, he's back."

"He's back?"

"Aye. I was about to call you when Junior rang. I spoke tae Roman today. He's sent oot word for the hit tae be cancelled."

"Well it's obviously not got fucking through, has it! Call him again. Tell him tae send another message."

"Dinnae worry. I will. You need tae go some place safe, mate. Do you ken anyone? I mean, someone no connected tae all of this?"

Her face was the first one that came to him. Emerald eyes sparkling. "Aye, I ken someone," he said.

"Good," said Rab. "I'll get in touch wae Roman. Get a message tae me when yer holed up. But don't call again. I'm no joking, mate! Tam was right! This is some seriously fucked up CIA shit! I dinnae ken how this cunt found ye."

"It doesnae matter," Barney said. "Just tell Roman tae get the hit taken off. And let Junior ken I'm alright."

"I will, mate. Good luck."

CHAPTER 56

THE HITMAN'S MESSAGE

When the hitman got back to his car, there was a message waiting for him in his special account on the dark web from the contact named, 'kingofthejungle'.

> *Cancel the hit. Repeat. Do NOT hit target*
> *Barnabas Wild. New information. New in-*
> *structions. New target. Will double money.*
> *Contact immediately to acknowledge.*

The man sniffed and blinked. It was the first time anyone had asked for a hit to be cancelled. This was turning out to be the most irregular job he'd ever taken. A black leather gloved finger touched the top of the screen and then slipped down to the order: *Cancel the hit.* The gloved finger caressed the words, curling around the C and sliding in a tender way across to the T, where it tapped three times and then stopped.

Something had changed, obviously. The man's fascination with Barnabas' ability to elude and escape and the disturbing way he'd missed his shot were engaging beyond sole professional interest. He wanted to know *what* had changed. And why it seemed acceptable to cancel a hit. This was his profession. What if it got out that he'd missed? Or that he'd let his target go? It didn't matter that the cancel had been called by the man who'd arranged it. Once he'd accepted a job and a target was on his list, that target was eliminated.

A slight twitch on the edge of his left nostril lifted that side of his lips to create what might have been called the faintest trace of a smile. Fascinating. He could not deny it was fascinating. The way life sometimes unfolded surprised even him. The gloved fingers curled and then closed into a fist. The black leather pulled taut around the knuckles, tightening into a smooth gleaming surface. The fist began to tremble from the strain before the gloved hand opened up and relaxed.

The man typed out a slow, deliberate reply:

Message acknowledged.

He sent it and closed his laptop.

CHAPTER 57

BACK TO GRACE

The Audi was a clear marker for the hitman and had to be gotten rid of. It'd been a long drive and more than enough time for him to come up with a suitable place to ditch it. Barney signalled to come off the city bypass at the Dreghorn Link on the South bound route into Edinburgh. He knew from his marathon training of a quiet slip road into the Pentland hills behind the army barracks where dog walkers and ramblers parked up. The place was obscured by thick fir trees and lay lower than the bypass itself, hidden from view. A top spot for doggers at night, he'd heard.

When Barney slowed into the parking area, he saw the sheep gate on the private road was open. Maybe there was a better spot to hide the car. No one was out today in the rain so he kept driving over a couple of cattle grids, rounding a corner to an abandoned, burned out farm building set within an eerie court-yard. Graffiti everywhere. Beer cans and Buckie bottles lay inside small fire pits with condom wrappers and sweetie papers; sure signs of kids who'd found a place to party.

One of the crumbling rooms appeared big enough for the car. He had only to shift a few large branches and broken blocks of cement to drive straight in. Trees and vegetation had found their way around every wall and between the gaps in the roof where tiles had fallen in. Barney used the branches to cover the Audi as best he could. Hopefully there were no parties planned this weekend and Rab could get to it before the vandals did.

It was a fifteen minute walk back to the Shell service station where he treated himself to a mars bar and a cup of tea before walking through the local estate and jumping on the 27 bus at the terminus. The driver, like most LRT employees, was in a permanent cream puff, and reluctantly told him, "Yes, the bus goes to Princes Street. That's why it says PRINCES STREET on the front."

Half an hour later, Barney got off at The Mound, making a quick call to Rab from a pay phone to tell him where he could find his car. Rab was furious, telling him he shouldn't be calling. He told Barney there'd been no update from Roman and made another point of telling him to stay away from Niddrie. It was far too dangerous. Barney thought it best to pick up a cheap pair of sunglasses, a baseball cap and a newspaper from the shops. Then he made his way to Grace's town house in Danube Street, waiting across the road by the railings until she came home from work.

She appeared on foot, walking with an easy posture, handbag over her right shoulder and a briefcase in the opposite hand. Her auburn hair was swept back from her forehead onto the collar of her long camel coloured, autumn coat. She had on brown leather boots up to her knees, a grey skirt and cream top. A sight for sore eyes indeed. Barney's stomach tingled. He smiled and fought the urge to grab her and carry her into the house. Instead he crossed the road unseen and came up behind as she took the four small steps to her front door.

"Grace," he whispered.

She screamed and whipped her handbag round, catching Barney square on the jaw. The force of it turned his head and his sunglasses went askew. She went for a low kick but Barney's old footwork got him out of the way just in time.

"Wait! It's me!" he said, pulling off his cap and dark glasses.

The fear and fight remained on her face even when her eyes had registered his face. "Barney!" she said, out of breath and flush in the cheeks. "Oh God!" She dropped her bags and put her arms around his neck, squeezing tight and kissing his cheek. Barney gave her a cuddle and took in the vanilla scent of her perfume.

"You gave me a fright!" Grace said, pulling back and looking him over. Her green eyes glazed by tears were angry and loyal. Beautiful to Barney. "Where have you been?" she said. "Why didn't you tell me about the cancer? And the HIT?"

Barney rubbed his jaw and gave a wry smile. "How do you ken aboot all that?"

"It's my job," said Grace, shaking her head. "Honestly, Barney! You've no idea what I've done trying to find you!"

CHAPTER 58

MIDNIGHT CALLER

R oman Rock's order to cancel the hit had been so out of place that the hitman thought it prudent to run another check of The Rock. There had been no need to go hacking into police files this time. Everything he wanted to know was plastered in the recent news.

Browsing through alarming internet pages alerted him to the astonishing fact that Roman Rock was a wanted man on the run from the authorities. The more he read about the events of the past few days, the more incredible this job became. One big mess.

Irrational was the word that came into the hitman's mind. Roman's transformation concerned him. Having the authorities involved at such close quarters concerned him too. People who made rushed decisions inevitably made mistakes. And those mistakes could affect other people around them.

Roman may have been able to stay hidden from the police thus far but his online security was dated and unsophisticated. It didn't take too long for the hitman to track Roman's internet use to a general area of a hundred square metres around his long term residence in Milton Road East. It wasn't a bad strategy. If you wanted to hide something, the best place was where everyone would consider too obvious to look. Or perhaps somewhere they'd already checked.

The security around Roman's house was even less impressive than his online systems. More a deterrent than anything else. The man took his bag of tools, pulled down his balaclava and went to a dark point where the night vision camera pictures would not overlap. From here, he used crocodile clips and a battery to keep the electric current in the fence running. The hole he cut out with his pliers went undetected and so he crawled through the gap onto a superbly kept lawn hosting a putting green and nine undulating holes.

From a prone position, the man brought out a custom made pistol with red-dot laser sight. He screwed on a silencer and fired four shots to knock out four security lights around an area leading to the upstairs balcony. He stood up and moved over the lawn to the house to wait and listen. When he was satisfied, he began climbing to the balcony with relative ease, using parts of the brickwork and drainpipe he'd scouted from the road outside.

The balcony window curtains were drawn behind a sliding glass door. A security sticker in the lower corner warned the door was alarmed. The hitman tested the frequency and determined the current had not been activated.

He put his stethoscope to the pane but there were no sounds from within. Placing a small suction cup on the glass next to the lock, he then used a diamond blade to scratch-cut a perfect circular pane, which he eased out of the patio door and placed onto the wooden decking without noise.

The hitman put a gloved hand through the circular hole and flicked the lock, sliding the door just enough to pull the curtain inside a few inches. Ambient light shining from the moon allowed him to scan the room. A book case lined the entire back wall behind a grand mahogany desk complete with green banker's lamp. The desk faced the sea-view patio doors where he now stood. The man's eyes swept over to a low-backed leather couch sitting in front of a fireplace at the end of the room. Next to it, there appeared to be a cage with a black sheet draped over it. There was nothing else of note. Presumably, this office was where Roman conducted his business.

The man listened. Waves from the sea and some passing cars in the road opposite. He entered and pushed the sliding door shut. Suddenly a dog barked from somewhere inside the house and a deep gravelled voice rebuked it. The walls were thick and the sounds muffled but the man understood that animals could often sense when things were not right. The dog barked again and this time the deep gravel voice did not admonish but instead asked a question.

The man took out a canister from his bag and moved quickly around the room, spraying something over the desk and chair and onto the floor in a snake trail leading around the bird cage to the fireplace and finally up the chimney. Then he moved back to the curtain, pulling it across but leaving a small gap, aware of footsteps and the panting of an eager animal scratching on a wall somewhere close by.

CHAPTER 59

ROMAN AND THE HITMAN - ROUND 1

"What is it, Boy?" said Roman. Floyd had got the wind up over something and was barking to get out. "What's the matter?" The big Alsatian scratched at the wall and whined. "Is it Monty? Dae ye want to say goodnight tae yer wee pal? Let's gie him some supper and say goodnight then." Roman pulled the heavy iron lever which clunked into place. Clutching the handle of the partition door in both hands, he then heaved it across his chest.

From behind the curtains the hitman watched the entire book shelf slide across the wall to reveal a secret room within the house.

An Alsatian dog trotted in and started sniffing around at the mahogany desk, picking up the spray scent on the chair and following it, nose to the floor, around the room to the couch and chimney where he whined and scratched and then stuck his nose up, trying to work out what was driving his senses nuts.

"Shut up Floyd," said Roman, as he removed the black cover from the bird cage. "You want some supper, Monty?" Monty turned on his perch and nodded his head as Roman offered a cracker through the bars of the cage. With his back to the window, Roman didn't notice the lean, dark figure emerging from the curtain. The hitman announced himself with a slight cough.

Roman turned his head at once to see a man dressed in black, wearing a balaclava. "Who the fuck are you?" he asked, still holding the piece of cracker to Monty's beak.

"Please restrain the dog," said the hitman.

"What?" said Roman.

Floyd's ears pricked up and he came from around the couch by Roman's feet. When he saw the intruder, he raised his head and barked three times. Roman caught him by the collar but never told him off, letting Floyd pull a few times as if he might let him go. Floyd bared his teeth and growled.

"My dog is hungry, so you'd better have a fucking good reason for being in ma hoose in the middle of the night."

"You asked for the job to cancelled," said the hitman. His voice was plain and had a mix of accents to make it undistinguishable from any particular place. Roman stared as Floyd barked once more. The hitman could see from Roman's delayed reaction that he'd now worked out who he was. The initial anger was dowsed by curiosity.

"So you're him, are you?" said Roman. And then the predictable question, "How the fuck did you get intae ma hoose?" as the famous temper rose up again. "In fact, how the fuck did ye ken I was even here?"

A long pause followed before the hitman spoke. "You gave a message instructing the job should be cancelled," he said calmly. "I acknowledged."

"I got your message," said Roman, firing back. "Ye were to await ma instructions."

Roman stared at the dark figure in the shadows. The man was making a point simply by being there. He'd bypassed the security systems and discovered Roman's hiding place, which the police and authorities had failed to do. He was showing Roman he could have done him if he'd wanted. But he hadn't. Nevertheless, Roman took it as a threat. If it'd been a game of chess, he'd have been checked early on and forced to move his king. "I dinnae gie explanations, pal, if that's what ye've come for," he said. "I gie orders."

The hitman sniffed twice. "In that case, there will be no cancellation."

"What the fuck are you talking aboot?"

The man did not reply. He stood still, watching Roman. More than watching. Observing. Mannerisms. Posture. Roman's answers brought about unconscious reactions in his body. The man had noted these.

His master's dislike of the man made Floyd anxious. He barked and growled. This was the intruder he'd sensed earlier. He fought to free himself. Roman let him forward a few inches.

"Listen tae me, pal," he said. "Make no mistake, the hit is cancelled. There's nae discussion. You're a businessman. I understand that. You've started the job. Maybe you've invested some time. That's fine, ye'll get yer fee. And ye'll get another fee for the new target which I'll gie you tonight. Less hassle for you. Everyone's a winner."

"You called a hit," said the man.

"Aye, and now I'm cancelling it."

The man turned his head to the left, producing three loud cracks of the upper vertebrae. "There will be no cancellation of this job," he said.

No one had talked to Roman like this in a long, long time. He straightened up. Floyd barked and rose up on his hind legs, trying to shake free but Roman twisted his collar to bring him down again. He took a moment to reason things out. He'd learned his temper could be a weakness if not controlled or used in specific situations. "Well, ye must've come here for a reason," he said.

"I came to ask why."

There was a certain depth and slow deliverance in the man's speech which intrigued Roman. A kind of detachment from what was happening around it. There was also something in his tone that gave Roman cause to think. Curiosity. Curiosity mixed with disgust. Or was it disappointment? The man wasn't interested in more money. In all likelihood, he wasn't doing it for the money. If he wasn't doing it for money then he was doing it for sport, or some greater sense of purpose. This was someone there was no bargaining with. Roman sighed. He saw now the man was a proper psychopath. Of course he was. No empathy. No common ground. Roman had been told by a psychologist years before of the particular traits he himself shared with some of history's famous psychopaths. But Roman, for all his sins, also had a heart. He could talk with people. Socialise. Negotiate, if he wanted to. He knew what the average person wanted. The creature standing in front of him was a machine without feeling. He would't take any explanations. His job was his life. And his life was deranged. A fucked up prick that needed stamped on. Roman would be doing the human race a favour.

"Fuck it," he said. "I cannae be arsed arguing wae someone so set in their ways." With his grip on Floyd's collar, Roman moved to the desk and sat down in his chair. "I was going tae let that cunt off the hook," he continued, "but finish the job if you want. What dae I care? However, I want this other cunt hit first. And I want it done fast. It's business."

The man watched Roman's whole attitude change. "Sit doon, Floyd," Roman said. The Alsatian settled beside the desk, though his ears were still up and his eyes fixed on the man in black.

The man sniffed and blinked twice.

"I can see you like a bit of Charlie," said Roman, noticing the man's habit of clearing his nasal passages. "Why don't we make medicine and get this all sorted?" Roman leaned forwards and the hitman's right hand glided to hover over his right hip where a pistol was holstered.

"Dinnae worry, pal," said Roman, "There's nae trapdoor below your feet." Roman reached forwards to turn on the desk lamp, illuminating the immediate area and some of the wall adjacent to the book shelf where hung photographs of himself with celebrities. Looking down his nose, he fiddled with a bullet shaped gold pendant hanging around his neck. The bottom section screwed off and he tapped out a single line of cocaine from the cap. "Must've gone through a bit mare that I thought yesterday... being in that room all day... But dinnae worry, pal, that's no the only stash in this hoose!"

The man watched as Roman picked up a gold pen from the desk above the blotter. "Police didnae find this," he said, removing the lid and taking it apart to reveal a secret compartment from which he tapped out another line of white powder. "Pure Columbian flake."

Roman put his hands face down on the desk, elbows resting either side of the cocaine. "Let's toast oor new arrangement," he said, pulling out a fifty pound note, which he straightened and then rolled into a tight straw. "Two lines, two hits... and here's tae big tits!"

"Big tits!" echoed Monty from his cage.

Roman sniffed up his coke and raised his head quickly, giving his nostril a wipe as he did so. "Here," he said, offering the note to the man. "Fuck me, that's good."

CHAPTER 60

ROMAN AND THE HITMAN - ROUND 2

In the brief pause between producing the cocaine and rolling the note, the hitman had analysed certain facts. There were too many contradictions between Roman's sentiment and his body language. Roman had wanted a job done for personal reasons. He'd then cancelled the job and refused to give a reasonable explanation, losing his temper, only to quickly change not only his decision but also his manner, going from angry to reasonable and then congenial in the space of a few seconds.

"Take a line," said Monty, momentarily breaking the man's thoughts. The man glanced at the African grey parrot nodding in its cage. "Take a line," it said again.

"See?" said Roman, "even the parrot knows it's good shit."

"No," said the man.

"Dinnae be so rude," said Roman. "Do you no ken it's bad manners tae refuse a drink or a line when you're in some'dy's hoose? Ma hoose of all places!" Roman waved the fifty pound note slowly from left to right between his fingers.

But the hitman wasn't affected by threats, banter, manners, or reputations, or the way things were, or the way Roman insisted they be. His ability to be impartial and unemotional was what distinguished and separated him from most of the human race whose brains, he knew, were functioning on a far lower frequency. The human sitting at the desk in front of him was trying to impose his will upon him. And he was doing it under the guise of mutual interest and trust, when in fact his body language was intent on overpowering. Cunning. Adaptable. Ruthless. And clever too, in his own way. A rare and fascinating case study of human behaviour.

Roman hadn't reckoned on the hitman's intellect, his ability to decipher subtle information at speed, or his doctrine in psychology. While Roman had taken pause to re-consider his options, assess the situation and change plans in what seemed like a very short time, the hitman's deductive reasoning was almost instant.

The first thing that struck him was that the two lines of cocaine had each come from a separate source. Roman's explanation for running out had been an obvious lie. The quick scratch on his nose afterwards had confirmed it. The second thing had been the photographs on Roman's wall, which had remained hidden until Roman turned on the lamp. In one of the pictures he noticed Roman standing next to a famous boxer. To the right of the boxer was Barnabas Wild. Both Roman and Barnabas were much younger, in their twenties, but it was them nonetheless, standing like brothers in arms.

The hitman took a step forward and removed his mask. Roman's dark brown eyes were glowing in the lamp light, and there was a slight but continuous nodding of his head, as he reeled in what he thought he'd hooked. The hitman put his finger and thumb onto the note and eased it from Roman's fingers. He leaned over the desk, his eyes meeting Roman's for a moment. Lowering his head, he put the note to his nose, and then onto the line, and then suddenly he put the note to his lips and blew the powder over the desk into Roman's face.

"Ya fucking bastard!" roared Roman, jumping up, spitting and wiping the powder from his eyes. The desk chair flew back and hit the bookcase whereby Floyd pounced, biting into the hitman's leg and causing a sharp sensation in the muscles of his left calf which cramped in the animal's canines. The solution was simple. The hitman drew his hunting knife and stuck it straight into the dog's neck. He took out the blade and plunged twice more. Floyd let go with a whine and lay down on his side, all of his fight gone. Thick red blood drenched his fur and poured onto the carpet as he panted in short breaths.

Roman's reaction surprised the man. He instantly knelt down beside Floyd, putting his hands over the wound and stroking the the Alsatian's head. "You're okay, wee pal," he said. Floyd's sad brown eyes looked at his master one last time. Then he whined softly and stopped breathing.

The internal eruption in Roman's body manifested itself as a soft growl in the pit of his stomach which seemed to affect the very air particles in the room. A heavy vibration. And then suddenly there was nothing except fire. The same fire that had killed his stepfather. Roman's spring was exaggerated by adren- aline. Roaring forwards, he smashed his shoulder into the hit- man's mid rift, taking him up into the air and then slamming into the ground. The knife came out of the hitman's hand as the force of the impact knocked the wind out of him. Roman gripped the hitman's throat and pushed his knees tight either side of his hips so he couldn't get his gun.

Huge hands squeezed the hitman's windpipe almost snap- ping his neck. The hitman knew to dip his chin as far as possible and bring air up from his chest but it had little effect. He put his own hands on Roman's fingers and snapped his left pinky but

Roman only squeezed harder. The pressure caused the man's eyes to push out of their sockets as three distinct lines of fury bulged on Roman's forehead. Nothing could stop him. The hitman could hear himself choking to death. Black spots appeared in his vision. He could feel his blood and air supply had stopped travelling into his brain. He kicked and threw his knees into Roman's lower back but his adversary was too far gone to feel anything. In all his studies, the hitman had never seen such rage. His vision was closing around the edges in a dark shroud. Soon it would be all over. In desperation, he waved his arms up and down on the carpet. His right hand hit and sliced against the razor edge of the hunting knife. Fumbling fingers spun the knife to take it by the hilt, cutting themselves in the process. Roman roared some unintelligible hate. Pure fury. Murder first hand. Gripping.

The hitman tightened his fingers around the hilt. It was imperative to get it right. There would be no second chances. He was about to pass out. One last effort, saw him contract his stomach muscles to rise up and then stick the bloody knife into Roman's neck, twisting through the jugular so the point came out the other side. A fountain of red spurted across the room as the man ripped the blade downwards out of Roman's throat. Threads of arteries and veins oozed air and blood from the wound. Roman's grip held for a few seconds more. The man could not break free and so faded out into the warm black ocean of unconsciousness. A surprising end to his life, he thought.

The deepest red dribbled from Roman's mouth, accompanied by a stuttered gurgling from his open throat; and then he fell face first onto his enemy, his hands loosening but still not quite letting go. Red lava continued to pour from his neck onto the hitman. The carpet was soaked with blood.

CHAPTER 61

SOUTER BAFFLED

It was Boneheed McCracken who discovered Roman's body the next day, lying face down in a pool of his and Floyd's blood. McCracken looked visibly pale when Ross Souter turned up to make the place a crime scene, not believing McCracken's story until he saw Roman for himself. McCracken, sickened by the sight of his boss in the office with his throat cut out, went outside to smoke a cigarette.

"The Rock's gone and you don't look too happy, Guv," said D.S. Weir.

"I'm not," replied Souter.

Souter knelt down and sighed. No doubt Roman had had it coming. But why did it have to happen now? He could already picture tomorrow's headlines:

Escaped "Houdini" Crime Boss Roman Rock Found Murdered
in House Under Cop's Noses. Detective Souter Baffled.

Souter baffled. Souter in deep shit more like. The superin-tendent would have something to say about this. And his boss too probably. They'd searched the house thoroughly and come back twice in surprise visits just in case they could catch him out. They'd even had men stationed outside on twenty-four hour surveillance. And all the time The Rock had been in a secret room right next door to his office, probably having a bloody good chuckle to himself while Souter had gone through his desk and books in search of clues. Sneaky bastard. Who the hell built secret rooms in their house these days?

Souter stepped inside the room-come-bunker and pulled the sliding bookcase door shut. He scanned the fully kitted out compartment complete with a bed, small kitchen, toilet, shower, TV and dog basket. When he slid the door open, McCracken was back in the room peering into the bird cage.

"The parrot's okay," he said.

"I don't care about the fucking parrot!" said Souter. "Did you know about this secret room, McCracken?"

"No, Mr. Souter," said McCracken, who'd dropped the grin and attitude, and was being as co-operative as he could.

Souter walked around the office examining things. "Did you know Roman was here?"

McCracken shook his head. "I'd no idea. I was just tellt tae look after the place until the boss got back. I came in every morning around eleven o'clock and left in the afternoon aboot four."

"Did he send you any messages?" said Souter.

McCracken grimaced.

"Did he or didn't he?"

"Aye. One or two. But from some unknown number. He didn't actually say it was himself."

"But you knew."

"Maybe I should speak to my lawyer..."

"Cut the crap, McCracken. I'm not looking to pin this on you. You've nothing to fear from the law. You can't be harbouring a fugitive if you didn't know where Roman was. What did he tell you?"

McCracken sighed. "Just to keep up appearances in the hoose and let you cunts, I mean, let the bizzies in if they came aroond. *Full access* is what he said. I was just following orders."

"Following orders," Souter repeated, fuming. "Well somebody knew he was here, that's for sure. Do you have any idea who could've done this?"

McCracken shrugged. "The Rock wasnae short of enemies."

Souter found a circular hole cut out of the balcony door glass. "This was a professional break-in," he said, and then uttered more quietly, "But not a professional hit..."

It was a bold move to take on The Rock at his own place. Especially with the law after him. What puzzled Souter was how this person had known Roman was here. Even McCracken, Roman's right hand goon, seemed clueless. Another search of the office and secret room had not turned up anything. It was likely that Roman's phone or phones had been picked up by whoever left him and the Alsatian on the floor.

The affair had certainly taken the big McCracken down a peg or two. He didn't stand so tall now. And there were none of the usual smirks or wisecracks.

Souter walked outside to the balcony. Nobody, not even his supposedly vigilant surveillance team, had seen a thing. He scratched his head and noticed bits of plastic glass on the decking. Security lights had been smashed. This was now a job for forensics. He ordered the room to be cordoned off with tape and then called the crew in the white suits, who soon appeared and began scouring the area for fingerprints, hairs, DNA and whatever else they could find.

Souter's morning was complete when a news van pulled up near the house and out stepped Mr. Warren Bailey, complete with his trademark Fedora, mocking grin and writing pad.

CHAPTER 62

ROMAN IN THE NEWS

Grace had told Barney not to leave the house until she got home. She was currently involved in an important case, though she'd do her best to get away early. They'd talked about Rab and Junior the night before, and her advice was not to contact them again until she'd been in touch with Roman to find out *first hand* what the situation was.

Barney flicked through the TV channels again and glanced over some of Grace's magazines in the vain hope of finding something that wasn't to do with fashion or house and home design. He was having to live like a fugitive. What about his business and the boxing gym? He'd be losing clients every day. The bills wouldn't stop just because a hitman was after him. The fighter in him wanted to walk out and face the danger head on.

But that's not how this game would play out. It was a coward's game. And he wouldn't see his opponent coming.

Grace had said to help himself to food. He opened a cupboard. Herbal teas, Swiss water-filtered coffee, organic muesli, gluten-free bread. Pish. All he wanted was a simple breakfast of beans-on-toast with a fried egg on top, preferably at a wee cafe where he could sit down and read the paper to catch up on all that had happened in the world since he'd been in the Highlands.

Fuck it. He put on his sunglasses and cap and went out the door into a fine Autumns morning. With the sun warming his face, he strolled down to the local shops in Stockbridge, taking the air and getting bolder with every stride. It felt good to be back in the normal world again. Dry brown leaves blew across the road and along the pavements. Mothers pushing prams tried to control toddlers, while a lollipop lady stopped traffic to let kids with sports bags cross at the lights on their way to football or probably rugby round these posh parts.

By the time he'd reached the row of local shops, he'd convinced himself there was no need to worry. Roman was out and had already tried to contact the hitman. Obviously there had been some miscommunication but it would get sorted. And there was no way anyone knew about Grace apart from him. He'd lost the hitman in the Highlands.

The door to the newsagents was stuck open by an angled block of wood. The place smelled of old leather school satchels and dust. Barney walked over to the rack and picked up a copy of The Sun. The headline gave him the sensation of missing a step in the dark on the way upstairs to bed.

Roman Rock Murdered at Home in Gangland Execution

Barney read it again with an open mouth, only glancing at the tits on page three as he flicked onto page four to read the full report. The article had almost no information other than what was conveyed in the headline.

"This isn't a public library, pal," said the Pakistani man behind the counter.

But Barney didn't hear him, unable to take his eyes from the description of his childhood friend brutally killed by an unknown assailant.

"Hey!" said the shopkeeper. "Are you going to buy that?"

Barney looked up, unsure at first as to where the voice had come from. "Erm... aye... I am." He walked over, digging into his pocket for change and scattering whatever he had on the wooden counter.

"That's too much," said the shopkeeper.

But Barney's eyes were back on the paper and he was walking out the shop.

The easy Autumn feeling had evaporated into the cooling air. His stomach tightened. He rolled up the newspaper and headed straight back to Grace's house, jumping when a car's breaks screeched behind him, and also when a man came running from around the corner to catch a bus. He turned around several times, sure that someone was following him as he scanned rooftops and windows. He even stood on the other side of the street, waiting until a delivery man had got back into his van and driven off before checking and crossing the road to Grace's town house, all the while fearing he may be shot in the back as he turned the key and let himself in.

His hands were shaking as he slid the bolt and clipped on the chain. He breathed out and became aware of the silence of the house. A sinister thought made him stiffen. What if the man had got into the house while he'd been out? Unable to get the idea out of his head, Barney took off his shoes and crept from room to room, hugging walls, shutting and locking the windows and doors of each room one by one, checking inside cupboards and under beds.

When he'd finished, he sat down at the bottom of the large hallway staircase opposite the front door and put his head in his hands. Roman was dead. And it was his fault. What the fuck was going on?

A quick treble knock on the door caused a hot surge of adrenaline to pulse through his neck. He looked to the back door, considering an escape route.

"Who's there?" he asked, in a high-pitched voice. He'd been trying to imitate a posh old woman but only succeeded in sounding like a pre-op tranny.

"It's Grace," came the reply. "Are you doing a funny voice? Let me in!"

She was home way too early. Barney tiptoed over to check the peephole. Grace was staring back. Barney opened the door, remaining hidden as Grace entered with a solemn face. "I have some news," she said. "I needed to tell you in person."

Barney shut the door, pulled the bolt and chain across and then stood with his back against the wall. He was white and panting. He leaned over and checked the peephole once more.

"It's Roman," said Grace.

"I know," Barney replied, holding up the newspaper. "He's been murdered."

"Roman was my friend," said Barney, leaning over the kitchen island table on his elbows. "Folk have no idea what kind of life he had. He wasn't always... *The Rock*. We were kids in a tough place. Roman had it the worst of anybody. His step father... and the things that happened to him... you wouldnae believe. Another time and place, he could've been someone different. Fuck! He was doing all this for me!" Grace put her arm around him. "I cannae stay here," he said. "I'm putting you in danger. What if he tracks me tae here?"

Grace didn't argue or tell him he was being over dramatic. "I know some people in London you could stay with," she said.

"No," said Barney. "I dinnae want anyone tae know where I'm going. I need tae think... and tae find a way to clear all this up."

"You've got to go to the police," said Grace. "If this is who killed Roman then the police are looking for him too."

Barney blew out a long sigh.

Grace persisted. "I know the detective leading the investigation. He was the one who arrested Roman in the first place."

"You're joking," said Barney.

"No. His name's Ross Souter. He's a decent guy."

"I'm no sure. Maybe this hitman's expecting me to run to the cops. What can they do anyway? Do I really want to be put under police protection? What if this guy has contacts in the force? It could be like walking into the lion's den thinking I'd found a good place to hide. You're a lawyer, you ken as well as I do, if someone wants to do someone else in, they will. And all the law, judges, silly wigs, and policemen in Scotland can't protect me forever."

Grace clicked a finger nail against her teeth. "I'll speak to Ross for you and ask what he could do. He'll know someone or something." Grace leaned over the table and gave Barney's hand a squeeze. "Life with Barnabas Wild..." she said.

"Aye," said Barney. "Some ride, eh?"

"You're not bad," said Grace.

Barney laughed.

Grace managed a smile. "In the meantime, I'll give you an old phone I've got upstairs. I bought it for my mum a while ago but she didn't want it. It's got a sim and credit in it. I'll call you once I've spoken to Ross Souter."

"Alright," said Barney, looking worried again. "I better go. It's no safe for you, me being here."

Grace slipped off her stool and moved close enough for a kiss. The scent of her hair and body enveloped Barney as they embraced and now she began clawing at his clothes. Barney lifted her onto the worktop, and it was a while before he actually left the house.

CHAPTER 63

ROSS SOUTER AND GRACE - ROUND 4

Sergeant Hume had one of those faces that was always rosy cheeked and in good spirits. "D.I. Souter's waiting for you in his office, Miss Farquhar," he said, giving a smile.

"Thank you," said Grace, as she walked down the corridor and knocked on the door.

"Enter," said Ross Souter, in his best school teacher voice. The atmosphere in the room was frosty. Grace too had read the reports in the press detailing Roman's escape and subsequent murder.

"Ross," she said, feeling it out.

"Grace," replied Souter, who was seated in an informal slouch over his desk.

"I need to speak to you," said Grace.

"Oh really? Last time you needed to speak to me you convinced me to let you talk to Roman Rock, whom you then decided to represent. That same evening, said villain escapes after a *feigned* heart attack and two days later, he's found dead in his house with his throat cut out."

"I heard," said Grace, not yet taking a seat. "That's why I'm here."

"Have you come to admit to being behind The Rock's *audacious* escape from custody?" Grace noted the headline '*Audacious Escape*' on a newspaper lying on Souter's desk.

"No," she replied, "I'm here to talk to you about who killed Roman."

Souter sat upright. "You know who killed Roman?"

"I'm pretty sure it was the hitman Roman employed for Barney."

"And what makes you think that?"

"Who else could have done it?"

Souter caught himself repeating Boneheed McCracken's sentiments, "The Rock wasn't short of enemies."

"No, maybe not. But he was short of people brave enough to stand up to him. Also, no one knew where he was. Not even you."

Souter winced. The Superintendent had said the same thing not a few hours before as Souter took a grilling about how the whole situation had been handled and whether his promotion had been justified. "I had the Rock here where he would've been safe," said Souter, through his teeth. "At the very least, your meddling made it a priority for him to get out. It was *you* that got him his phone calls, remember? No doubt that's how he arranged it."

"I'm not here to argue," said Grace.

"That's good. Because I've not got the time."

Grace sat down and put her bag on Souter's desk. "Roman needed to make contact with the hitman to save Barney's life," she said. "Think about it. Maybe they met at his house. Maybe they---"

Souter shook his head. "They didn't arrange to meet."

Grace's eyes asked the obvious question.

"It was a break-in," said Souter. "Roman's security fence was cut, outside lights shot out and a pane of glass cut from the balcony door."

"Maybe the hitman did that afterwards, to make it look like a burglary," suggested Grace.

"An elaborate cover up? I don't think so. The whole thing was too messy."

Grace frowned. It didn't make sense. If the hitman hadn't arranged to meet Roman, then what was he doing there?

"Roman told me he needed to contact this hitman," Grace said. "So what if he sends a message to cancel the hit and the hitman somehow tracks the laptop or connection to Roman's house. Have you looked into his laptop?"

"There was no laptop in Roman's house," said Souter.

"You're sure?"

"Positive."

Grace sighed. "So we can presume whoever killed Roman probably has his laptop."

Souter laughed and leaned back in his chair. "Even if you're right, even if this is indeed the work of some mysterious hitman called in by Roman, why would he kill Roman?"

"Maybe they had an argument," said Grace.

"About what?"

"About the hit." Grace's eyes wandered onto the table as if reading signs Souter could not yet see. She began voicing her thoughts. "Barney said Roman ordered the hit to be cancelled. And then he was shot at. He got away---"

"Woa! Woa! Woa!" said Souter raising his palm as if back on traffic duty. "Go back a bit there. Barney was shot at? Where? When? And by whom?"

"Three days ago. In the Highlands. By the hitman, who else? Barney was in hiding, waiting for Roman to make the call to cancel the hit."

"And did Roman cancel it?"

"Apparently so."

"And this guy got the message?" asked Souter.

"I'm hoping not," said Grace. "Because if he did... it would mean he wasn't cancelling anything."

Souter stared at Grace and put his finger tips together in a bridge over his mouth and nose. He was interested. "You've been in touch with Barney?"

Grace nodded.

"Where is he?"

"I don't know," said Grace. "He came to see me yesterday but left when he heard about Roman. He's in hiding again and he wouldn't tell me where he was going."

"So what are we saying here?" asked Souter. "That some rogue hitman is on the loose, roaming Scotland with no intention of stopping until he bumps off Barnabas Wild?" Ross considered the possibility and then leaned back in his chair and directed a mocking laugh at the ceiling. "Uch, come on Grace! You had me going for a minute there but this is ridiculous. Roman's dead. All bets are off. The hitman's got his money. Or maybe he hasn't..."

he added, tailing off into his own thoughts. "...maybe that's what they were arguing about... if it even *was* a hitman..."

"Ross, please. Look at the facts."

"I have," snapped Souter, "and they don't stack up with your theory. A professional hitman wouldn't go visit The Rock for a wee conversation at two in the morning. He'd only go there to kill him. And a professional hitman wouldn't make the mess I had to go and see yesterday morning. Put me right off my bacon sandwich, so it did. Now, if it was a professional burglar who'd been taken by surprise by Roman, who incidentally was living in a secret *bloody* room behind a bookshelf in his office, well, that'd be more plausible and in keeping with the evidence we found. Perhaps Roman's Alsatian spooked the burglar, and somehow during the commotion, Roman and the dog got stabbed."

"You said Roman had his throat cut out," said Grace, not liking the callousness of Souter's descriptions.

"Yes, it was."

"And the dog also killed."

"Stabbed in the neck. Similar injuries."

"Similar injuries..."

Souter could see what she was driving at. The murder had been messy but the culprit had made sure of his kills with some accuracy. Not an amateur, that was for sure. He'd gone for the jugular, killing a big man and a big Alsatian by himself. For a moment Souter considered whether Barney might have killed Roman. That would certainly tie in with the facts better. And DNA samples from Roman's office would confirm it. All this hitman stuff was too far fetched for Souter's liking. But if Barney and Roman were actually gunning for each other... Maybe Barney wasn't the innocent Grace believed him to be. Maybe Grace wasn't either. They might both be in on it. The thought made Souter sit upright in his seat as if recoiling from a snake. "I'm guessing you can contact Barney if you need to?" he said, trying not to sound different.

"I'm hoping he contacts me this evening," said Grace.

"Why didn't he come here and tell me all this himself?"

"He thought he'd be better off alone. He said he was going somewhere no one would be able to find him."

"Didn't trust us, eh?"

"Can you blame him? The most feared Crime Boss in Scotland has just been murdered in his own home. I came here to ask for your help. Can you guarantee his protection?"

"Of course," said Souter, unconvincingly.

"And for how long? Until you run out of resources or your superintendent decides the situation has all blown over? From what I can gather, this guy will wait. He tracked Barney to a place in the Highlands only two people knew existed. And he found Roman when the police couldn't. Can you really promise Barney he'd be better off with you lot?"

Souter smarted, shaking his head. "So what do you want me to do? I've nothing to go on. The killer's DNA didn't come up on any databases."

"Put out a press report," suggested Grace. "The vultures are itching for a story. There's about a dozen of them out there waiting for you to give them an update, including your pal, Mr. Bailey."

Souter groaned.

Grace went on, "Tell them you believe it's a professional hit-man who had business with Roman. This hitman, whoever he is, will likely be following the case. It's his business. It sounds like it might even mean more to him than that. Roman told us he was a psychopath, remember? But this guy's already slipped up. He missed Barney in the Highlands. And like you said, Roman was a messy kill. Something went wrong. Let him think you're onto him. Say you've got DNA on him and he's known to sources you're working with. Maybe he'll make a mistake or someone will come forward. *Someone* must know who he is."

Souter listened. Grace wasn't the kind of person to get worked up over nothing. The situation was strange and violent. But he'd got used to that working in CID. Gangsters and drug dealers.

That was their way. If Grace was right, the hit had gone bad. But who was the worse for it? Roman Rock had paid the piper. How many people had he killed or had killed, over the years? Karma was what Souter called it. He also wanted time to think over his new theory. This Barnabas Wild character had got to Grace. She was too emotionally invested. Besides, if some hitman *had* been responsible for Roman's murder then it made sense Barney would now be safe. What good would it do a hitman to bump off Barney after slaughtering Roman? There was no money in it. And a hitman wasn't a danger to the general public.

"I'm sorry Grace," he said. "It's just too fanciful. I don't have enough evidence or the resources to warrant putting Barney in protection. And I'm already up to my neck with the Superintendent. As far as I'm concerned, the Rock's dead and we'll probably never find out who did it."

"And Barney?" asked Grace.

Souter shrugged. "I think he'll be fine."

Grace's green eyes went through Souter. Either he really was too dumb to see, or just didn't want to listen. Probably a bit of both. "I hope you don't live to regret that," she said. And then she stood up and left his office.

CHAPTER 64

GRACE'S VISITOR

Barney's manly odour was still on her pillow. Grace breathed it in and smiled before rolling over and switching off her bedside lamp. It'd felt so good having his strong arms around her, snuggling into his warm chest, feeling safe and protected.

She pictured his keen blue eyes; engaging, laced with humour. He came out with old expressions her granddad used when she was a child and had since forgotten. What would her friends think of him? A bit rough around the edges perhaps? But there was a strength in him that her ex Martin had never possessed. Something from boxing maybe. Some of the things he did, like taking her arm as they walked, reminded her of her dad. He was a throwback to another time. A better time. And he made her laugh. Who else would have taken her on a first date to a boxing gym? Barney's whole body was giving. They'd only shared two nights together but already she knew she missed him. She thought of his surprise at the Scott Monument, the view from the top and the castle all lit up as he pulled her into his arms to kiss her.

She was almost asleep when a leather gloved hand covered her nose and mouth. Instinctively she tensed and tried to turn her head but cold metal pressed against her temple forcing her to lie still. A man's voice warned her not to move or scream. The voice was calm. Controlled. Frightening. "If you lie to me, I'll know," it said.

The shock of the intruder had rendered Grace unable to speak even if she'd wanted to.

"Grace Farquhar," it said. "You were Roman's lawyer, until recently." Grace didn't answer. His gloved fingers squeezed her cheeks together. The skin inside Grace's mouth was trapped against her teeth and she let out a whimpering moan.

"Do you know who I am?" asked the voice.

It was obvious to Grace this was him. The hitman sent to kill Barney. How had he found her?

The man watched as she attempted to speak but something seemed to catch in her chest before the words formed. She was trembling. The man smiled.

The metal object pressed harder into Grace's temple until she gave a slight shake of her head in response. There was a double sniff and then another question. "When did you last speak to Roman Rock?"

"I don't know..." she said, her voice fading into a whisper.

The gloved hand tightened like a vice around her jaw.

"The... the day... before he escaped," she moaned, struggling to form the words with her mouth forced open. The hand relaxed and pulled away. The metal that she took to be a gun slid from her temple to her cheek.

"Tell me what else you know about him," said the man.

Despite her shock, Grace began to calm herself by breathing slowly. The initial fright had passed and now her natural fire and curiosity were aroused.

"I... I was... Roman's lawyer," she said, exaggerating her tears. "I was representing him after his arrest. I didn't hear from him... after he escaped."

The hitman took pause to consider, noting her impaired speech and the way she blurted out the details without thinking. Hostages invariably tried to help their captors for the simple reason they wanted the ordeal to end. Often, they'd give out information purely from fear and sensory overload.

However Grace wasn't a normal victim. She'd already worked out he wasn't here to kill her. It was information he was after.

She herself had used manipulative psychology to gain information from people, though never through violence or threats. An instinctive anger rose up inside. How dare this bastard break into her house. Hiding behind a gun in the dark. But it wouldn't do to fight back or show her real feelings, and so she kept up the pretence of being in shock, still quivering and stuttering her way through his interrogation.

"Where is Barnabas Wild?" asked the hitman suddenly, watching and observing how her body gave a slight shiver.

Even with a gun to her head Grace had the presence of mind to know this was a very clever question. If he knew that she and Barney had spoken, she would be used as bait to get to Barney. But how *could* he know anything about them? He had to be testing the waters. But what if he wasn't? The metal moved onto her temple again. She was taking too long to answer.

It was then Grace had the idea to play a more dangerous game. She took a breath and threw the dice. "Who? What are you talking about?"

The gun was shoved into her face with such force she thought it would break her cheekbone.

"Stop!" Grace cried.

"I'll ask you one more time," said the man, raising his voice. "Where is *Barnabas Wild?*"

"I don't know any Barnabas Wild! Please! I'm telling you the truth!"

The leather gloved hand covered her mouth and nose. She tried to pull them away but couldn't. She kicked under the covers but the gun went back to her temple as a warning and so she stopped resisting.

The man sniffed. The slight twitch in his right nostril had spread up to encompass his eye, which winked involuntarily. A tremor he could not deny. This job had turned into a professional disaster and the one lead he had from Roman's laptop and phone records had come to nothing. A gamble that hadn't paid off.

"Don't turn around," he said, "I'll be watching you."

The mattress rose up when the man took his knee off the bed. Grace's head was turned to the bay windows but she dared not move. She started to count the seconds. After a couple of minutes silence the front door banged in the wind. Grace turned her head slowly, inch by inch, and then sat up. The room was empty. She immediately flicked on the lamp and called the police.

CHAPTER 65

SOUTER PERPLEXED

Ross Souter had told his team he was to be notified immediately of any developments related to Roman Rock's murder.

The call came in just after midnight. Grace Farquhar had been attacked in her home by an intruder. Souter jumped off the couch where he'd fallen asleep watching the snooker highlights and instructed headquarters to have two CID officers meet him at Grace's house.

When he got there Grace looked shaken but she wasn't marked up, apart from a slight bruising on her temple where she said the intruder had put a gun to her head.

"You saw a gun?" asked Ross, handing her a cup of tea.

"No," Grace admitted, taking a sip. "He had his hand pushing down on my face to turn my head away. But I felt it."

Ross nodded. "Did he say anything else? Or give any clue as to who he was?"

"Ross, he's the hitman. He made it bloody obvious he wanted to know where Barney was, *and* if I knew him. That's all. Just see if you can find any evidence or DNA that matches what you found in Roman's house."

"Forensics are on their way," said Ross, watching Grace clasp her hands around her mug for warmth. She seemed OK considering what she'd just been through.

When the white suit crew had finished their data gathering, Ross came back into the living room to find Grace asleep on the couch under the blanket he'd given her. He gave her a gentle shake and she awoke with a start. "Oh, God!" she said, when she saw someone standing over her.

"It's me," said Ross. "Forensics are done. Are you okay? Do you want me to take you to your mum's?"

Grace nodded, wiping the sleep from her eyes. "I'm fine. Yeah, I'll give her a phone first."

Grace packed a few things into a travel case and Souter drove her to Colinton on the other side of the city where her mother lived. Before he left, he gave her his personal number and told her to call if she needed anything.

Souter pondered on the night's activities on his way back to the station. There were only two explanations as far as he could see. One, Grace was a natural actress who'd broken bad and was now in cahoots with the elusive Barnabas Wild, or two, there really was a hitman on the loose who'd done for Roman Rock and was now on the prowl for Barney. Either way, the Superintendent wasn't going to like it. Not one bit.

"Fuck," Ross said, hitting his palm against the steering wheel.

CHAPTER 66

CROSSING THE LINE

The hitman parked his car in a quiet country road. His twitch was becoming more frequent and had now spread up to his eyelid, which every so often gave an annoying wink. He sniffed and slid his index finger along the bottom eyelashes pulling the skin at the corner. It seemed Grace Farquhar had no link to Barnabas Wild. She was just a lawyer looking to make a name for herself by taking on a big case for a well known gangster and got more than she bargained for.

Though the job was far from finished, he brought out his metal canister and tapped out a line of cocaine. Breaking his own code, he snorted the white powder. A quick internal rush, rising through his head and then... clarity.

He sniffed and wiped the residue from his nose and then proceeded to tap out another line. He snorted again. Afterwards his twitch stopped.

The hitman closed his eyes. Collateral damage had given the authorities DNA samples belonging to him. It was professional ineptitude and his reputation, if it got out, would be tainted, possibly ruined in certain circles.

After waking up under Roman's dead body, he'd been physically sick at the smell and taste of iron from the blood that had poured into his mouth and nose whilst he'd lain unconscious. His debilitating fear of germs, especially germs from other people, caused an uncontrollable revulsion and temporary loss of both presence and time. Paranoid and unable to stop from retching, he'd fled, wiping his face and spitting, when he should have set the room on fire and burned the bodies and evidence. On a whim, he'd grabbed Roman's laptop and phone. That was something, at least. Later, when he'd scrubbed himself down, gargled and then swallowed three cups of mouthwash, he'd contemplated going back to rectify the situation, but the idea was tactically unsound at best.

The man closed his eyes and let the effects of the cocaine filter through his body.

Yes, it would be best to wait. He took in five seconds of cool air through his nostrils, pausing at the top of his breath, before letting out on a slow count of eight.

There were no witnesses to identify him.

His data was not on any police or government records.

Barnabas Wild couldn't hide forever.

He could still finish the job.

And when he did, everything would go back to normal.

As long as he hit the target, everything would be OK.

CHAPTER 67

GRACE CALLS BARNEY

Grace dialled the number from a pay phone near her mother's house. With the world having gone mobile it'd been a mission to find one. Barney answered before the second ring. "Hello?" He sounded nervous.

"Hey, it's me," said Grace.

"I've been trying to reach you," said Barney. "You're phone's been off."

"Sorry," said Grace."I'm at my mum's."

"Is she okay?"

Grace smiled. Even now, with everything going on Barney still thought of other people first. "Yeah, she's fine."

"Are you?"

Grace sighed.

"What's up?" asked Barney.

"I had a visitor last night," Grace said. "A man... in my room."

Barney's heart dropped into his stomach. "You're seeing someone else?"

"No, Barney. An intruder! Who put a gun to my head and asked if I knew where you were."

"*What*? The hitman?"

"Yes," said Grace.

"Fuck! Are you okay?"

"I'm fine. I called the police. Ross Souter came round with some other officers."

"I shouldnae have come to see you. I'm so sorry. Fuck. Grace, I'm---"

"It's not your fault. He didn't know about us. Somehow he knew I was Roman's lawyer. I didn't tell him anything. He must've been desperate if he's having to question Roman's lawyer to find you."

Grace heard a deep sigh from down the line. "Grace, if anything was to happen to you..."

"I'm fine," she said. "I asked Ross to take me to my mum's because I didn't want to spend the night alone. God, I don't know if I ever want to go back there now."

"You know I'd come and see you if you---"

"I know. But I don't want you to. It wouldn't do any good and it's not smart now, is it?"

Another deep breath told her Barney was in turmoil, not knowing what to do as his heart fought with his head. "What did Souter say about it?" he asked.

Grace gave a sardonic laugh. "Yesterday he had a *theory* Roman's death was a botched burglary. I'm hoping this changed his mind."

"Grace..." began Barney. "I... well, I *care* for you darlin'. More than I can say."

"Me too," said Grace. I want you to know that yesterday, I really felt something. Something I've never felt with anyone."

"Was that before or after you clocked me on the jaw?"

Grace smiled and took a breath before continuing. "You make me laugh, Barney. You have this glow. You see the truth, like my dad and my granddad. I love being with you."

Barney could feel what was coming next.

"But... I can't live like this. That *man* breaking into my house. With a gun! This whole thing, it's too much. Look at us now. I'm on a bloody payphone just to speak to you! And this hitman, whoever he is, he's not going to stop. I heard his voice. He's cold. And clever. Just like Roman said. If they don't catch him, you'll be running your whole life, or until..."

"Grace," said Barney, his voice carrying a resolve he hadn't shown her until now. "I'm going to say *two* things. One, I'm going to sort this oot. I'm no running away all my life or having some hitman turn up at your hoose and threaten you. I've got tae think about this and work it oot. It'll be alright. But dinnae contact me again. It's too risky. I'll be in touch when I can."

"What's the second thing?" asked Grace.

"Eh?" said Barney.

"You said there were two things. That was only one."

"Oh, aye. Second thing is, I love you."

And with that, Barney hung up the phone, leaving his finger on the end call button for a moment and letting out a breath. Inside he was rolling with anger, fear, and a call to action. He needed to find this guy. This bastard who'd killed Roman and put a gun to Grace's head. But he couldn't get wild. Junior had warned against it. This would never be a square-go in a Niddrie street or a showdown between two men at high-noon like in the movies.

No, he had to be clever. He had to outsmart this guy.

Therein lay the trouble. Barney wasn't devious by nature. He'd been a fighter, not a tactician. When it came down to it, he knew his limitations. He couldn't do this by himself. He put his face in his hands, letting his fingers slip down his cheeks. When he opened his eyes, he saw Freddie's wig and the other pieces of the disguise the Ladbrokes Mafia had given him hanging on a peg by the door. Between the four of them, those old boys had seen and done it all. The cogs began to turn. Barney put on the wig and overcoat.

It was time to call in a few favours.

CHAPTER 68

WAR COUNCIL

They met at an abandoned air strip south of the city. Tesco Tam and Rab were standing by the old Audi as the Ladbrokes mafia pulled up in Freddie's classic silver Jaguar. Tam had a good chuckle watching the heavyweight Basher trying to squeeze out from the low-set rear passenger door. Freddie donned a curly black wig, possibly in memory of Roman.

Barney scanned the overgrown field, knee high grass and wild flowers, thistles and bracken. Freddie waved an arm and said, "You can still make oot the runway by the way the grass is a different shade. See how it runs in the one direction?"

A few old horses stood grazing near the outer fence. Freddie explained they'd all been racehorses saved from the knackers yard. He had an arrangement with the stables nearby for grazing rights in return for a small rent and free riding lessons for his grandkids.

"Aye," said Freddie, brown eyes lost in some distant memory, "this is where it all used tae happen back in the good old days."

"Bit of the old import-export was it?" asked Rab.

Freddie gave him a wink. "More like import-import," he said.

"We should have a wee talk later," said Rab, "This's given me an idea..."

The master thief Sykes showed them to an old hut by the strip, which he said used to be the reception and mess for pilots and ground staff. "A place to have a cup of tea and talk aviation," he told them.

"Cup o' tea would be ideal, like," said Tam, rubbing his hands together.

"Well volunteered," said Sykes, who put a key in the lock and opened the door. Barney entered and was hit by the pungent odour of mould and stale cigar smoke. The windows were covered in grime and the mildewed floral wallpaper pealed from various places. Barney gave an audible tut at the state of the carpet. Fag burns, damp patches and poor quality fittings all round. Two scratched oxblood leather couches, four old armchairs and some tables were all that remained of the former flying club. Bob turned on the radiators to give some heat.

"Kettle's up there next tae the sink," said Sykes, guiding Tam along to the small kitchen at the far end of the hut. "And here's some tea bags and sugar."

Tam mumbled something but went to his work, his lowly position as lackey already established in the group dynamics.

Rab opened a window to allow some air in. "Place reeks like an old folks home. When's the last time you were here?"

"Two thousand," said Sykes, "for Hogmanay."

"Ye had a shindig *here*?"

"No, but the bizzies were always so stretched with the street party, it was a perfect time for pilots to come in under the radar."

Rab smiled approvingly.

The rest of the crew helped Basher move around the tables, fitting them together to construct a makeshift operations room, or '*council of war*', as Bob put it. Everyone took a seat. Freddie was about to speak when the sound of a car entering into the airfield stopped him. The Ladbrokes mafia looked about, ears tuned as a car door opened and closed. A few puzzled glances from the group at the sound of footsteps on the slabs approaching the hut. Only Rab seemed unconcerned.

"You expecting guests?" asked Freddie.

"As a matter of fact, I am." Rab stood up and opened the door.

To everyone's surprise, in walked Junior, scarred face and all. Barney sprang up and gave Junior a man-hug, making sure to slap him twice on the back to show he wasn't gay. "It's good tae see you again, pal!"

"And you mate," said Junior, showing no return in affection as he pulled out Tam's seat to take his place at the table. The sight of Junior's face had quietened the party.

"You might as well all have a good look," Junior said. "Get it over wae."

Tam was staring with his mouth open, pouring water into an already full cup that was spilling all over the counter.

Freddie broke the silence. "If yer referring tae yer face, then I dinnae see much except a wee scrape and a bit of a burn. Spare a thought for Tam over there. He's had to walk aroond wae *his* face all his life."

The men all laughed.

"At least I'm no wearing Tom Jones' curly fuckin pubes on ma heid!" said Tam.

"Now, now," said Bob, "Is that anyway to talk to your elders?"

"Aye," said Sykes. "That wig cost Freddie over two hundred quid. Or would've done had I not half inched it fae the shop."

Tam brought over the tray and a bag of sugar. Sykes produced some milk and biscuits that he'd stolen from a newsagent on the way over.

"Tunnocks tea cakes!" said Tam, delighted. "Barry!"

"And some caramel wafers," said Sykes, emptying his other pocket and throwing two packets onto the table. "Plus some daft cunt's wallet tae boot!"

"Hey! That's ma wallet!" said Tam, snatching it back. "There better still be two quid in there."

Greedy hands ripped open the packaging and snatched at the goodies as Basher pushed up his cap at Junior. "Good tae see you again, lad," he said, in his husky, half-whispering voice. He held out a huge paw.

Junior shook it.

"You still boxing, Big Man? When's your next fight?"

Basher grinned, appreciating the joke, and Junior remembered the giant he'd always feared as a kid in the gym. The huge man who could make the heavy bag swing almost horizontally under punches that some of the other kids said could kill normal people.

Freddie took a sip of his tea, clapped his hands, and rubbed them together. "Well now, if we're all done wanking each other off, how aboot we get doon tae the matter in hand?" Heads nodded, tea was sipped and biscuits munched. "As we all ken, our good and loyal pal, Barnabas Wild here, is knee deep in the shite."

"Baw deep!" shouted Tam.

"Aye," Freddie continued. "There's a hitman after him. The same psychotic cunt who killed our *friend* Roman and also threatened Barney's new bird at gunpoint."

The tea cups went up in respect when Freddie mentioned Roman.

"Rumour has it this lawyer bird of yours is quite a woman," said Freddie, with a wink. "Hot totty. Well done, son."

Barney nodded.

"Barney's always punched above his weight," said Rab.

The men laughed and Freddie went on, "Now, Roman may have been a sick psychotic bastard himself but he was fae Niddrie, and proud of it, just like us. Like it or no, he kept order aroond Edinburgh. Fact is, the bizzies aren't going tae dae fuck all aboot it, so it's up tae us tae sort this hitman oot before Barney gets a bullet through his heid."

"Or up his arse," said Tam.

The heads turned. No one laughed. An awkward silence. Freddie gave a treble tut before going on. "Fae what we ken, this sick cunt isnae going tae stop. So that's why we're all here today, tae come up with ideas and hopefully a plan tae put an end tae it all, if possible."

The heads nodded. More tea was sipped. A few ideas went round and were either dismissed or aye-maybe'd.

"If it was me, I'd have someone do this bastard in," said Tam.

"Aye, good idea," said Rab. "Have you forgotten we dinnae ken who he is, *or* what he looks like?"

"Or *where* he is," added Junior.

"And we're no likely to either," said Sykes.

"So how dae we find oot that sort of stuff?" Tam asked.

Shoulders shrugged. Blank faces looked to other blank faces for an answer.

"Herein lies the problem," said Freddie.

"T-R-A-P-P-E-R."

The heads turned to Bob, who was voicing the letters of his crossword as he jotted them down. "Trapper," he said.

"Do you think you could gie this meeting a bit mare of your attention, Bob?" said Freddie. "It's only Barney's life at stake after all. Unless your crossword's mare important?"

Bob cleared his throat. "My apologies gentlemen. But I have been listening to your predicament, Barney lad. And in fact, this crossword has just given me the answer."

Freddie knew better than to interrupt Bob when he was being clever and mysterious. Bob went on in his theatrical way. "As some of you may already know, I used to make plans for... well... all sorts of projects."

"Aye, after 'oor cash withdrawals fae the Royal Bank of Scotland," said Sykes.

"And during business 'oors too," said Freddie. "And no just the Royal Bank."

"If I could finish, please," said Bob. "Now, from what you've told us, Barney lad, we don't have many options in how we go about things. In my opinion, this hitman character isn't going to surface unless he knows, or at least *thinks* he knows where you are going to be at a specific place and time. Therefore, any plan we concoct would necessarily involve you being presented as, for want of a better word, *bait*."

Bob peered over his half-moon reading glasses at Barney who simply opened his palms and gave a look of resignation. "I cannae run anymare," he said. "I've made up ma mind. There's no other way. I need help setting it up but I have to face this guy. I caused all this. I was the one who asked Roman tae organise the hit. And I dinnae want anyone else fighting my battles. And I woudnae ask either."

"That's well said," said Sykes, "as I dinnae think anyone here particularly wants tae fight this one for you anyway."

A few chuckles.

"But we are here to help," said Bob. "Though I think, Barney, you should be prepared for... well, how can I put it... some... *dirty* work?"

A few raised eyebrows around the tables.

Freddie cleared his throat. "I think what Bob's trying tae say in his fake educated way, is that you might have tae dae this cunt in and get rid of the body."

Eyebrows went down and the heads nodded again.

"Unless we get the jump on him first," said Tam. "Bring'im in tae the bizzies. If they have his DNA they can link him tae Roman's murder and maybe also tae Barney's *very* tidy bird's hoose."

All faces turned to Tam.

"And how do you propose we do that?" asked Rab.

Tam shrugged and took a bite out of his wafer.

"Is that your *second* wafer?" asked Rab.

"Oh for fuck's sake," said Tam, cheeks bulging.

"Going back tae Bob's idea," said Freddie. "we need a situation where this cunt knows, or at least *thinks*, Barney is going tae definitely be some place."

Junior shook his head. "This guy's no fool. I've seen his work first hand. He's not going tae be lured into a trap. Not unless it seems legit."

"A public gathering or similar event would be the ideal scenario," said Bob.

"Like a funeral," said Tam, thinking aloud.

"Aye, like a fu– – –" Freddie stopped.

The jaws stopped munching and the cups went down on the tables.

"Roman Rock's funeral!" said everyone together.

The heads nodded in agreement.

Rab gave Tam a pat on the back. "You've actually contributed something useful to this meeting," he said.

"Fuck off ya cunt!" replied Tam. "I made the tea as well."

"It's good," said Junior.

"Ta," said Tam. "I put extra sugar in your one."

"I meant the plan," said Junior. "If we could somehow get this hitman inside the church. And then cut off his exits."

"It'd have tae be after the mass," said Freddie. "When everyone's left."

"Except Barney," said Bob. "Sorry Barney, but he'd have to know you were there. Paying respects at the end, maybe?"

"Aye, I could dae that."

"The church itself is going tae be as important as anything," said Sykes. "We want it tae have more than one way in and oot. Otherwise this hitman might think it's too risky. And it cannae have an upstairs balcony. That's just asking for trouble."

"Picture the church inside," said Junior bringing out some paper and a pen. "We need to simplify everything." Junior drew a crude diagram as he described the ideal scenario. "An altar, two rows of pews, nothing too big, a coffin at the front..."

"A big coffin," said Tam. "I mean, Roman was a big dude. Just think of the size of coffin Basher would need. They'd have tae cut doon half a forest for that."

Basher stared at Tam without the grin before dunking his wafer into his tea and crushing it between his teeth.

Tam dipped his head. "I was just saying..."

"The boy's actually got a point," said Freddie. "A *big* coffin is exactly what we need... Sykes, is your son still a carpenter?"

"Aye, doing well for himself too."

"Barney, Junior," said Freddie, "Stand up lads."

"What?"

"Go on, up ye's get!"

Barney and Junior pushed back their chairs and stood side by side. "Perfect," said Freddie. "You and Barney are almost exactly the same height. Similar build too."

Rab was enjoying Freddie's enthusiasm. The old boy's big brown eyes were dancing. He was a character alright. No wonder the ladies loved him.

"It's a beauty!" Freddie said, slapping the table with his hand. "An absolute beauty! Could be one of my finest."

The men looked at each other, confused and amused, waiting for an explanation. Basher started to grin.

"It'll take cool heids," said Freddie, "and *big* baws..." he added. "But I think it might just work."

CHAPTER 69

FUNERAL ARRANGEMENTS

Freddie made a few calls until he was put in touch with the lawyer in charge of Roman's estate, a Mr. Mathew Pinnons. Mr. Pinnons and his upturned nose had been at a loss over what to do regarding the infamous Roman Rock's funeral. Pinnons was a busy man and had so far been unable to locate a living friend or relative willing to take charge of the arrangements.

Freddie knew just how to deal with posh cunts like him. Soft boys who'd been silver spooned up the arse all the way through Heriot's or Stewart Melville's or whatever poncey private school they'd been sent too.

He put on a pristine pinstriped suit and flamboyant pink tie as well as a rather distinguished looking grey combed-back wig. In a well spoken accent, he introduced himself as Frederick D.

Brown, 'a dear friend' of Roman's, who'd known him for many years, both having come from the same part of Edinburgh.

"I myself was fortunate enough to attend Fettes for my secondary education, curtesy of my well-meaning uncle," said Freddie, to which Mr. Pinnons nodded approvingly.

"Yes," Freddie went on, pulling out a polkadot handkerchief from his breast pocket and wiping his brow, "by the time I was twenty-two, I was already a successful entrepreneur and international business man."

Mr. Pinnons was impressed with Freddie's manners and acumen, and was only too happy to pass the buck. He had his secretary bring in tea as he informed Freddie that Roman had left a good sum of money for the occasion.

"How much exactly?" Freddie asked.

"Mr. Pinnons paused and then said, "Twenty-five thousands pounds."

Freddie waved a hand. "Dear, dear, is that all? I'll have to make up the rest myself then."

Mr. Pinnons' eyebrows went up ever so slightly. "Yes, well," he said, "you will still be required to provide an itemised bill and receipts of all expenses."

"I'll have my man do it," said Freddie, nonchalantly.

"Indeed," said the lawyer with a polite smile. Mr. Pinnons looked through some papers. "Roman also made some stipulations regarding an ornament on the lid of the coffin. A golden lion's head no less. Some other items are also to be placed *inside* the coffin. I'll have a list drawn up and sent to you. I believe Mr. Rock intended at least half of the money for a reception afterwards, with anything left over going back into the estate."

Freddie cleared his throat. "Who is the estate being left to, if I may ask?"

Mr. Pinnons gave an apologetic tilt of his head. "I'm afraid I can't discuss that at the moment. We're still trying to trace the relevant parties, who appear to be out-with the UK."

"I see," said Freddie. "How mysterious."

"Yes," said Mr. Pinnons.

"Well, I won't take up any more of your time," said Freddie, offering his hand to the lawyer. "We'll do our best to give our dear Roman a grand send off. "

Mr. Pinnons stood up to shake Freddie's hand.

"And do let me know if you need help with finding relatives," said Freddie, handing Mr. Pinnons his business card. "I know a company who are *very* good at finding people and have assisted me in the past on some very important business."

Mr. Pinnons nodded again, quickly gazing at the card. "Thank you very much, Mr. Brown. I might very well take you up on that."

Freddie left Mr. Pinnons' office and went whistling down the New Town street. His first task was to get Sykes' son working on the coffin. Next, he'd get in touch with that drunk degenerate, Father Michael of Saint Teresa's Chapel in Niddrie. That priest would do anything for a bit of fast cash, plus he had debts with the Ladbrokes Mafia for the gee-gees. Bob would handle the funeral costs in the usual way, faking invoices and payment notes, so that none of the twenty-five grand went back into the estate. Freddie rubbed his hands together and smiled at the world. This whole enterprise was proving quite a lucrative wee venture.

CHAPTER 70

FUNERAL NOTICE

The notice in the Evening News read:

> *Funeral mass of Roman Rock to be held at*
> *10am on the 28th October at*
> *St. Teresa's Chapel, Niddrie.*
> *A chance for friends and acquaintances to pay*
> *respects and say farewell to a well-known and*
> *proud Edinburgh man.*
> *All are welcome.*
> **All grudges past or present to be put on hold*
> *in honour of "The Rock".*

The last line was specifically intended for the hitman.

CHAPTER 71

FUNERAL SERVICE

It was a fresh October morning with the first touch of winter biting in the air. The hitman pulled up his coat collar and blended into the congregation of mourners gathered in St. Teresa's church car park for the funeral of Roman Rock. Just another face awaiting the hearse, his grey eyes skimmed the crowd unnoticed, yet noticing everything.

Hard faces smoking cigarettes, scars, missing teeth, thick eyebrows, old grey faces in long black coats protected by younger faces in black or grey suits and jackets, bull necks stuffed into shirts and ties; game wild eyes, steady eyes, angry eyes, a few handshakes, a few nods, a few stare-downs and malicious smiles, but no trouble so far.

Some reporters and cameramen hung around outside but
there had been some angry words and warnings given out earlier by the faces and so the newspaper people had decided to
stay back on the pavement behind the low black rail, away from
the actual proceedings. A few uniform cops stood near the entrance gate and across the road in groups of twos and threes,
their presence serving as a warning.

A scrunch and squeak of tyres turned the many faces as a
long white funeral hearse bumped up the kerb into the car park
from Greendykes Road, greeted by a storm of camera flashes.
The long side window of the funeral car contained a floral reef
spelling out *The Rock.*

Six men exited from the procession cars and helped lift
out a huge, deep set mahogany coffin with solid gold handles
and plating that brought a few laughs and comments from the
crowd. There was a golden lion's head roaring on the lid near
the top. The Rock, it appeared, was just as extravagant in death
as he was in life.

The hitman recognised some of the faces who bore the coffin
or walked beside it. The four older men were from the bookies in Niddrie. He recognised the big one with the flat cap and
the one with the obvious wig. Roman's goons, AKA Boneheed
McCracken, Hatchet and Billy Blow were easily identifiable.

But there was another man, wearing a baseball cap, scarf and sunglasses. The scarf pulled up over his mouth and nose in the manner of a football hooligan. A man who didn't want to be identified. There might be plenty at a gathering such as this but this man insisted on carrying Roman's coffin. That was suggestive.

The hitman's eye twitched, making him wink. The character in the baseball cap was of the same height and build as Barnabas Wild. The hitman sniffed three times and ran a gloved finger over the edge of his eyelid. Just then something caught his attention. Something out of place. A movement, and then a face that didn't fit. Ross Souter. The inept detective leading the investigation into Roman's death had just spoken into a microphone hidden inside his sleeve. He pinged two more cops by their tiny ear pieces. There would be others lurking about, no doubt. Risky to enter the church as a member of the congregation. He'd scrutinised the building and location as soon as he'd seen the notice in the newspaper. Four stairs up to the arched stone entranceway which led into the vestibule. Only two other exits, one at the side, one at the rear. Inside, there was room for a good hundred and fifty people, possibly two hundred if you included standing room at the back and sides. The front entrance comprised two large oak doors, wide enough for four men to pass shoulder to shoulder. However, as he predicted, it was bottle necked by the crowd; eager faces straining to see in, some on tiptoes, some still smoking. A few whispers, a few jokes and a few sly winks as the coffin disappeared inside with Ross Souter following.

The man's eye gave a double twitch.

Crowded. Difficult to get out if things went wrong. He moved up to the top of the steps, just another grim face in funeral attire but with eyes surveying, gathering and then homing in. He went no further than the entrance way, taking a position with his back against the wall. From here he could see the coffin being placed on the bier in the centre aisle. Both rows and the altar were visible. Sitting in the very front row on the left hand side was the peculiar sight of the man in the baseball cap and sunglasses.

CHAPTER 72

ROSS SOUTER UNDERCOVER

Ross Souter moved in amongst the long coats and strong aftershaves to take a pew as near to the front as he could get. Souter scowled. The ridiculously large casket was facing sideways below the altar with the lid open and was big enough to store an elephant. Roman himself had been cleaned and suited up. A high collared shirt and tie concealed his horrific injuries, since stitched up by the coroner's talented apprentice. Sporting his favourite Elvis sunglasses and all his gold, the funeral director's make-up artist had gone to town on the fake tan and rosy cheeks making him look like a waxworks model of his former self.

Souter clocked about fifty guys he'd lifted over the years. A who's who of Edinburgh gangsters, hard men, bank robbers, thieves, and general dodgy bastards. Quite a send off for The

Rock. But it was the figure dressed as a football casual sitting in the front row that intrigued Souter the most.

Barnabas Wild. Who else could it be?

He was the only one conspicuous by his absence. Quite a gamble to think a hitman wouldn't take him out just because he was at a funeral. Then again, it would be unlikely anyone would attempt a hit in a crowded church with only two possible exits and a host of people to get through and police outside. Souter stroked his chin. Maybe it wasn't such a gamble after all.

The mass bell sounded, resonating through the church to quell the murmurs of the congregation. Sharp whispers told those beyond the entrance way that proceedings had begun and soon the faces that had only managed to get a place on the steps outside or looking in from the car park, all quietened down.

The decrepit alcoholic clergyman, Father Michael, appeared from the vestry, assisted onto the altar by a pair of altar boys who held his elbows to make sure he didn't trip over his vestments. The boys both had their heads turned away. Souter knew only too well the sweet stench of sherry on Father Michael's breath. Souter had personally pulled over the old bastard on two separate occasions for being drunk at the wheel, only to let him go with a warning because Souter's mum was a devout catholic who'd never forgive her son for arresting a servant of God.

Father Michael's big red nose shone under the lights as he began the service. "We are gathered here today for the funeral of one of Edinburgh's best known sons, Roman Rock..."

Bla-bla-bla. It was amusing to watch how even the articulate and educated Father Michael struggled to paint Roman in a good light. "Roman was perhaps not what we might call a saintly man, though he did do some good things, erm... on occasion. For instance, he was only too happy to donate a sum of two thousand pounds to his friend Barnabas Wild, to help raise money for a children's charity in this year's Edinburgh marathon."

Father Michael held out an open palm and looked over in the direction of the football casual. So it *was* Barnabas Wild. The silly old bastard had just identified him to any would-be hitman who might be in attendance.

Souter whispered into his sleeve. "Sierra-one to cover groups, that's Wild in the baseball cap alright. Are the front and back doors covered, over?"

"Roger that, Guv," came the first reply. "Sierra-two on the front door now."

"Romeo-one covering side entrance, Boss," came the next message in his ear.

Souter awaited confirmation of the last exit. A crackle and then nothing. And then another crackle. "Sergeant Hume reporting on the walkie-talkie. The rear door is covered."

Hume kept a hold of the button well after he'd finished his message so everyone else with a radio was forced to listen to him humming to himself and other background noises from the rear exit.

Souter shook his head. Staff cuts had forced him to take what he could get regarding man power. However, if there *was* a hitman and he was foolish enough to go for his man inside, Souter would have him. Part of him wanted it to happen, just so he could collar the guy and restore his reputation in the force. Even that prick Warren Bailey would have to write something good about him then. Either way, Barnabas Wild wasn't getting out of this one. Souter had instructed his men in the briefing room earlier that Wild was a possible suspect. He'd also made it plain that he was going hands-on with this one. No more fuck ups. That's why he was sitting inside the church instead of conducting things from outside. He was taking no chances. The superintendent had warned him.

Souter tuned in as the old priest went on with some readings from the bible. Some pish about forgiveness and how it was never too late to redeems one's soul. Maybe it was for the benefit of the crooked congregation, sitting row upon rotten row all the way to the back of the church and spilling onto the steps outside like diarrhea. Certainly it couldn't have been for The Rock. He'd sold his soul a long time ago.

Next, Father Michael invited some old boy in a cowboy hat, suede tassel jacket and pure white beard to come up to the front where the altar boys brought over a chair and a microphone stand. The old boy had a guitar and tapped the microphone to make sure it was working. He gave his strings a pluck to check they were in tune and then said, "This was one of Roman's favourite songs," before belting out a pretty good rendition of 'Little ole Wine Drinker Me.'

The words, '*I'm sitting in a Honky in Chicago cause my baby left for Florida on a Train*,' were changed to '*I'm sitting in a pub in Craigmillar cause my baby left for Niddrie on a bus*,' much to the crowd's delight. Big roar and applause.

Father Michael's head bobbed to the music. He had his eyes closed and a big drunken smile on his lips as if he'd been at the holy wine prior to coming out. Either that or he was imagining the moment the mass was over and he could go back to the parish house to open another bottle.

The old boy finished and got a standing ovation. It was a disgrace. There was no respect at all. "More!" they cried, as if it was a gig at the Usher Hall. "Encore!" And "G'on yersel, big man!"

Father Michael said, "Perhaps we could have just one more, seeing as though it's Roman?"

The old boy took his seat and strummed out, "San Quentin," by Johnny Cash but again changed the lyrics to "*Saughton*

Prison, I hate every inch of you. You held me since two thousand and two."

More wild cries and claps, but this time Father Michael waved his hand and got back to his job, changing the mood with mention of Roman's gentler side and love of his pet alsatian, Floyd, who'd died trying to defend his master, "on the night of the heinous act that brought us all here on this sad occasion.

"Floyd's ashes will be placed into Roman's coffin along with a few personal items set out by Roman in his will," said Father Michael. A few murmurs in the rows as Father Michael said they would now have a moment's silence to reflect on Roman's life and also their own mortality.

"That's my son that made up the coffin," whispered Sykes to Rab, who was seated next to him.

"Must've cost a fair bit," replied Rab. "Is that lion's head solid gold?"

"Aye, and so are the handles. But Roman left mare than enough to cover it. You should see how much he put away for the bar bill at the reception after..."

"I'm looking forward tae it," said Rab. "I hear a few of Roman's treasures are being buried wae him."

Sykes said, "The will was *very* specific."

"Shame for all that loot tae go six-foot doon, never tae be seen again though, eh?"

Sykes nodded, sensing a proposal.

"Maybe we can talk aboot a wee salvage operation later, eh Sykes?"

Sykes turned his head to Rab. "A bit of the old Burke and Hare, ye mean?"

Rab grinned.

"Disgraceful," said Sykes. "Sacrilegious."

"Aye," said Rab, "that it is. So, are you in?"

"I'll bring my shovel and lantern."

Souter instructed his men to get ready as Father Michael said a few closing words. Thanking those who'd come, he raised his hands in a theatrical way to give a final blessing to, "Our dear departed brother, Roman. May he rest in peace."

Father Michael exited with the altar boys, and Souter almost spat as the song 'My Way' by Frank Sinatra began playing over the speakers.

The congregation stood up, many of them tapping the coffin and giving their best to *The Rock* before they left. On Father Michael's orders, the two altar boys ran around to the entrance doors where they stood, holding out wooden collection boxes for the exiting crowd. These were soon stuffed with notes as the gangsters and hard men all left to smoke and talk outside.

Father Michael peeped around from the vestry and smiled. The amount he'd make from those boxes would keep him in sherry for at least a year.

CHAPTER 73

FUNERAL BRAWL

The hitman let the crowd of faces flow past him, spilling through the doorway and down the steps into the car park and grounds. The big man and the one with the wig came down centre aisle behind everyone else, ushering people out of the church while mentioning the reception at the White House Pub. Rab Lawrie and his housemate assisted by moving down the outer aisles between the four stone pillars.

The two altar boys carried their boxes to the altar with the same slow reverence they had displayed throughout the mass. They handed their collections to Father Michael, who nodded, and then all three disappeared into the vestry at the back of the church.

The hitman spied Detective Souter approaching. It wouldn't be wise to be the only person left hanging around inside, or for Souter to see his face, and so he walked outside to the top of the steps beside some old faces smoking cigarettes with yellow teeth and scratching voices. Leaning around the exterior wall, he could see the rear exit guarded by a heavy-set uniformed officer. The two altar boys burst out behind the officer, kicking a football up into the air and then chasing it through the gate and away down the street.

It was Freddie who recognised Souter standing at the back. "Hello Mr. Souter," he said, cordially. "I wouldnae have expected tae see you here. Didnae think you and Roman were that close."

"Very amusing," said Souter. "However, I'm not here for Roman. Is that Barnabas Wild at the front?"

"Who?" asked Freddie, turning his ear to the detective and touching his hearing aid.

"Don't come it with me, Freddie. I know you hear well enough when you want to. It doesn't matter anyway. I'm going to speak to him whether you like it or not."

"Mr. Souter, have some respect for the dead. Give friends and relatives time to grieve. What would the press out there think if they foond oot you were harassing mourners at the funeral of the man you recently let *escape* from custody? That reporter, Mr. Bailey, seems particularly fond of you. Have ye seen some of the nasty things he's written lately?" Freddie gave a double tut. "Oh, look over there, if that isn't the very man himself waiting by the road for a wee bit to put in his column!"

They all gazed over to see the notorious Bailey in his trademark fedora hat, holding a notepad and pen. Freddie smiled and gave a wave which was returned by Bailey, who pointed at his watch and gave an open-palmed shrug.

"Ten minutes," shouted Freddie, extending the fingers and thumbs on both hands. Bailey gave a thumbs up in reply.

Ross Souter inhaled through his nostrils before turning back to Freddie. "You tell Wild, I'll be waiting," he said. "If he tries to do a runner without speaking to me, I'll arrest him *and* you!"

"Right you are, Mr. Souter." Freddie exchanged a grin with Basher as they closed one side of the large wooden entrance doorway.

Souter went outside to survey the scene. His superintendent had instructed him to make sure things went smoothly. Local media will be watching, he was warned. No more cock-ups. Souter stuffed his hands in his coat pockets. There must've been around two hundred faces you wouldn't want to bump into in a dark alley. He noted the uniformed officers standing in clusters on the pavement behind a waist high iron boundary fence. A small, low cost deterrent. He'd had to argue just to get them because of the recent cutbacks. Souter checked his watch. By the time he looked up again it had all kicked off.

Hatchet had been picking up what he called 'negative vibes' and 'bad looks' all morning. A voice behind him said, "Aye, that daft wee cunt's no so big now The Rock's gone." Hatchet spun around, caught some face growling at him, and threw a punch. The face stumbled backwards into a few other faces. A cigarette accidentally got stubbed out in a cheek, and a shout of, "Ya fucking radge!" caused another punch to be thrown. The kindle was lit. A few of the faces had a bit of history and grabbed each other, their pals jumped in, and in a matter of seconds, two of Edinburgh's most feared gangs – along with everyone else – were going at it hell for leather in the car park. Souter watched helpless as the fighting escalated before his eyes. He could almost hear his superintendent sighing above the screams and war cries as reporters ran to the fence and the cameras turned to the action. Flashes, shouts and bodies colliding. Fists, kicks and roaring voices.

Sergeant Hume heard the shouting but couldn't see what was going on from his position. A message came over the radio. "Holy shit! World War Three's going off out here!" Sergeant Hume plodded around front and saw the mourners battling in the grounds. He radioed Souter but got no response. Carnage.

Hume's eyes darted from one part of the melee to the next. Unsure as to what he should do, he radioed Souter again. "Sergeant Hume on the walkie talkie. Guv, what are your orders? Is anyone there?"

By now, folk were on the ground getting their heads kicked in. Sergeant Hume didn't like it. Where was Detective Inspector Souter? Maybe he was one of the poor devils on the ground. It didn't look good, and so the old school cop took out his truncheon and went steaming into the fray.

Souter wanted no part of the mass brawl taking place. He didn't have the bodies to cope with a riot. He radioed his men and the uniformed officers to hold back. "Let the bastards sort themselves out and we'll mop up," he said. That's when he saw Sergeant Hume running into the mix. What the hell was he doing? With a cruel swipe to the ear, the heavy cop sent a thug crashing to the ground. Four guys quickly surrounded the big sergeant. Souter sighed. Oh well, traffic duty wasn't so bad. At least he wouldn't have to deal with the Super ever again.

"All officers to the front at the corner of Niddrie Mains Road and Greendykes!" he said into his radio. "Sergeant Hume and I are in urgent need of assistance!"

Souter got his baton to hand and ran down the steps smashing into the back of some deadbeat who went flat into the tarmac. When a hardened face next to him turned to see what had just happened, Souter brought his truncheon down through the protruding jaw, noting the sweetness of the strike and how the body of the man went limp on contact.

Blood poured out onto the cobbles from various sources. Souter reached the red faced Sergeant Hume who threw a man to the ground and gave him a boot up the arse for dessert. He was blowing hard through his cheeks. "Ah, there you are, Guv!"

In the central mix, Basher had seen Bob knocked down by a cowardly punch to the back of his head. Sykes was being set upon by four young lads but had his razor out and was just about holding them off with wild swipes that sang through the air. One of his slashes caught somebody's best coat and popped a button off. "Old cunt!" the owner cried, snatching up the button as if it had been a pound coin.

The block-shaped Basher jogged down the steps and began clearing a path with shoves and shoulder barges that sent bodies flying and crashing into each other like ten pins. Freddie was right behind with a snooker ball in a sock and a duster on his left hand. He punched the first face that stood around Bob, and as the man reeled, Freddie swung the snooker ball once around his head and then into the man's eye socket. Down he went. "Yer oot the game, pal!" Freddie said.

A rat-like face booted Bob twice in the guts. But Bob didn't groan or move. He was out cold. Freddie had once been a semi-professional footballer and showed a natural balance as he stepped froward and brought his shin up into the rat's nuts. Rat-man bent over from the kick to his testicles and, in one flowing strike, Freddie hammer-punched the back of his head using the edge of the duster. "Two nil, ya cunts!"

Basher put one foot either side of Bob, throwing haymakers that cracked two skulls and dropped four men in a semi-circle in front of him. A voice cried, "Get that big cunt!" and a wave of black coats and faces ran at him, Sykes slashed one across the neck, sending a spray of vino across the crowd from a cut artery as Freddie templed another sleekit face with his snooker ball.

Rab had been inside the church talking to some bird on his phone when the commotion started and he strolled outside to have a look. "Fuck me!" he said, cancelling the call.

Basher was about to get charged by two big bastards. Despite all the self-improvement books he'd read, the mad streak and violence were always too close to the surface for Crazy Horse to attain Nirvana. There were no enlightened thoughts going through Rab's head as he ran across the upper landing, screaming "YNT ya bastards!" and leapt off the highest step, propelling his body like some stage-diving rock star into the goons.

In the midst of the madness, Basher caught sight of something big flying through the air and landing on two guys who were about to flank him. The weight of the impact snapped one of the attackers' knees in a crunch that could be heard above the roars and shouts. The downed man screamed, and he screamed louder when Crazy grabbed his ankle and stirred the man's leg around the knee joint. "Ya like that ya cunt?"

Basher grinned at Rab and then KO'd some face with a monster uppercut that took the man's feet out of his shoes. The Ladbrokes Mafia and Rab had cleared a good space around the unconscious Bob, and were now back to back, dug in and holding position.

Souter and the uniform police who had joined him were only adding to the number of participants involved in the mayhem. Fists everywhere. Guys getting punched and kicked. Rugby tackles, body slams, head stomping, people being dragged out and into the mix. Coshes, knives, bottles, even a heavy chain swung around a head which whipped into Billy Blow's back.

Billy gasped and fell onto all fours. Six pairs of boots all went in and he felt the thuds all over his body. Boneheed McCracken put his fist through the chain swinger's face and then went to work on the kicking boots gang. He loved a good karate chop to the neck. He got two of them without reply. And then a big lad, not as big as him, but big, turned with too wide a stance for McCracken to ignore. McCracken toe punted his ball sack and watched the tower crumble, a fantastic look of morbid pain on the man's face as he dropped to his knees and lay in the foetal position, whimpering. Two of the others made for McCracken and then thought better of it, taunting him instead as they watched their mate get round the big man's back without him noticing. The goon was about to stick his chib up McCracken's arse when he was poleaxed by a hatchet through the collar bone.

Hatchet's wild eyes had gone the colour of a gas flame. The melee's instigator gave a mad cry and then put his foot on his fallen foe's neck to pull his axe out. His face was stained with blood as he nodded to Boneheed. Each got a hand under Billy Blow's pits to drag him away and onto the grass, which had become an unofficial safety zone where injuries were nursed and bodies lay unconscious.

Hatchet wiped his face with his sleeve, smearing human war paint in horizontal lines above and below his eyes. Centuries before, he might have done the same as a Pictish warrior.

"Thanks for that, wee man," said McCracken.

"This is fuckin great!" said Hatchet, his words rising up into a scream as he revelled in a world of bloodlust.

"Aye," said McCracken. "Too bad Roman couldnae be here tae see it."

"We'll dae some more cunts for the big man!" said Hatchet. "Come on! Let's get back in there!"

Onlookers watched what would later be described by the reporter, Warren Bailey, as a pitched battle in honour of the Crime

Boss, Roman Rock. A crowd of violent men giving perhaps the most violent man of our time the kind of fighting send-off he would have been proud of.

Meanwhile the hitman slipped along the wall of the vestibule behind a stone pillar at the the top of the stairs. Watching the mass brawl with a certain detached interest, he'd witnessed Ross Souter engaging in the chaos, along with other officers. Chaos was indeed the word for it. A spontaneous outbreak, which had led to a singular opportunity he could not otherwise have hoped for.

Everyone was out of the church and involved in the brawling, including the police. His eye twitched. He sniffed. It was worth a look. He walked in through the half open doorway unnoticed, closing over the other half of the wooden entrance door and barring it with the substantial wooden latch.

The church fell into respectful silence again. Just then a toilet flushed and a door he hadn't seen before opened in the vestibule to his left. Out came Rab Lawrie's housemate, Tam. The sound of water re-filling in a tank was muffled as Tam closed the toilet door and spied the stranger. Water dripped from Tam's fingers as he zipped up his flies.

The hitman twitched in disgust.

"Sorry mate," Tam said. "Naebdy's allowed in the church the now. We're getting ready for the burial, ken?"

The man nodded his understanding, half turned from the hips as if to leave and then used the momentum to swing back and crack Tam's neck with a forearm blow, rendering him unconscious in a heap. The man put his hands under Tam's armpits and dragged him into the stinking toilet.

CHAPTER 74

THE TRAP

The hitman scanned the empty church and then began walking down the central aisle, eyes fixed on the baseball cap of Barnabas Wild who had his head bowed, oblivious to the fracas outside as the priest cleared up and folded white sacramental cloths into neat piles at the altar. The hitman slipped his hand into his overcoat, gloved fingers resting on the grip of a silenced 9mm pistol. Father Michael noticed him only when he reached the coffin. "Hello, my son. Five minutes until we go for burial."

The hitman nodded. He took two steps back and knelt down, making the sign of the cross. A twitch, blink, and sniff.

It would end here.

CHAPTER 75

THE SURPRISE

The baseball cap and scarf were causing a severe itching on his face but he kept his head bowed – not out of respect for Roman or even god – but because of the phone screen hidden between the pages of the bible in his hands. On it, he'd watched the grey haired man in the dark overcoat enter the church and take a knee at the end of the row in front of the coffin.

It'd been Tam's idea to fit a camera above the doors so they could see anyone coming. But neither Rab nor Tam were at their stations. He'd sent them both a message and got no reply. Where the fuck were they? And what the hell was going on outside? It would've been nice for someone to have given a situation report. Fucking amateurs. He should've known. There was no option but to stick to the plan, hoping the Ladbrokes Mafia were still doing their job and covering the exits.

The stranger with the grey hair was still on his knee, looking at him. He could see it in his screen but he could also feel
it. It might be an innocent member of the crowd come to pay
respects to Roman. It was plausible the stranger was intrigued
by the sight of him in a baseball cap, scarf and sunglasses. But
he was staring and wouldn't stop staring. And then the stranger
stood up and spoke. "Barnabas Wild," he said, sure of his man.

He closed the bible in his hands but did not turn his head.
Freddie had been adamant on the hitman's need to know it was
him. "Surprise is everything," he'd said. It was the very last moment that would count.

On his mobile screen, he watched the stranger draw a pistol
from his overcoat and point it towards him. "Barnabas Wild,"
the grey haired man said again, in a forceful voice which carried
through the natural acoustics of the church with its high ceiling,
stone floors and pillars.

The time of reckoning had come. The old feeling of knowing
when things were about to get serious was followed by an inner
slowing down and a heightening of the senses. The adrenaline
began to flow but he'd been here before and so remained cool
and collected. With a deep breath, he closed the bible and stood
up slowly. Still looking forward, refusing to acknowledge the
stranger or his pistol, he took off the sunglasses and placed his

hands either side of his neck, pulling his scarf down and removing his baseball cap. The badly burned face turned to the stranger, and Junior said the words, "Roman Rock is RESURRECTED!"

That was the cue for Father Michael to duck and Barney to act.

Barney sat up in the coffin, raising the pistol point blank to the man in the centre aisle. A man with a grey face and a gun. A man he'd never seen before. Junior had given him the moment's confusion and space to act. They'd practised the movement a hundred times, drawing from a seated position, making sure not to rush but also to fire within two seconds after sitting up.

He used both hands to steady his aim, took one breath but couldn't squeeze the trigger. "Don't move!" he said, instead. "Put down the gun!"

With his pistol on Junior, the hitman slowly turned his head to see Roman Rock sitting up in his coffin pointing a gun at him. He twitched in disbelief.

"I'll shoot!" said Barney, but his voice was unsure. "Drop the gun!" Barney's arm tensed, his grip tightened and sweat trickled down from under the hot wig. The hitman watched the pistol shaking in Barney's hands.

Junior understood Barney had frozen. The hitman was now in control, not him. Junior opened his coat and drew his own pistol. He'd almost brought it to bare when the hitman caught the movement in the corner of his eye and snap-fired without looking. No aim but too close to miss. The shot impacted Junior's chest, knocking him back into the pillar where he fell to the ground. The hitman was already turning to Barney.

Another loud bang, immediately followed by a sharp ping as the hitman's gun jumped from his hands to clatter on the stone floor. The deflecting bullet zipped into the ceiling, pinging against a girder and then slicing through one of the tension wires connecting a life-sized crucifix to the ceiling. Whitewash paint fell as snowflakes and the front of the cross dropped only to catch and swing precariously as a pendulum on the one remaining wire. Jesus' anguished face looked down on them.

The hitman examined his hands with utter confusion. He looked to Barnabas and the muzzle smoke that told him he'd just been shot at. He sniffed in the pungent smell of nitroglycerin mixed with incense.

Barney's ears were ringing from the shots. He took off the Elvis sunglasses and the wig. "You killed Junior, ya bastard!" he cried.

The man showed Barney his palms, extending his fingers in a gesture of surrender but the rage in Barney overpowered him. He squeezed the trigger and screwed his face in preparation for the bang... but this time nothing happened.

The hitman's twitching eye blinked repeatedly. Barney pulled the trigger again, and again, but it was stuck. The gun had jammed.

The hitman gave a knowing smile, almost sympathetic, had it not been for the delight in his eyes. He pulled the skin around his twitch and then crouched down to pick up the customised silver 9mm, turning the weapon over in his hands to observe where the bullet had glanced off the barrel. His gloved index finger ran over the scrape and indentation, visible evidence of the miracle.

A miracle in a church.

Something about that made him laugh. Or almost laugh. The surprising spasm of his abdomen had produced a single note of joy that had been caught and stifled just as it had come out of his mouth. He stared inwardly like a kitten who had just coughed up a fur ball.

This whole job had been jinxed from the outset. But now his luck had miraculously changed. Shot and hit without injury. He lifted his gaze to the ridiculous image of Barnabas Wild sitting there in an over-sized coffin dressed as Roman Rock, complete with curly black wig. A small, rebellious tingle manifested itself inside his stomach, tickling its way up into in his throat as a breathy staccato before suddenly jumping loose in a high-pitched shrill he could not control. Cruel, menacing and strangely childlike, his laughter reigned in a voice clearly un-used to such expression.

In an attempt to control himself, the hitman stood up, but his hysteria proved overpowering. With streaming eyes he tried to focus on the idiot Barnabas Wild still sitting there like an imbe-cile in the coffin. Barney's confused face sent him into convul-sions. The sound of the tension wire straining to its limit and the plug pulling in its socket were drowned out by his insane laughter which bounced off the walls and rose in volume like voices in a choir.

Barney watched mesmerised as the hitman doubled up in the aisle and the giant cross twirled above. More plaster dust drifted down from the ceiling to land on the hitman's head and shoul-ders as he leaned over and held his stomach. But the hitman didn't notice.

Just then, the heavy wooden entrance door shook and Rab's voice shouted from outside, "Barney! Junior! What the fuck's going on in there?" Fists pummelled on the door as a single strand of wire snapped. The crucifix gave a centimetre jolt but did not fall. "Tam?" cried Rab. "Is anyone in there?"

The interruption brought the man to his senses. Something clicked and his hilarity wound down, tailing off into a long,

"Aaaah." He'd read essays on laughter being medically therapeutic but until now had never been able to.

Back to business. There was just enough time to finish the job and make his escape. The perfect finale to an epic opera. One he'd never forget. He smiled and raised his pistol to the adversary, Barnabas Wild, who could only sit there watching it happen.

All of a sudden there came a curious sound from the ceiling. A pop and twang. A snap and splitting of wood and plaster. The man looked up as the giant cross plummeted down and the last thing he saw was Jesus Christ himself who flattened him into the stone floor. A terrific boom resonated through the building as if a tomb had been sealed over by some giant rock.

Father Michael jumped and then gulped some holy wine straight from the bottle. "Let it all be over," he prayed.

CHAPTER 76

PROBLEM SOLVED?

Barney dropped out the coffin onto the stone floor. Picking himself up, he walked tentatively over to the hitman. The hitman's grey eyes were open but there was nothing inside. Thick red blood trickled from his mouth and ears. His neck had snapped at a right angle and his chest was crushed. Barney kicked the gun out of his hand, just in case.

A groan from the pillar gave Barney a start and he turned to see Junior sitting up. "I thought you were dead!" he said, running over.

"Where's the hitman?" asked Junior, whose question caused a sharp pain in his chest.

"Dead," said Barney.

"You're sure?"

Barney nodded.

"You shot him?"

"Aye, well, sort of," said Barney. "The bullet ricocheted off his gun into the ceiling and the crucifix came down on him."

"What? Show me!"

With Barney's help, Junior stood up to examine the body crushed under the crucifix. "I've never seen the like of it," he said, lifting his eyes to the ceiling. "That type of luck... it's not normal."

Barney shrugged. "What aboot you?" he asked. "I thought you got hit, didn't you?"

Junior opened his shirt to reveal a black ballistic vest with a silver bullet squashed into the size of a coin directly in the centre of his chest. He tapped it. "Thought this might come in handy," he said. "Fucking heavy shot though. Knocked the wind right oot of me. Stunned me tae fuck."

"You were wearing a bullet proof vest?" said Barney. "Why did I no get one?"

"Because you were supposed tae shoot the cunt before he even saw you. I was the one he'd be aiming at! The one taking the biggest risk."

"Sorry aboot that," said Barney, looking sheepish. "I froze."

"I noticed."

"I just couldn't pull the trigger wae him not even looking at me."

"So ye had tae wait until he shot me before it was okay tae shoot him?"

Just then footsteps sounded from the rear exit of the church and Rab came running in. Father Michael was still crouched behind the altar gulping wine.

"Junior! Barney!" Rab said. "I couldnae get in. The door's barred. What's happening?"

"That's what I'd like tae know," said Junior, with an acid tone. "Where the *fuck* were you lot?"

"Eh, ootside in the pagger of the *fucking* century! Aboot a hundred cunts going at it! Bizzies n' all! It's still going! Do ye no hear the sirens? Holy Fuck!" said Rab, noticing the crucifix and a man underneath. "Who's that?"

"Who dae you think it is?" said Junior.

Father Michael's head appeared above the altar. He stood up but had to put his hands onto the altar to balance.

Rab was crouched next to the hitman. He'd seen a few dead bodies in his time but none with the anguished face of Jesus resting on top, as if both had died together, in some sort of pseudo-homosexual tragedy. "There's something very fucked up aboot that," he said.

The rear door banged against the wall and echoed through the church. In came Freddie and Basher, each with an arm around Bob who had a bloodstained handkerchief tied around his head. Sykes brought up the rear.

"Here come the fucking cavalry," said Junior.

CHAPTER 77

A COFFIN MADE FOR TWO

"We've nae time tae argue," said Freddie. "Okay, it may no have gone *exactly* tae plan- - -"

"Exactly to plan?" said Junior. "You lot were supposed tae jump him before he got tae the coffin, never mind before he pulled a *fucking* gun and shot me!" Junior glared at Barney.

"I wasn't supposed to have to shoot him," said Barney.

"But we kent it was possible," said Freddie.

"Fine shot it was too," said Rab, looking up to the rafters. "What are the chances of that happening?"

"Divine intervention," said Bob.

"Jammy bastard, mare like," said Sykes.

Freddie brought them together. "Look on the bright side. This psychotic cunt will never trouble *you* or anyone else ever again.

Think aboot it. What if he hadnae gone tae jail? Or what if he got oot and came after ye tae finish it? Trust me, pal, it's for the best."

The crew looked down at the gruesome scene under the cross. The figure of Jesus had one of it's arms broken off. A foot had also been smashed to pieces.

"And who's going to pay for that?" asked Father Michael.

"Insurance," answered Freddie. "The mare pressing question is, what tae dae aboot the body..."

Tam was sitting on a pew, rubbing his neck. "Stick the cunt in the coe-ffin wae The Rock," he said, sounding slow and concussed. "Be done wae it."

"That is grim as fuck," said Rab.

"It's actually no a bad idea," said Sykes.

"Hold on!" Barney said. "We cannae put the man who killed Roman in the same coffin wae him. Father Michael, is it no against God or something?"

"This whole situation is against God!" said Father Michael.

"So is accumulating gambling debts, womanising and alcoholism," Freddie reminded him.

The priest swigged some more holy wine. "We'll all burn in eternal damnation."

Junior was the next to speak. "Two bodies in one coffin would save a lot of trouble," he said. "And we dinnae exactly have much time."

Sykes and Bob agreed. Basher grinned.

"It's no right," Barney protested.

"Do you want to try disposing of this guy with all these cops around?" Junior asked him. "Do you have any *idea* how difficult that is? Or how long ye'll go doon for if yer caught?"

Barney only sighed.

"It's for the best," said Freddie, putting his arm around Barney's shoulder. "And Roman wouldnae mind. It's a big coffin. We'll put Roman on top and arrange it so his arse is in that cunt's face for eternity."

"Wait a second," said Barney. "Is that why you got this coffin made up so deep?"

Freddie winked. "Always be prepared. Scouts' motto. I had tae assume things might get a bit dirty with this cunt."

Barney sighed. "Seems we dinnae have much choice," he said.

The men set to work. The hitman went into the coffin with his legs bent and his face under Roman's arse. Roman himself was set on top of an expensive Burgundy robe provided by Father Michael. Father Michael also brought in some cleaning products so they could get the blood stains off the floor. The cross was wiped clean and stored in the vestry where it could be disposed of later when everything had calmed down.

The nine men stood around the open grave with bowed heads as sirens blared all around. The brawl was over. Police reinforcements and the heavy mob had arrived en-mass and most participants had scarpered, been chucked head first into meat wagons with their hands cuffed, or been carted off into ambulances on stretchers. Most were just too knackered to continue fighting and so lit up and took to smoking and rubbing their knuckles instead, pretending to be uninvolved with the fighting.

Barney's crew had got the coffin into the grave easily enough but Barney had insisted on proper funeral rites for Roman. "Make it short and sweet," said Freddie. "The bizzies might turn up any minute."

Father Michael opened his black prayer book and went into Priest mode. "We commit the body of Roman Rock, our dear departed friend and brother, to the earth and his eternal sleep. May he rest in peace." Father Michael drew the sign of the cross in front of his body and then spoke something in Latin, whereupon everyone said, "Amen."

"Alright," said Rab, "let's get it finished."

Basher, Barney, Rab and Sykes started shovelling earth into the grave. They went at it hard, sweat dripping down their foreheads until it was done. The last of the sirens stopped and a few minutes later Detective Inspector Ross Souter came running into the small cemetery to see Freddie patting down a mound of earth with a spade in front of the tombstone of Roman.

"Ah, Mr. Souter," he said, "you've just missed the burial. Father Michael did a *lovely* service."

"Is that right?" said Souter, eyeing each of them in turn and then inspecting the grave and headstone.

Roman Rock

Proud Edinburgh man and King of the Jungle.

There was nothing obviously wrong, however, Souter's cop instinct told him something sinister was happening. Possibly it was just the sight of these crooks and their dodgy faces being trusted with something as ritualistic as burying a body. Basher's grin had always made him feel uneasy.

Freddie spoke again, "We have a certain Barnabas Wild here to speak with you, Mr. Souter, as promised."

Barney stepped forward.

"No disguise this time?" said Souter.

Barney shook his head. "That's all finished with."

"Is it indeed? Well I'd like to hear more... at the station if you don't mind."

CHAPTER 78

THE FINAL ROUND

Grace received the call from Barney to say he was at the police station and needed a lawyer. He hadn't told her anything else. She phoned a taxi and got them a private interview room, the same one she'd been in with Roman. Her eyes told him she was worried. When the officer shut the door, Barney put his arms around her and whispered in her ear that it was all over.

By the time Souter called them into the interrogation room, their story was watertight. Grace advised Barney to use Souter's own theory about the hitman being finished with him when Roman was killed. It gave her a sense of satisfaction to see Souter now so unsure of his own reasoning.

"There was a message left on Roman's coffin saying I wasn't a target anymore," explained Barney.

"Where is this message?" asked Souter.

"He burned it," said Grace, "on a prayer candle after the mass."

"How convenient," said Souter. "Don't take me for a fool, Grace. I know there's more to this."

"Barney has told you everything he knows," said Grace, defiant.

Souter drummed his fingers on the desk, sat back in his chair and folded his arms. "I'll be wanting DNA samples from you," he said, glaring at Barney.

"What for?" asked Grace.

"To eliminate him as a suspect in the murder investigation of Roman Rock."

"What?" said Barney.

"That is ridiculous," said Grace.

"Are your refusing to take the tests?" asked Souter, daring them to try it.

"Of course not," said Grace. "But how can you think Barney might have killed Roman?"

"It's a possibility until proved otherwise," Souter said.

"Then you'd also have to believe I was..." Grace stopped. Souter's stare said it all. She looked him straight in the eye. "After everything I've been through..."

Souter's official defensive wall was up and impenetrable. "We have to investigate all possible suspects and scenarios," he said, echoing the very words the Superintendent had spoken to him during his latest dressing down. But even Souter saw the disappointment in Grace's face. He'd just crossed a line he could not go back from.

"So you trust this is all over?" he said, wanting to move out from the uncomfortable silence. Grace didn't answer. Her emerald eyes cried betrayal. Souter shifted in his seat and fiddled with his collar. "Even after this *hitman* broke into your house and threatened you with a gun in order to find out where Barney was?"

But Grace had become a stone faced lawyer. "Like you said, Ross," she said, cool and collected, "there's no *real* evidence to say a hitman killed Roman. A botched burglary seems to make more sense. The guy in my house could have been anyone."

Souter gave a poor attempt at a laugh and shook his head before addressing Barney. "So this hitman just disappears and gets off Scot-free, does he? After he's killed Roman and taken a pot shot at you?"

Barney gave a shrug.

"Aye, well, I hope for your sake that your DNA doesn't match the blood we found in Roman's house."

"It won't," said Barney.

"And what if your little note from the hitman wasn't genuine? Have you considered that? What if he comes back for you?"

"It's over," said Barney with a conviction Souter did not understand.

Detective Inspector Souter sighed. Grace and Barney were two clams in cahoots. Something wasn't right but he couldn't work out what. There was nothing else to do, and so he made the time honoured gesture of washing his hands and told Barney to wait there while they got ready for DNA testing.

CHAPTER 79

ALL'S WELL THAT ENDS WELL

There were more than a few battered faces in the White House Pub that afternoon, with some of the mourners coming back from the cells and hospital just for the piss up, all in good spirits now with the free bar flowing and snacks on offer.

Barney handed Grace a gin and tonic and clinked his glass against hers. "Cheers," he said.

"Cheers to you, Mr. Wild," Grace replied.

Posters around the pub advertised the upcoming Halloween fancy dress party:

ALCOHOLIC DOOKIN PARTY

TICKETS £20 - Dook and Drink - Win a prize

Fancy Dress Only

Junior and Tam were leaning against the bar, steaming. "I'm g-g-gone as Count Drunkula, and you go as Alchenstine," said Tam.

Bob, Sykes and Rab were sharing a forty-five year old single malt, whilst discussing Edinburgh history. Burke and Hare as far as Barney could make out. The bulk of Basher swayed happily on a bar stool with his flat cap pulled low on his head and a near empty brandy glass in his hand. Father Michael burped, and all of a sudden came a cry from Freddie, "G'on yersel The Hitman!"

The heads turned to see Freddie staring up at the horse racing on the television. The Hitman was two lengths ahead and charging to the line. He crossed in first place and Freddie jumped off his stool. "Ya fucking beauty! I put that money I got fae Hatchet on "The Hitman" at twenty-five tae one! That's five grand in ma poe-kit!"

"As long as that's the only hitman to come in a winner," said Grace.

"Almost gave me a bloody heart attack," said Barney, holding his chest.

Freddie came over and gave Grace a wink. "If I were only five years younger, darlin," he said, tipping his wig to her. "Now listen Barney, ma wee pal, you've been through a lot lately. I ken you and Roman went way back. And I ken nothing can bring the big man back, God rest his soul. But I want tae gie you some money fae ma winnings there. Maybe ye can have a wee holiday." Freddie put his finger to Barney's chest. "And I willnae take no for an answer," he added. "Ye deserve a bit luck, pal. Two grand, courtesy of me and the boys. Just pop in the bookies on Monday, first thing. I'll have it there for ye, in cash."

"What can I say?" said Barney. "That's really decent of you Freddie, ta very much, mate."

Freddie gave Barney a wink and a pat on the back, and then walked up to see Bob about the funeral accounts.

"He's a right character, isn't he?" said Grace.

"You dinnae ken the half of it," said Barney. "Anyway, he's right. We have been through a lot recently. A holiday would be just what the doctor ordered. Somewhere nice. Exotic. Somewhere I've never been before. How about it? You and me. We'll use that dosh Freddie promised me as spending money."

"Sounds interesting," said Grace, putting her arm around him. "So... on the phone last week... before you hung up... you said something..."

"Did I?" said Barney.

Grace was looking up with her green eyes glinting and swimming in gin. Playful and eager. "Something about loving me," she reminded him.

Barney took a quick sip of his beer.

"Well?" she said.

Barney smiled. "Oh, aye. I did."

"Did?" said grace, feigning insult.

"I do," said Barney.

"You do? That's good." said Grace. "And now you want to take me on some sort of romantic holiday?"

"Aye," said Barney, unsure exactly where she was going with this.

"Somewhere you've never been before?" Grace said.

Barney nodded.

"Somewhere *exotic*?" said Grace, in a low, sultry voice. Barney blushed as she whispered into his ear, "Where were you thinking, *Mr. Wild*? The *Maldives*? The *Caribbean*?"

Barney looked up at the ceiling. His eyes narrowed and then opened wide as the answer came to him. "Benidorm!" he said. "Got tae be!"

Just then a coin dropped into the juke box and an old record was snatched by the robotic arm inside which flipped it over and put the needle to the thread. Runrigs' version of "Loch Lomand" started playing and so Doug the barman cranked the speakers up to full volume.

"This was one of Roman's favourites," he announced.

The clientele began crossing arms, holding hands and forming circles; voices sang, bodies swayed and the hairs on the backs of the necks went up as by the Bonnie Banks, and in the best of Scottish traditions, the good old White House went wild.

GLOSSARY

ane	own
bag off	kiss/snog
bairn	child
bampot	person of low intelligence
banter	talk/chat
barry	good/great
baws	balls
braw	brilliant/good
bizzies	police
cannae	can't
chore	steal
clarty	disgusting/dirty
coffin dodger	old person
couldnae	couldn't
dae	do
daein	doing
deid	dead
didnae	didn't
dinnae	don't
doesnae	doesn't
doon	down
fae	from
get wide	be cheeky/insulting
gie	give
gonnae	going to
greet	cry

heid/heed	head
hame	home
hoose	house
isnae	isn't
jobby	poo
ken	know
kent	knew
ma	my
ma'sel	myself
mare	more
McGee	person who thinks of others
McTack	selfish person
naebdy	nobody
nae	no/not
nash	run, scarper
noo	now
nowt	nothing
oot	out
pished	drunk
radge	wild/crazy person
scratcher	bed
shindig	festive party
some'dy	somebody
stardy	jail
steaming	drunk
tae	to
thay	those
ya/ye	you
yersel	yourself
wae	with

ABOUT THE AUTHOR

Alex Brown describes himself as a family man, son, brother, husband, father and grandfather.

He's a proud Scot, born and raised in Edinburgh. As a child, Alex was an exceptional young amateur boxer whose professional career appeared to be laid out in front of him until he collapsed at a bus stop on his way to a bout and was rushed to hospital. After waking up from surgery for an emergency appendicitis, Alex was told by doctors he had tuberculosis. He underwent pioneering medical treatment, which is still in use today. Although Alex made a full recovery the illness meant missing years of boxing training and school.

Alex returned to the ring many years later but said his passion for boxing had transferred to coaching. He opened his own gym and started to coach many talented young boxers whom he says, "became like sons to him."

Alex is also a business man and entrepreneur who is well known in the community for his children's charity fund raising exploits. He's completed five marathons for good causes, including Edinburgh, London and New York.

A natural entertainer and musician, Alex has been known to pick up the guitar and give impromptu performances of Neil Diamond and other artists. He is available to give motivational talks at schools, clubs and events though may insist on bringing his guitar...

So watch out!